BOOK FIVE IN THE *TORN* SERIES

NEW YORK TIMES AND **USA TODAY** BESTSELLING AUTHOR

K.A. ROBINSON

ISBN-13: 978-1502739933

OTHER BOOKS BY

NEW YORK TIMES AND *USA TODAY* BESTSELLING AUTHOR

K.A. ROBINSON

THE TORN SERIES
TORN
TWISTED
TAINTED
TOXIC
TAMED

The Ties Series
SHATTERED TIES
TWISTED TIES

BREAKING ALEXANDRIA

Taming Alec

DECEPTION

contents

Prologue... 1
Chapter One... 3
Chapter Two 11
Chapter Three 23
Chapter Four... 35
Chapter Five 55
Chapter Six 67
Chapter Seven.. 83
Chapter Eight... 91
Chapter Nine.. 105
Chapter Ten 121
Chapter Eleven 135
Chapter Twelve 145
Chapter Thirteen.. 157
Chapter Fourteen 169
Chapter Fifteen 173
Chapter Sixteen 185
Chapter Seventeen 201
Chapter Eighteen 215
Chapter Nineteen 225
Chapter Twenty 243
Chapter Twenty-One 251
Chapter Twenty-Two.. 261
Epilogue... 273
Broken and Screwed Teaser by Tijan................ 275
Other Books by K.A. Robinson........................ 285
About the Author.. 289
Acknowledgments 291

prologue

I hated the word *whore*. It sounded so…filthy. I'd been called a hundred different names before—slut, skank, ho, bitch, just to name a few—but when someone called me a whore, it would set my blood on fire.

As I stared down at my fate, I realized that they'd all been right. I was a whore.

There was no coming back from this.

I closed my eyes and willed myself not to cry. I'd done this to myself. This was what I deserved.

I hadn't always been this way. Once, a really long time ago, I'd been innocent. I'd worn my heart on my sleeve. I'd looked at every day like it was a gift instead of the plague that it really was.

Life was so damn hard. I hated it. I'd hated it for years. More than once, I'd wished that I hadn't had to deal with it, that I hadn't had to deal with *him*. But fate had laughed at me, repeatedly throwing him in my face just when I thought I'd healed.

How could I tell him this when he seemed to hate me more and more every time we saw each other? How could I tell him this after what she'd done? I was no better than her.

What was once innocent love and attraction had morphed into something…volatile and ugly. By now, it was almost unrecognizable.

Who am I kidding?

It had never been innocent. We'd seemed to be incapable of innocence, especially him.

I would never survive this. The moment I'd seen him, even though I hadn't wanted to admit it, I'd known that I would never survive *him*.

Tears fell down my cheeks, but I brushed them away as I stood and walked out of the room. When I reached my bedroom, I picked up my cell phone and dialed the only person I knew I could trust, the only person who knew every secret of mine—my best friend.

"Hey, Amber. What's up?"

"Chloe, I need you," I whispered.

one

Four Years Earlier—May

Charleston, West Virginia

I ran a brush through my dark brown hair and looked in the rearview mirror, making sure that my makeup was still flawless. Bright green eyes stared back at me, outlined perfectly with black eyeliner. My tanned skin was practically glowing from happiness. I smiled to myself as I adjusted my low-cut tank top so that it revealed even more of my cleavage. I climbed from my car and tugged on my shorts, inching them up my legs bit by bit.

I'd fought with myself for almost an hour as I debated on what to wear to surprise Chad, my boyfriend for the past year. Today felt special for some reason. I wasn't sure why, but it did, and I wanted to look perfect.

Along with my two best friends, Logan and Chloe, Chad and I had graduated from high school just last week. We only had two months to spend together before we would head off for West Virginia University in the fall. He'd be there with me, but I knew things wouldn't be the same, so I wanted to make sure that this would be a summer he'd remember.

I'd grown up alongside Chad in Charleston, West Virginia. We'd been in classes together since kindergarten, but it wasn't until last year when I'd really noticed him. I wasn't the only one who had taken notice either. He'd come back to school a good two inches taller and heavier with several pounds of all muscle. Girls who had barely looked at him before had started hanging around him, flirting their hearts out, but he hadn't paid them any attention. Instead, his eyes had watched me.

Two weeks after school had started, we had officially become an item. Since then, we'd been inseparable. He'd even earned bonus points by winning over Chloe and Logan.

I was a lucky girl, and I knew it.

I grabbed a grocery bag out of the backseat and locked my car before walking up the sidewalk to his parents' two-story brick home. I grinned as I slipped my key into the lock and quietly opened the door. After closing it behind me, I put my bag down by in the entryway and crept up the stairs to Chad's room.

His parents were on vacation this week, and instead of going with them, he'd decided to stay home and spend some quality time with me. Unfortunately, he had called early this morning to let me know that he had to cancel our plans because he'd ended up with food poisoning.

Instead of letting him wallow in misery alone, I'd decided to surprise him and nurse him back to health with some soup, and I would do it all while looking fabulous, of course.

When I reached his room, I grabbed the doorknob and slowly opened the door. I didn't want to wake him if he was sleeping.

The smile left my face when I saw his bed. He definitely wasn't asleep. My world crashed around me as I watched him fucking Carrie Jenkins, head cheerleader and complete whore. I stood there, frozen in shock, while he let out a groan as he came. He kissed her forehead before pulling out and standing, his back still facing me.

He slipped on a pair of basketball shorts. "As usual, that was great, babe."

Carrie mumbled something before burrowing underneath his covers. When he turned around, facing my direction, he had a satisfied smirk on his face, but it died instantly when he saw me standing in the doorway.

"Amber!"

I shook my head as he took a step closer.

"Don't come any closer, or I'll rip your dick off."

"It's not what it looks like," Chad said, his voice pleading.

I laughed. "It's not?"

"It's exactly what it looks like," Carrie said from the bed.

I looked over to see her sitting up and stretching her arms above her head, putting her breasts on full display.

I rolled my eyes. "At least one of you is honest." I turned to leave.

"Amber, wait. Please," Chad said.

I ignored him. I hurried through the hallway and down the stairs to the front door. He caught up to me just as I was getting ready to open the front door.

"Amber, please."

I jerked my arm out of his grasp and leveled him with a death glare. "We're finished, Chad."

"I know I messed up, but it won't happen again."

"How many times?" I asked quietly.

"What?"

"How many times have you slept with her?"

"This was the first time, I swear. She's been coming on to me for months, and I finally caved. It was the stupidest thing I've ever done. You mean the world to me, Amber."

I laughed. "You're lying through your fucking teeth, Chad. I heard what you told her. The sex was great—*as usual.* This wasn't the first

5

time you've slept with her, and I doubt that it will be the last. Enjoy each other. I can't think of two people who deserve each other more."

His mouth hung open, obviously shocked that I'd caught him in another lie. I stared at him, truly seeing him for the lying asshole that he was.

"I can't believe I thought I loved you." I laughed bitterly. "Never again will I give you the power to hurt me. Stay away from me, Chad, or you'll regret it."

I turned and threw open the door, and then my eyes landed on the bag I'd put down earlier. "By the way, I brought you some soup and crackers to help your stomach."

I picked up the bag and tossed it at his head. It missed and crashed into the wall, knocking several pictures onto the floor. I watched as the glass in the frames shattered, but I didn't even care.

I turned and walked out of his house. I promised myself that I would never look back, but I'd always remember this day. It had changed everything for me. I wasn't naive and innocent anymore. Chad had stolen that from me, and I'd never forgive him.

Maybe I should've thanked him. He'd shown me what the world was really like.

He was the beginning of the end for me.

—— —— ‑ ——

I walked into my parents' house, wiping my tears away.

"Oh my God! What happened to you?" Chloe shrieked.

I looked up at my best friend. How many times had I comforted her while she cried over her abusive mother? It was more than I could count. We'd been best friends for years, but I couldn't think of a time when I'd cried in front of her. I was sure it had been a shock to see me walking through the door, sobbing, with my makeup destroyed.

"Chad," I whispered, sitting down on a barstool in the kitchen.

I rested my elbows on the counter and willed myself to stop crying. He wasn't worth all this pain. He wasn't worth anything.

"What did he do?" Chloe pulled out a stool and sat down next to me.

She reached out and pulled me to her. I cried into her shoulder for a few minutes before pulling away. I winced when I saw the black stain, courtesy of my eye makeup, on her white shirt.

She looked down and frowned when she saw what I was looking at. "I don't care about my damn shirt, Amber. Now, tell me what happened."

I stared at her, almost smiling at the fierce look on her face. It seemed foreign on her delicate face. Despite the way she'd been raised, Chloe was fragile. I always told her that she reminded me of a porcelain doll. She thought it was because of her blonde hair, blue eyes, tiny frame, and creamy pale skin. It wasn't the reason, but I let her believe it. No, it was because she was so damn breakable. I was always the strong one, the one who defended her and offered to crack skulls whenever she needed it.

I wondered how I'd fair with a porcelain doll coming to my rescue. We might both end up broken by the end of this conversation.

"He cheated on me. I caught him screwing Carrie Jenkins about half an hour ago."

Her eyes widened in shock. "Chad? You can't be serious. He's so...nice."

I nodded. "I wouldn't have believed it if I hadn't seen it with my own eyes. He called me this morning to tell me that he was sick, so he couldn't meet up for our plans. I thought I'd surprise him and help him get better, but I was the one who got the surprise."

Chloe shook her head. "I'm so sorry, Amber. I really thought he was a good guy."

"It's not your fault. I didn't see it, and neither did Logan."

She gave me a small smile. "We could always call Logan. I bet he could kick Chad's ass. Logan is bigger, and he'd probably even enjoy doing it for you."

I shook my head. "There's no point. Logan would end up in trouble. And for what? A lying, cheating asshole who doesn't deserve even a second of our attention."

"You're right," Chloe said finally. "Are you going to be okay? I've never…it's just…you never cry."

Her voice was so soft and gentle that it nearly brought me to tears again.

"I'm not okay right now, but I will be. I'll survive."

She pulled me into another hug. "I'm right here. I'll make sure everything gets better for you." She took out her cell phone, one that my parents had paid for, and started texting.

"What are you doing?" I asked.

"Texting Logan," she said as if it were the most obvious thing in the world.

Truthfully, it was. The three of us were inseparable. We would be best friends forever—or at least until Chloe realized that Logan was in love with her. Then, I wasn't sure where our terrible threesome would end up.

"He'll be here in a few." She stood and walked to the fridge.

I watched as she opened the freezer and pulled out a tub of ice cream.

She grabbed three spoons out of a drawer and turned to face me. "Come on, I know just what you need."

"What?" I asked wearily.

"An ice cream party while we watch the hottest man alive slay evil things."

I smiled. "*Buffy* marathon?"

She nodded. "*Buffy* marathon."

When Logan arrived twenty minutes later, we'd already put a huge dent in the ice cream. He took one look at the television and sighed before dropping down on the couch beside me.

I handed him a spoon. "We're going to spend the day getting fat. You might as well join us."

He smiled before glancing over at Chloe. His eyes were still on her when he took the spoon from my hand.

Finally, he looked back at me. "You good?"

Chloe had obviously told Logan what was going on.

"I'll survive. Now, shut up, and let me watch Angel. I think he takes his shirt off in this one."

He rolled his baby-blue eyes. "Oh, goody, I can't wait."

I laughed as I elbowed him in the stomach. He'd obviously been working out more. My elbow felt like it had collided with solid steel.

Asshole.

Logan was one of the prettiest guys I'd ever seen but not in a feminine way. No, no one could describe him as feminine, that was for sure. His sandy blond hair was cut shorter than normal for summer, but he pulled it off well. His eyes were a bright blue, and his lips were full but not overly so.

I'd watched him for the past four years. His once round baby face had gradually sharpened into the strong face of a man. Once upon a time, I'd thought that I cared about Logan as more than just a friend.

I'd even tried to act on those feelings, but he'd kindly told me no. I'd been hurt until he explained how in love he was with Chloe. Once he'd admitted his feelings, I wasn't sure how I'd been so blind to them. From then on, I'd notice him watching her daily with a desperate look in his eyes.

Even though he'd shot me down, I never held it against him. He'd been sincere with his regret. That had been much easier to handle than watching my boyfriend of over a year fuck someone else.

Tears welled up in my eyes again, and I silently cursed myself. I tried to hide them, but Logan missed nothing. He wrapped his arm around my shoulders and pulled me tight against him.

"This show isn't all bad. At least Buffy is hot," he said without taking his eyes off the TV.

Jesus, I love this boy. Leave it to him to let me deal with my tears without drawing more attention to myself.

I glanced over at Chloe. I only wished she could love him the way he wanted her to. Out of all of us, Logan deserved happiness the most.

two

Three Months Later—August

West Virginia University Campus,

Morgantown, West Virginia

As I stepped out of the building after class, I shielded my eyes with my hand to block out the glare of the sun. Once I could see, I noticed Chloe, and I waved as I headed toward her.

"Hey, girl! How did your classes go?" I asked once I was next to her.

She smiled as she stood, and we started walking toward our dorm. "They were good. It was mainly a bunch of boring stuff over and over."

I nodded as she walked alongside me. "Yeah, mine were the same. I'm so glad we decided to only take a few classes this semester until we get adjusted."

Both of us had decided to go easy on the classes our first semester, so we were squeezing by with the bare minimum to be considered full-time students—unlike Logan, who had enough classes for two people. He was always the overachiever, that one.

"Anyway, have you seen some of these guys walking around here? I think I'm in love!" I said, thinking of the hot guy I'd sat next to during my first class.

He'd eye-fucked me for ninety minutes straight. That had to be a new record.

Since the day I'd caught Chad in bed with Carrie, my outlook on men had changed. They were no longer something I desired. The only reason I would pay any attention to them was for the simple fact that I enjoyed sex. I'd promised myself that I would never again give my heart to a man. Would I toy with them the way Chad had toyed with me? Without a doubt.

Unfortunately, I'd spent most of my summer avoiding men at all costs—with the exception of Logan. Now that I was on a campus filled with thousands of college guys, my long-lost libido was now wide-awake and raring to go.

"Yeah, I noticed a couple," Chloe mumbled, pulling me from my thoughts.

I stopped dead in my tracks and spun to face her. "What? You noticed someone? I thought for sure you were a nun in hiding!"

The fact that Chloe had noticed someone was huge. While I'd spent most of my high school years flirting with any cute guy I could find, Chloe had stayed away from men altogether, claiming that she wasn't interested in any of them.

She elbowed me in the ribs. "I am not a nun. There just hasn't been anyone to catch my interest. We can't all be as boy crazy as you are."

"Whatever. So, who is this guy?" I asked.

Chloe fidgeted a little and glanced at her shoes, which was a total mistake. I knew the shoe-staring was her thing when she was trying to keep something from me.

"Don't you dare look at your shoes, woman! Spill!"

She sighed and looked up at me. "I don't know his name or anything. He was just a guy who was sitting in the seat next to me this morning."

I raised my eyebrows at her. "And what does this mystery guy look like?"

12

She glanced around, making sure that no one was near us. "He's cute, I guess. His hair is so dark that it's almost black, and he has these beautiful piercing eyes. Oh, and these really hot piercings in his lip and eyebrow. And he had some tattoos peeking out from the sleeves of his shirt, but I couldn't tell what they were."

As she spoke, I felt my mouth dropping in slow motion. "You don't like just any guy. You like a bad boy. Holy shit, I'm pretty sure hell just froze over. My little Chloe is crushing on a bad boy!"

I pretended to faint, and she elbowed me.

"Shut up. I don't like him. I just find him kind of attractive. What is this—middle school?"

I busted out laughing at her, unable to stop myself. "Touchy, aren't we? Sorry, I'll stop bothering you about the tattooed, pierced, and kind of attractive bad boy."

Underneath all my teasing, I secretly worried about this new development. Chloe had never once paid attention to any guy. That alone had allowed Logan to keep his sanity. If Chloe fell for someone else, I wasn't sure what he would do. Logan was so in love with her that I truly worried he'd do something stupid.

We started making our way across campus again, and we were nearly to the dorm.

"So, I know it's a Monday and all, but some girl in my English class invited me to a party across campus at one of the fraternity houses. Will you please come with me? I need my wingwoman!"

"I really shouldn't. I still have a couple of boxes to unpack, but I'm sure your roommate would be glad to go with you," Chloe said.

I stuck my lower lip out and pleaded with my eyes. "Please, Chloe? I saw Chad today, and I really need a night out. We won't even have to stay late, I promise!"

I really had seen Chad today, but it had been from several yards away. Still, even with that much distance, I would know him anywhere. Surprisingly, I hadn't felt like crying when my eyes landed on him. Instead, I'd felt a hate so deep that I feared I would start breathing fire. My pain was gone now, but it had been replaced by something even more wicked—pure anger.

She sighed and pulled me into a hug. "All right, Amber, I'll go, but only because I have that super cute dress I've been dying to wear."

I squealed and started jumping up and down. "Yay! I love that dress. I told you so when I bought it for you! Plus, I have the cutest shoes to go with it!"

I grabbed her arm and pulled her into the dorm and up to her room. As soon as we were inside, I started rummaging through boxes in my closet, and I pulled out a pair of killer red heels.

She gave me a half-smile as I handed them to her. "Thanks. I'm going to head to my room and try to get the rest of my stuff unpacked before tonight. I'll meet you back here around eight o'clock, okay?"

"That works for me," I said as I watched her leave.

I felt like tonight was going to be the start of something great. I just hoped it wouldn't turn out to be like the last time I'd had this feeling. That hadn't ended well at all.

This is amazing! I thought to myself as Chloe and I climbed the steps to the fraternity house.

Drunk people were everywhere, all of them laughing and having the time of their lives. This was what I'd needed—freedom. Chloe and Logan had been great to me over the summer, but *this* was what I'd been longing for all along. I wanted to be around other people. I wanted to dance and drink and act like a stupid college freshman.

We pushed through the doors and looked around. I smiled as I watched the massive group of people in front of me. My eyes skimmed over the live band playing Chevelle's "The Red" and landed on a table full of alcohol.

Bingo.

I motioned for Chloe to follow as I walked over to the table. I grabbed two cups and filled them up with beer from a keg. I handed one cup to Chloe before taking a sip of mine. I looked around to see several guys standing around us, all of them staring at Chloe and me. I had to admit, we looked good. Chloe pulled off that dress like a pro, and I wasn't doing too bad myself in a tight micro-mini and a bright yellow tank top.

When two guys stopped in front of us, I looked up. I couldn't hide my smile when I realized that one of the guys was the one who had been eye-fucking me in class earlier. "Pour Some Sugar on Me" started playing, and his companion smiled down at Chloe.

"Hey, I'm Ben. This is Alex. Care to dance?"

Alex. I liked that name. I also didn't mind the way he was looking at me. He was attractive with light-blond hair and blue eyes. His nose was a bit too big, but it didn't take away from his overall appeal. His body wasn't built like Logan's, but Alex was solid.

I smiled at Alex before tossing my cup in the garbage and taking his hand. He led me out to the dance floor with Chloe and Ben following close behind. Once we found a spot in the crowd, Alex stopped and pulled my back up tight against him. I ground my hips against his pelvis, loving the feel of him behind me. He was the first man I'd allowed to touch me since that day with Chad. I hadn't realized how much I missed being pressed up against a man until now. His fingers gripped my hips as we continued to move against each other. I lost myself in the music, enjoying both its sound and the way Alex's body felt against mine.

When the song ended, Alex grabbed my hand and pushed his way through the crowd. I followed him, checking out his ass as we went. It was nice to look at. When we reached the far corner of the room, he pulled me down on a couch beside him.

I gasped in shock as he pulled me over to him and kissed me deeply. I almost slapped him, but something stopped me. The feel of his lips on mine were incredible. I felt nothing for him, except lust. I expected that to disappoint me, but it didn't. Instead, it made me feel powerful. This man could do nothing to me that would cause me pain. I was the one in control this time even if he didn't realize it.

When he pulled away, he stared hungrily at me. "I've wanted to do that all day."

I pulled him closer, a faint smile on my lips. "Then, why did you stop?"

He pushed me down onto the couch as our mouths collided again. I should've felt ashamed that I was letting him kiss me in public like this, but I didn't. I was past caring about what people thought of me. I was tired of holding back from what I wanted. Tonight, I wanted to be in this man's bed. Tomorrow, I would disappear, satisfied, before he woke up.

He groaned into my mouth and thrust his hips against mine. "Do you want to go upstairs with me?"

He was asking, not demanding, leaving the decision up to me. I nodded, and he kissed me once more before sitting up. He stood and helped me to my feet. I held his hand as he led me upstairs, away from the party. We passed several doors, all of them closed with a sock on the door handle. I assumed that was code for, *Stay the fuck out. I'm getting laid.*

Alex led me to a room at the end of the hall. I stepped in first and looked around as he closed the door behind us. The room was small but still bigger than the dorm I slept in. A full-sized bed sat in the corner. A computer desk sat against the far wall, covered by a computer and several textbooks.

I didn't get a chance to look further because Alex picked me up and carried me to the bed. He dropped me, and I laughed as I lightly bounced across the bed.

"I don't even know your name," he said as he pulled off his shirt, revealing a lean but muscular chest and stomach.

"I'm Amber." I pulled my tank top over my head and tossed it onto the floor. I stood and slipped my skirt and panties down my legs to the floor. I kicked them aside as I unclasped my bra and tossed it aside.

Alex's gaze traveled down my body as he pulled his boxers off. I glanced down at his hard dick as it jutted away from him. Yeah, this boy would entertain me for sure.

"It's nice to meet you," Alex said as he walked across the room.

I fell back onto the bed, and he climbed on top of me.

"Shut up, and fuck me," I mumbled as he kissed a trail across my breasts.

He chuckled. "I think we're going to get along just fine, Amber."

"Mmhmm," I mumbled as he ran his tongue across my nipple.

He sucked it into his mouth as his fingers found my clit. I arched off the bed and grasped his arms. He grinned down at me before plunging two fingers inside me.

"Damn, you're tight," he said as he finger-fucked me.

My hips rolled, meeting his every thrust. Quicker than I'd thought possible, I felt my orgasm overtake me. I cried out as I rode the wave of ecstasy. Alex pulled away from me long enough to grab a condom from his drawer. He slid it on, and in one swift movement, he slammed into me. I gasped, my body trying to adjust to his sudden intrusion after over three months of no sex whatsoever.

"Jesus," he muttered as he pulled out and shoved into me again.

It didn't hurt as bad this time. I wrapped my legs around his waist, allowing him to go deeper. He kept up a steady stream of hard and fast thrusts. Soon, I felt myself building again. Just as he came, my second orgasm took over. I cried out as I dug my nails into his arms.

When we both came back down, I opened my eyes to see him smiling at me.

"That was everything I expected and more," he said as he pulled out and stood. "I knew there was something about you the moment I laid eyes on you."

I gave him a weak smile as I sat up. "Do you want me to go now?"

He paused for a moment. "Nah, you can stay the night."

I nodded, relieved that I wouldn't have to walk home by myself. My thoughts flipped to Chloe, and I grabbed off of the nightstand where I'd placed it earlier. I sighed in relief when I saw her text, telling me that she was going back to the dorm. I knew Logan would pick her up and make sure she made it home safely.

I lay back down in Alex's bed and pulled the covers up to my chin. A few seconds later, I felt the bed move as Alex climbed in behind me. I was surprised when he wrapped his arm around me and pulled my back tight against his chest.

"Night, Amber," he mumbled. Within seconds, he was asleep.

He was still asleep the next morning when I crept from his bed and got dressed. I gave him one last look and headed for the door. I wasn't sure whether I should be happy or sad over the fact that I felt absolutely nothing for the man I'd had sex with hours before.

I decided on being happy. This, whatever it was I'd shared with Alex, was much easier to walk away from.

⸺ ⸺ ⸺ ⸺

I looked up when Alex sat down next to me in class. I was surprised to see him in another one of my classes, but I was even more surprised that he'd decided to sit by me again after he'd gotten what he wanted.

"Where did you disappear off to last night?" he asked.

I shrugged. "I went back to my dorm this morning to get ready for class."

He nodded. "You should've let me know that you were leaving."

"I didn't want to bug you. Besides, it wasn't like I had to walk far. My dorm is close to the fraternity house."

He stared at me, his hesitation clear. "Listen, Amber—"

I held up my hand. "You don't have to give me the whole it-was-just-for-fun speech, Alex. I already know that."

He grinned. "I'm glad you do, but that wasn't what I was going to say."

"Oh?" I asked, raising an eyebrow.

"We had a lot of fun last night, and you seem like you're not the type of girl who gets clingy after sex. I wanted to know if you'd like to hook up again tonight?"

"Again?" I asked, completely shocked. When I'd slept with him last night, I'd gone in knowing that it was a one-time thing, and I was totally okay with that.

"Yeah, again. Maybe even more than once, if you're up for it."

"You want me to be your fuck buddy?" I asked.

He grinned. "I guess so. It sounds bad when you say it like that though."

"You want just sex. No relationship, no dates, nothing besides sex, right?"

"Well, we could be friends if you want."

I stared at him, debating on what I should say. Part of me was offended by his offer, but the other part—the majority part—thought that this was a brilliant idea. I wanted sex, and Alex could give it to me, free of any emotions.

"Would we be exclusive? Sexually, I mean," I asked.

He stared at me for a moment. "If you want to be, then sure. I'm okay with just fucking you for a while."

I grinned. At least the guy was honest. "All right, I'm cool with this if it's just the two of us." I felt like I should shake his hand to seal the deal, but I refrained.

"I knew you'd be down for it." He leaned forward and kissed me gently on the lips. "I'll see you tonight then."

"I can't tonight," I lied. "I have plans."

I didn't, not yet anyway, but I also didn't want to spend two nights in a row with him. I didn't want this to feel anything like a relationship.

"Tomorrow night?" he asked hopefully.

"Sure."

Just then, the professor walked in, effectively ending our conversation. I stared straight ahead for the rest of class, refusing to look at him. I should have felt embarrassment over agreeing to something like this, but I didn't. I wasn't sure what that said about the person I was becoming.

I did know that I could never tell Chloe or Logan about my agreement with Alex. Neither of them would understand. I hated that I would have to keep a secret from them, but I couldn't stand the thought of the judgment and disgust I would surely see in their eyes.

When class ended, Alex handed me a piece of paper.

"Call me tomorrow night before you come over," he said before standing and walking away.

I clutched the note in my hand as I threw my things into my bag and stood.

Welcome to your new life, Amber, I thought as I headed for the door.

three

Two Months Later—October

Morgantown, West Virginia

I'd spent the last two months loving every minute of college. I hated the actual classes, but everything else was amazing. I'd always felt held back by my parents when I was in high school. Now that I was a couple of hours away from them, I no longer had to live by their rules. Instead, I did what I wanted.

I still spent most of my time with Chloe and Logan. Unfortunately, things had slowly—emphasize on *slowly*—progressed romantically between the two of them, and I had forced myself to take a step back from our threesome. They always tried to include me in things, but I felt like I was intruding on their lives.

The guy Chloe had mentioned to me on the first day of class, Drake, had ended up not being an issue for Logan. After I'd dropped a few subtle hints about Drake to him, Logan had seemed to realize that he was about to lose Chloe without any fight at all. After more than four years of secretly loving her, he'd finally come clean. The two of them were well on their way to a permanent relationship.

Drake would still hang out with us but only as a friend to Chloe. At least, that was what he'd claimed to be, according to her. I didn't buy it. More than once, I'd caught him staring at her with lust-filled eyes. The guy wanted her even if she was with someone else. I just hoped she would have enough sense to turn down his advances if he tried anything with her.

I'd ended my *relationship* with Alex after only a few weeks. It wasn't that I didn't like the guy because I did. I'd realized that he wasn't an asshole like I'd expected. In fact, he was a truly nice guy. We'd become friends, but we'd barely hung out outside of his bedroom.

The reason I'd ended it was because Chloe had asked too many questions. She'd noticed my absence and asked about where I was always sneaking off to. Finally, I'd lied and told her I was dating Alex. I'd told him as well. He hadn't seemed to care that I claimed him, which had made me wary because I didn't want a relationship. When Chloe had constantly tried to get me to bring Alex to places with us, I'd finally told her that we'd broken up. It was easier that way.

Shortly after, I'd truly ended things with him. Sneaking around with him had just been too hard, and I'd grown bored with the sex. Alex wasn't bad at it. He'd just seemed to like things one way only. He had instantly shot down any suggestion to change it up. That had ended up being a deal-breaker for me.

Tonight, I was going to the bar where Drake's band played—Gold's Pub. I was excited for a night out with Chloe, Logan, and Rachel, who was Chloe's roommate. I was wearing a sexy black dress, hoping to catch at least one guy's attention. It had been too long since I had sex. Calling Alex crossed my mind, but I decided against it. We were finished, and I didn't want to go back to him, no matter how desperate I was starting to feel.

I left my hair down and applied my dark eyeliner and shadow with a heavy hand. After a few adjustments, I had the dark look I was going for. I gave myself one more glance in the mirror before heading up to Chloe's room. We were all meeting there, including Drake. I couldn't help but wonder how that car ride was going to go. Logan and Drake would act like asses when they were around each other. The last time we'd all gone somewhere together, Logan had ended up drunk and tried to beat the shit out of Drake, and that was *before* Logan had finally come clean to Chloe.

I shook my head. If Chloe let it, that whole situation would become a disaster.

I knocked on Chloe's door once before walking into her dorm room. Logan and Chloe were sitting on her bed, talking to Rachel.

"Hey!" I said cheerfully as I dropped down onto Rachel's bed next to her. "Are we leaving soon?"

"Just waiting on Drake," Chloe said.

We all chatted as we waited for Drake to show up.

After almost twenty minutes, Logan glanced at his phone. "Chloe, it's eight now. The band goes on at nine. Call him, and see where he is."

She pulled out her phone and dialed Drake's number. After a few seconds of conversation, she hung up.

"We have to pick him up at the library," she said, clearly annoyed over him not showing up.

We walked downstairs and out of the building to where Chloe's car was parked. Logan climbed into the passenger seat before I had a chance. I hid my smile as I slid into the backseat with Rachel. Before Chloe even pulled out of the lot, Logan had her hand tightly grasped in his. Yeah, the boy had it bad.

When we reached the library, Chloe popped the trunk, so Drake could toss his guitar in the back. Rachel scooted over closer to me to make room for Drake in the backseat. He climbed in and gave us a quick smile before glancing up at Chloe. His gaze hardened when he saw Chloe's hand in Logan's.

He shook his head before turning his attention back to Rachel and me. I had to admit, the boy was sex on a stick. His hair was black and hung in his eyes. His eyes were just as dark. He had a piercing in his eyebrow and another in his lip. Tattoos poked out from underneath the sleeves of his tight T-shirt. If he weren't Chloe's friend, I would've totally made a pass at him.

I felt Rachel tense beside me as he looked at her.

"I don't think we've met. I'm Drake," he said, giving her the flirtiest look I'd ever seen.

Player.

"I know who you are. I'm Chloe's roommate, Rachel."

Rachel seemed to eat up the attention Drake was giving her as he continued to flirt with her. She was so caught up in it that she didn't notice Drake's gaze constantly moving to Chloe. My stomach dropped. He was using Rachel to make Chloe jealous.

I leaned back against the seat and closed my eyes. With a guy like Drake, Chloe would have to be made of steel to ignore his advances. I needed to talk to her since it was obvious that Drake had a thing for her. *Stupid, stupid men. They always have to complicate things.*

When we pulled into the parking lot of the bar, Drake climbed out and grabbed his guitar from the trunk. The rest of us climbed out and headed for the bar. I looped my arm through Logan's. I felt the need to hug him and tell him everything would be okay, but I couldn't, so this would have to do.

Once we were inside the bar, we stopped by the door to wait for Drake. This was his place, not ours, and he would tell us where to sit. I looked around as we waited for him and Chloe to appear. She had apparently hung back to walk with him.

The bar was older but clean. A while back, Morgantown had banned smoking in bars, but I could still detect the subtle scent of cigarette smoke in the air. Where we stood in the back of the bar were several tables, all of them full. At the front was a stage. A large space had been cleared out in front of it so that the patrons could stand in front of the stage.

Drake appeared and motioned for us to follow him. Chloe wasn't with him, but she came through the door a few seconds later. Once she joined our group, we followed him to the front of the bar where an empty table sat.

"I had them save this one for you guys. I've got to go to the back and meet up with the guys and Jade."

We all sat down at the table as Drake walked away. I noticed Rachel staring at him with a look of longing on her face.

"Earth to Rachel. Come in, Rachel," Chloe said as she snapped her fingers in front of Rachel's face.

"What? Oh, sorry," Rachel said as her cheeks flushed bright red.

I shook my head as Logan chuckled. This wasn't going to end well.

"Don't go there, Rachel. If you have sex with him, you'll make it awkward for me when he kicks you to the curb," Chloe bit out.

My eyes widened in surprise. Chloe was pissed. She never got pissed, especially over a guy.

Rachel frowned. "I wasn't planning on having sex with him."

Chloe gave her an incredulous look. "Could've fooled me."

I jumped up before Rachel could reply. "Chloe, why don't you come to the bar with me and help me get us drinks?"

She stood and followed me to the bar.

I spun around to face her as soon as we were out of earshot. "What the hell was that?"

She looked at me, confusion written clearly over her face. "What are you talking about?"

"You know exactly what I'm talking about. You blew up at Rachel for no reason."

She shrugged as she ordered our beers. "No, I didn't. I just saw the way she was looking at Drake. If they hook up, it'll be awkward every time we're all together."

"Are you sure that's all it is? I saw the way you were looking at him. For God's sake, Chloe, get your act together. You were just holding hands with Logan earlier."

"You're imagining things. I'm over Drake, and I haven't given Logan an answer. We're taking things slow."

I shook my head. "I'm not blind, Chloe. You can lie to yourself, but you can't lie to me. You still care about Drake, and you're stringing Logan along. Do you even have feelings for Logan? Or are you just trying to get over Drake?"

She grabbed the beers and turned to glare at me. "Yes, I do fucking care about Logan. I'm trying to get my shit together. I want to give Logan a chance, but I'm afraid, okay? I don't want to lose him."

"Do you really think Logan would abandon you if things went south with him? He cares too much about you to let that happen. You need to get your head out of Drake's ass and see what's standing right in front of you."

"You think I don't know how amazing Logan is? Because I do, so stop trying to push me to him, and let things happen!" she practically shouted as we walked back to the table. She set Logan's beer in front of him and forced a smile onto her face.

I watched them as I sat down. Logan pulled Chloe's chair closer to him and rested his hand on her thigh. I swore that I could see panic in Chloe's eyes.

"What took you guys so long?" Logan asked.

She glanced at me, but I looked away. There was no way I was going to help her out.

"We had to wait forever. Sorry," she said.

We sat and talked as we waited for Drake and the other members of his band to take the stage. My eyes kept landing on Chloe and Logan. Chloe tried to keep her attention on Logan, but her eyes kept darting to the stage. This whole thing was a bigger problem than I'd realized.

When the lights dimmed and the band climbed onto the stage, people started shouting. A large group of people were already standing in front of the stage, but more shoved in, hoping to get closer to the front. I raised an eyebrow. I'd barely paid attention to Drake's band play at the fraternity party. If their groupies were any indication, I obviously needed to pay closer attention this time.

"Are you guys ready to fuckin' rock?" Drake roared into the mic when the lights came up.

The crowd roared their approval.

"We're Breaking the Hunger, and we're about to tear this place down!" he shouted into the mic.

I watched as he turned and nodded to the girl behind the drums. She was so small that I could barely see her.

She started a steady beat. A few seconds later, the other two guys in the band came into the song. I glanced at the one on the opposite side of the stage from me as he played his bass. He reminded me of Drake from this distance—same haircut, same build. He didn't carry himself the way Drake did though. There was less…arrogance and cockiness. He never once glanced up from his instrument. It was as if he was trying to avoid the crowd altogether.

My eyes flashed to the guy closest to me, and I froze. *Holy shit.*

He was the most attractive man I'd ever seen. He was also the wildest. His hair was dyed an electric blue, and it was styled into a Mohawk that stood several inches high. His eyebrows were both pierced twice, and he had a set of snakebites. He was shirtless, revealing full sleeve tattoos on both of his arms. His chest was covered in tattoos as well. My eyes dropped to the tight six-pack abs. *What I wouldn't give to run my hands over them.*

I stared at him, unable to pay attention to anything happening around me. I didn't even hear the music playing. One glance at this man, and I was completely captivated. He kept shooting flirty looks at the women in the crowd, obviously enjoying the attention of being on stage. My mouth dropped open in awe when he played a solo. The man knew his way around a guitar. He played the solo flawlessly, his forehead crinkling in concentration.

I was pulled back to earth when I noticed Chloe and Logan stand. I gave him a questioning look, but he just shook his head as he led Chloe onto the dance floor. He pulled her against him, and they began dancing to the slow melody of the song. I looked around to realize that several other couples were dancing together as well.

I turned my attention back to the band. My eyes fell on Drake first. He had a look of pure rage on his face as he watched something out on the dance floor. I had a good idea what, or rather whom, he was staring at. Sure enough, when I turned back to look, Chloe and Logan had stopped dancing, and they were now kissing.

I sighed. Those three were going to be the death of me. I could feel it.

"I want to thank all of you for coming out tonight. We hope you enjoyed the show," Drake said once the song had ended. He looked anywhere but at Chloe and Logan.

Wait, what? They just started, I thought to myself before glancing down at my phone. *Holy shit, it's already ten.* Had I really been staring at that guy for over an hour? There was no way.

My eyes snapped up when Chloe and Logan sat back down at our table. A few seconds later, the tiny drummer chick dropped down into the seat next to Chloe. I looked up to see the other three members of the band grabbing chairs from a neighboring table. We all scooted closer together to give them room to sit down. My breath caught when the guitarist with the Mohawk ended up in the chair next to me.

He was even more gorgeous up close. His eyes were the richest brown I'd ever seen. He had a strong jaw covered in dark stubble. He'd grabbed a shirt somewhere between the stage and our table. Despite that, I wanted to reach out and touch him more than I'd ever wanted anything else in my life.

"Guys, this is Chloe, Logan, Rachel, and Amber. These two idiots are Eric and Adam. Jade is the tiny chick," Drake said, motioning to each of us as he called out our names.

Adam. I even loved his name.

I glanced over at him again, but he was looking away from me. He was in a deep conversation with Eric. I frowned. I wasn't used to men ignoring me, especially when I was sitting right next to them.

I felt someone give me a hard kick under the table. I looked away from Adam to see Chloe watching me closely. Her eyes darted to Adam before returning to me. I shrugged my shoulders, and she rolled her eyes.

The table fell into easy conversations. Adam continued to ignore me as he talked to Drake and Eric. Chloe was focused on Jade. Logan didn't talk to anyone. Instead, he kept his focus on Chloe. Rachel tried to keep my attention, but my eyes kept drifting back to Adam.

A few minutes later, three scantily dressed chicks surrounded the guys. Without breaking eye contact with Eric, Adam grabbed one of them and pulled her onto his lap. His hand cupped her ass and squeezed. My eyes widened.

Seriously? He had a girlfriend. I almost groaned out loud. No wonder he'd ignored me completely.

"I'm Stacey," the girl said as her other two friends made themselves comfortable in Drake's and Eric's laps.

Eric looked uncomfortable, but Drake seemed at ease.

"I don't need to know your name," Adam said as he finally looked at her.

Hold the fucking train. He doesn't even know her?

I was so confused. *What kind of asshole gropes a chick he doesn't even know? Oh yeah, Alex had done that to me.*

My eyes flashed back to the girl. She had a hungry look in her eyes. She was a fucking groupie. That was all. She just wanted Adam to fuck her.

Why the hell did that make me clench my hands into fists under the table? I was losing my damn mind.

I looked over at Chloe. She was staring at Drake's hand, which was currently slipping up the skirt of the girl on his lap. Pain flashed across her face before she looked away. I glanced back at Drake and saw him watching Chloe's every move. *What was up with those two?*

As the night wore on, Adam and the girl on his lap became even more annoying. I hated myself every time I glanced in their direction. I didn't want anything more than this girl did. I had no right to feel jealous over the fact that she had decided to take a chance and came out the winner.

Jade, the drummer chick, started talking to Rachel. I joined in, desperate to distract myself from what was happening six inches away from me. It turned out that Jade was actually pretty nice. She asked about our classes and stupid things like that to keep the conversation flowing. She had the cutest Southern accent I'd ever heard.

When she asked about our favorite bands, we got into a huge debate. I declared Avenged Sevenfold as my favorite, and Jade said that Korn was way better. Rachel didn't have a clue who we were even talking about.

I looked up when Chloe abruptly stood.

Logan quickly did the same and glanced over at Rachel and me. "You guys ready?"

I told Jade, "Good night," before standing and following them to the exit. Unable to stop myself, I glanced back at Adam one more time, still struck by how drawn I was to him.

It was too bad he was a bigger asshole than even I could handle. I might be a little more open-minded than most women, but I sure as hell wasn't a fucking groupie.

four

Three Months Later—January

From Charleston to Morgantown, West Virginia

"I love you, too," I said as I hugged my mom.

I waved once more before climbing in my car. I smiled as I watched my mom pull Chloe into a tight embrace. Chloe had spent most of our teenage years practically living with me. My parents considered her their second daughter.

"You need anything—anything at all—you call me, okay?" my mom said to Chloe.

I couldn't help but wonder what she meant by that. It wasn't the words but the tone she'd used that concerned me.

"You ready?" I asked as Chloe climbed into my car.

"Yeah," she whispered, her voice thick with emotion.

I pulled away from my childhood home, my thoughts still on Chloe. We'd spent winter break with my parents. It had been nice to come back and visit, but I was excited to get back to Morgantown. I told myself it was simply because I missed college, but even I knew that was a lie. I wanted to get back because I planned on watching Drake's band perform again tonight.

Over the past three months, I'd spent every Friday night at Gold's, desperate to get a glimpse of Adam. Even after Chloe had been forced to work Friday nights at her job at Starbucks, I would still go with Rachel or by myself. It was getting ridiculous. I'd obsessed over him since that first night, and he had yet to even say hello to me. He was always too busy with groupies to pay attention to anyone else.

I knew my infatuation with him was unhealthy. While I wasn't looking for a relationship, even I knew getting involved with Adam for sex would be a bad idea. I'd paid too much attention to him already. If he threw me a bone, there would be no going back for me. Obsession could be managed much easier than addiction. I knew Adam could easily become an addiction, one that I wouldn't be able to handle.

I'd watched him leave the bar with over a dozen different women, but none of them were ever repeats. A few had approached our table, hoping for seconds, but he'd completely ignored them. To sum it up, Adam would use me once and toss me aside with no chance for seconds. He wasn't exactly the best guy to form an addiction for.

I forced my thoughts away from Adam and back to Chloe. During our time in Charleston, she had seemed withdrawn and sad. I'd even heard her crying in her room the first night we stayed with my parents. My mom had been in there with her, but neither of them wouldn't tell me what was going on. Logan had stayed back in Morgantown to work over break, so I wondered if maybe that was the reason for her sudden depression.

"Want to tell me what that was about?"

"What was what about?" Chloe asked.

I rolled my eyes as I turned my attention back to the road. "Don't play me, Chloe. I heard what Mom said, and I know you were crying that first night, and she was in your room with you, so spill."

She bit her lip, an obvious sign that something was bothering her. It hurt that she hadn't come to me first with whatever it was.

"My mom is trying to find me. She came to your house a while back, searching for me. It wasn't exactly a happy occasion from what your mom told me."

"Why didn't you tell me? What did she want?" I asked as I tightly gripped the steering wheel.

Anytime Chloe's mom came around, things would end badly. She'd mentally and physically abused Chloe for years before finally disappearing from her life. That was when Chloe had moved in with me. I hated her mom more than anyone else in this world. The things she'd said and done to Chloe were inexcusable, especially coming from a parent.

"I have no idea. She wouldn't tell your parents. She just wanted to know where I was. We didn't tell you because I know how you worry when it comes to her."

I sighed. "You're right. I do worry about you when it comes to that crazy bitch after everything she put you through. But that doesn't mean I don't want to know what's happening with you. You know I care about you, right?"

"Yeah, I know. I'm sorry I didn't tell you. I just didn't want to bother you with it."

"Chloe, you're such a dummy. You can bother me with anything—except your sex life with Logan. I draw the line there."

She laughed as I merged onto the interstate.

"You mean, my nonexistent sex life with Logan."

My head spun around in her direction. "*What?* You mean, you two haven't done the deed yet?"

They'd been official for a few weeks now. The way Logan looked at her—well, I'd assumed that they'd had sex about two-point-five seconds after they made it official.

"No, we have, but it was when we got together. We haven't done anything since. It just doesn't feel right."

"How can sex with Logan not feel right? He's my friend, but I'm not afraid to say that he's smoking hot. I bet he's great in bed! Is he? Tell me! Oh, wait, don't tell me. Ah, I have to know."

She laughed as I fought with myself. "You done yet?"

I giggled. "I can't help it! I want to know, but then he's my friend, too, so I don't want to know. Oh, I give up! Just spill it already!"

"It was…it was nice."

I raised an eyebrow. "Just *nice*? Oh shit, he's bad in bed, isn't he?"

She shook her head. "No, he's not bad, honest."

I stayed silent for a minute, milling over what she'd just told me. Something wasn't adding up.

"Chloe, is everything okay with you guys? You barely mentioned him over break, and you seem less than enthused with this conversation."

"We're fine. But that's the problem. Everything about him is just fine. I love him, but I don't know if I share his feelings or if I'm mistaking friendship for something more because that's what I'm supposed to do."

"Don't you think you should have figured that out before you decided to get into a relationship with him? Actually, I distinctly remember telling you to get your shit together."

"Yeah, I know. I'm a dumbass. Point made," Chloe said, her voice trembling.

I gave her a sympathetic smile. "Sorry, but you've got to figure this out. It's not fair to string him along like this if you aren't sure."

Chloe groaned and sank further back into her seat. "Trust me, I know. You have no idea how much I know."

We made it back to Morgantown in record time, mostly due to my crazy driving. I'd wanted to make sure we made it back in time for the show. I'd laughed as people blew their horns at us. Chloe had repeatedly asked me what the hell was wrong with me, but I'd just laughed and continued my NASCAR driving.

I stepped out of the car and opened the trunk to start pulling our bags out.

"What. The. Hell?" Chloe yelled.

I threw her bags at her and grinned. "What's your problem?"

"My...wha—*you tried to kill us!*" she screeched.

"You're such a baby! I was just trying to make it back in time for Drake's show with the guys. Since you're off, you can go, too! You haven't been to one in forever!"

A look of horror crossed Chloe's face. "Um...I can't. I have to go pick up my work schedule and put away all this stuff."

I rolled my eyes as we walked inside our dorm. "You can do that tomorrow. Tonight, we party! Let's meet down here in two hours, and I will hunt you down if you try to get out of it!"

There was no way I was going to give her a chance to get out of tonight, so I turned and walked down the hallway to my room. No matter what had been bothering her, I would make sure she had a blast tonight.

I made it to the entrance before Chloe did. I'd been waiting for almost ten minutes when she finally decided to make an appearance.

"It's about damn ti—whoa! Holy shit, Chloe, you look amazing!" I said when I caught sight of her.

She was wearing a little black dress that left very little to the imagination. It was so very…un-Chloe-like that my mouth dropped open in surprise.

She glanced down at my super short miniskirt and ripped stockings. "You don't look too bad yourself. You ready?"

We chatted all the way to the bar, both of us full of nervous energy.

"What's got you so wound up tonight, Amber? Let me guess. Does it start with an *A* and end with an *M*?" Chloe finally asked.

I giggled like I was fifteen, unable to stop myself. "Shut up! It does not. Well, maybe a little bit. Do you think he'll notice me in this outfit?"

She gave me a bewildered look. "Are you kidding me? Every male in the whole damn place will be begging at your feet. He'd have to be blind not to notice those legs."

I smiled. "I hope so. He's barely even glanced my way." At this point, I was starting to feel desperate for his attention—hence, the super slutty outfit tonight.

"Amber, I'm only saying this because I love you. I have no doubt he will notice you, but he's not the type to stick with one girl. I just don't want you to get your hopes up for something that is pretty much impossible."

I snorted as I pulled the car into the parking lot and maneuvered into a space far too small. "You think I don't know that? I don't want to marry the guy. Have some fun? Sure, why not? I'm done with relationships for a while. I just want to have a good time!"

I hoped that was all this was. Maybe if I had him, even once, it would be enough.

"All right then. That changes things. Go get him!" Chloe said as we climbed from my car.

We linked arms and giggled as we made our way into the bar. Heads turned as soon as we walked in, and I felt a smug grin curve my lips. Breaking the Hunger was already playing as we made our way to our usual table. Despite our absence the last couple of weeks during break, it was still empty, waiting on us. The heat of a hundred male stares engulfed my body as I took a seat and looked up at the band playing onstage. I just hoped Adam would notice me for once.

I felt my heart constrict at the sight of Adam. He was wearing nothing but a pair of faded blue jeans. I never once saw him perform with his shirt on. No matter how many times I saw him, my body still responded like it was the first time. He did things to me that even I didn't understand. I could only imagine what it would feel like if he actually gave me the time of day.

Drake finished out the final line of the song with a scream before opening his eyes and smiling at the crowd. "All right, guys, one more song, and you get to pick. Tell me what you want!"

The crowd went wild as people began shouting song titles up at him. I looked up when Chloe suddenly stood and walked to the front of the stage. Drake's eyes instantly snapped to her. Even I could feel the heat from his gaze as he took in her outfit for the night.

"I have a request!" Chloe shouted over the crowd, who had quieted slightly when they noticed the looks Drake was giving her.

He walked over and leaned down until they were eye level. "And what would that be?"

Chloe gave him her sweetest smile. My stomach dropped. This wasn't going to end well.

"'Gentleman' by Theory of a Deadman. You know that one, right?"

His eyebrows disappeared into his hair as the women in the crowd started whistling. I wanted to drop my head down onto the table. She couldn't be serious. What the fuck was going on with them? And why hadn't I thought to text Logan and ask him to come with us?

"Sure do. I'm a pro at it." He walked back to the center of the stage and motioned for the band to start.

Chloe sat back down next to me, a mischievous grin on her face. As Drake sang, he constantly glanced at our table with a defeated look on his face. I almost felt sorry for him.

The band finished their set and made their way to our table, fighting women as they went.

When Drake neared Chloe, he leaned down and whispered in her ear, "You think you're hilarious, don't you?"

She grinned and gave him a look of complete innocence. "I have no idea what you're talking about."

He chuckled as he sat down across from me. "I'm sure you don't."

I almost opened my mouth to ask what the hell was going on, but I was distracted when Adam sat down next to me. I instantly wanted to groan when I realized he was wearing a shirt.

Unlike every other time he'd sat with me, he finally turned to look at me. "Amber, right?"

"Yeah, and you're Eric?" I asked as I fought not to squeal. It was about damn time he noticed me. I wasn't going to make this easy for him.

Eric, who had just sat down next to Jade and Drake, choked on his beer. "Dude, you just got burned. You've been sitting at the same table as her, drooling in her lap for months, and she doesn't even know your name!"

Drooling over me for months? Doubtful.

Adam flipped Eric off. He turned back to me and smiled. "Nah, that douche over there is Eric. I'm Adam."

I gave him the fakest embarrassed smile I could manage. "Whoops. Sorry, Adam."

"It's all right. Let me buy you a beer?" he asked.

I nodded as he motioned for the waitress to bring a round over to our table. Since we were with the band, the waitress appeared in front of us almost instantly. Adam opened his mouth to say something, but he was cut off when Drake growled like a caged animal. I looked up to see a stranger sitting down next to Chloe.

"Hey, I'm Chris," the guy said as he stared at Chloe.

She gave him a small smile. "Hi, Chris. I'm Chloe."

The guy was attractive, but something about him bothered me. I couldn't put my finger on it. His hair was a light brown, and he had amazing green eyes. He was built with muscles bulging out of his tight white shirt.

"Can I buy you a drink?"

Chloe shook her head and held up the half-empty bottle in her hand. "No, thanks. I'm good."

"Come on, that one's almost empty. Just one."

Before Chloe could speak, Drake broke into the conversation. "She said no, buddy. Why don't you take the hint and go back to your table?"

Chris glared at Drake. "I don't remember asking for your opinion, *buddy.*"

"Well, you got it. Move along."

Chris glanced back at Chloe. "You with this asshole?"

She shook her head. "No, definitely not."

Chris turned to give Drake a smug smile. "Looks like you don't have a say then."

Drake clenched his fist on the table before pointing to the door. "You need to leave—now. Or I'm going to help you leave."

Chris laughed as he threw his arm around Chloe's shoulders. "I'd like to see you try."

Everyone at the table was deathly quiet as Drake stood so fast that he knocked over his chair.

Chloe quickly removed herself out from underneath Chris's arm. "Guys, chill out. Drake, sit back down. Chris, thank you for the offer but no thanks. I have a boyfriend who isn't him." She pointed at Drake, who was still standing and shooting murderous glares across the table at the guy.

Chris frowned but stood to leave. "That's too bad. I'll be over there if you change your mind." He gave Drake one last glare as he walked back to his table.

"Asshole," Drake muttered as he picked his chair up and sat back down.

Everyone was staring at him as Eric started laughing hysterically. "I have seen it all. Drake Allen just took up for a girl."

Chloe rolled her eyes as everyone started laughing with Eric. "Shush. And you"—she turned her gaze to Drake—"I don't need you to take up for me. I can fight my own battles."

His eyes turned hard. "Sure you can. Sorry, it won't happen again."

I couldn't stop looking back and forth between the two of them. *Oh shit.* Drake was in love with Chloe. I could see it in his eyes. I looked back at Chloe, and the look on her face made me think she knew it, too.

"Those two need to get laid," Adam mumbled under his breath.

I glanced over to see him watching Chloe and Drake as well.

"As long as it's not with each other, I'm cool with it," I said.

He turned so that he was looking at me. He flashed me a smile that set my body on fire. I stared at him, taking in every little detail. *God, he was perfect.*

"So, Amber, tell me more about yourself."

I grinned. "Do you really care?"

He scooted closer to me. "I've been watching you for over three months, but I know nothing about you. Call me curious."

I leaned closer to him. "There's nothing interesting about me. I'm sure you have more on your mind than my birthday, my favorite color, and what classes I'm taking."

I rested my hand on his upper thigh, catching myself by surprise. I'd wanted to touch him for months, and now that I had even a little bit of his attention, I couldn't help myself. His breath hitched as my hand slid higher up his leg. My hand would have been shaking from nerves if it hadn't been resting against him.

Adam's eyes flashed to Chloe and Drake before returning to me. "I don't fuck my friends' friends anymore. It always turns out bad."

I grinned, my pulse racing, as I stared into his eyes. I wanted this man more than anything else. "Do I look like I'm the type to cause problems?" I asked.

"No, but you look like a fucking angel. That's almost just as bad." He rested his hand on top of mine.

I almost groaned at the skin-on-skin contact.

I jumped when Chloe poked me in the ribs and motioned to the door. "You ready?"

I glanced back and forth between Adam and Chloe. "Actually, I was going to hang out here with Adam for a little longer." I pulled my keys out of my purse and handed them to her. "Take my car. I'll catch a ride back with someone."

Chloe looked back and forth between Adam and me before winking. I watched as she told everyone good-bye and left. As soon as she disappeared, Drake stood.

"I'm out of here," he said without looking at any of us. He stormed to the door and disappeared.

I hoped he wasn't trying to stop Chloe.

"I'm tired, too. You ready to head home, Jade?" Eric asked.

I'd only recently learned that those two lived together. I'd assumed they were a couple, but Jade had laughed it off.

"Yep. We'll see you guys later," Jade said, flashing a smile at Adam and me.

"Guess we know how to clear a room," I joked.

Adam turned his attention back to me. He studied me so intently that I shifted uncomfortably in my seat.

"Why do you keep staring at me?" I finally asked.

He shrugged. "I'm just trying to figure you out."

"I hate to break it to you, but I'm not exactly a mystery." I removed my hand from underneath his.

"Oh, I think you are." He paused for a moment. "I can't figure out your end game. Most women want me because they think I'm the key to getting close to the band. Thanks to whatever fucked-up relationship Chloe and Drake have, you're already in."

I frowned. "If you know those women are only using you, why do you let them?"

"Why wouldn't I? They get their five minutes with the band, and I get laid."

I had never expected this part of Adam. I'd seen him for what I thought he was—a wild, sex-crazed guitarist who only wanted women for sex. I'd never really thought about the way other women saw him. It made me sad to think about the way others used him.

"I never expected to have this type of conversation with you," I said after a minute of silence.

He grinned. "I don't usually talk this much. I'm no good at conversation, but I'm very good at other things."

"I can only imagine," I mumbled.

He leaned closer until our lips were almost touching. "What do you want from me? Besides a fuck, of course."

"Who said I wanted to fuck you?" I teased.

"I can see it in your eyes and the way your lips part when you stare at me. I know women, Amber."

"So, maybe I do," I said, my eyes darting to his lips. I wanted him to kiss me right here for the world to see.

"But what else do you want?"

"Nothing," I said, surprised when I realized the statement was true. I didn't want a thing from him other than sex. This man was under my skin already without even trying. I knew I'd never find relief unless I had a taste of him.

"Nothing," he echoed, his eyes never leaving mine.

I jumped when he suddenly pushed his chair back and stood. I gave him a questioning look, but instead of speaking, he held out his hand. I took it without a second thought and let him lead me to the door.

Once we were outside, he led me across the lot to an older model Ford Escort. It wasn't a dream car by any means, but I hadn't picked him because of the car he drove.

"Where are we going?" I finally asked as he unlocked his car.

"My place." He paused. "Unless you'd rather sneak me into your dorm room."

I thought of my super boring roommate, Eva, and shook my head. She'd shit herself if I brought a guy home. "Let's go to your place."

He opened his door and climbed behind the wheel. I hurried to open my door, and then I slid down into the passenger seat. The car rumbled as it started, the sound so loud that I felt my body vibrate as he pressed on the gas.

He tore out of the parking spot and hit the main road, going faster than even I drove. I stayed silent as we drove across town to an older apartment building. After pulling into a parking spot, Adam shut off the car. I stared up at the three-story brick building next to us.

"This is where you live?" I asked.

"Yeah. It's not much, but it's home."

We climbed out of the car and walked to the building. I grinned when Adam held the door open for me.

"Look at you, acting like a gentleman," I said as I walked past him into the lobby of the building.

"Don't get used to it," he mumbled as we climbed a set of stairs. "I have no intention of being a gentleman to you for the rest of the night."

We stopped on the second floor. The hallway was dimly lit, but I could make out the dark carpet beneath our feet. Adam stopped in front of the second door in the hallway and shoved his key in the door. He stepped in and flipped on a light. I followed closely behind him, curious to see where he lived.

I looked around his apartment. It was obvious that a single guy lived here. The walls were bare with the exception of a flat screen television mounted against the far wall. The living room had an older gray couch and matching chair, but that was all. The kitchen opened up behind the couch. White appliances, older-styled countertops, and a sink full of dishes made up the kitchen. A tiny table sat in the center, only big enough to fit one or two people.

Before I had a chance to look around further, Adam grabbed me and pushed me up against the wall. I sucked in a surprised breath as his lips crushed mine. I moaned as every part of my body came alive.

I'd imagined Adam's kiss a thousand times, but I'd never once done him justice. The power, the sheer force of his kiss, stopped me in my tracks. I tasted cigarettes along with a hint of beer on his breath. On anyone else, the taste would have been revolting. On him, it only added to his appeal. I tasted raw need as our tongues tangled together.

He pulled away briefly, his expression turning serious. "No expectations?"

"No expectations," I mumbled.

"Just wanted to make sure that we were both on the same page."

He shoved his body closer against mine. His hard length pressed against me, and any rational thought about what we were going to do left me. I wrapped my arms around his neck, my nails digging into his back. He grabbed one of my legs and lifted it to wrap around his waist. I wrapped my other leg around him without a second thought. His hands slipped under my short skirt and cupped my ass as he pulled us away from the door. I kissed him deeply as he carried me through his apartment. When we reached his bedroom, he dropped me down onto the bed. His hands found my top and pulled it over my head before I could blink.

I stared up at him, wearing only my short skirt, ripped stockings, and a black lacy bra. I thought about covering myself, but the look in his eyes stopped me. Raw hunger. He wanted me more than I had realized.

"Fuckin' hell, woman. You're sitting there like a fucking dream." His eyes scanned my body.

I stood and gripped the bottom of his shirt. I lifted it up inch by inch until the hard planes of his chest and stomach were revealed to me. He grabbed the shirt from my hands and pulled it over his head. He tossed it across the room before his hands moved to his pants. I watched with rapt attention as he unzipped them and shoved them over his hips. They dropped to the floor, and he kicked them aside.

My eyes trailed downward, taking in every dip and plane of his body. He was still wearing a pair of black boxers, and his hard cock was barely contained by the thin fabric. I reached out and ran my fingers along the skin above his boxers. He shivered, a look of longing crossing his face. I gripped the fabric and slowly pulled it down.

His erection sprang free, jutting from his body. I raised an eyebrow, impressed with his size. Next to him, Chad and Alex looked like little boys. I hoped he would be gentle at first, or sex with him would hurt like a bitch. I swallowed roughly as I stared at it. I reached out and ran my fingertips across the smooth skin. He shuddered, his hands balling up into tight fists.

"Suck me," he commanded, his voice rough, as he fought for control.

I sank down onto my knees in front of him, a smile creeping onto my face from the mere thought of tasting him. I grasped him, my hand sliding up and down his shaft. He groaned and thrust his hips forward. I leaned forward, and his breath caught as I took him into my mouth. I closed my eyes as the tip of his cock touched the back of my throat. I sucked as I slowly slid him back out until only his tip was still in my mouth. I rolled my tongue over the tip, tasting his pre-cum. It only spurred on my need for him. I started moving my mouth back and forth as I reached up and grabbed him. I squeezed tightly, causing him to thrust his hips forward. His fingers found my hair and pulled roughly. Instead of pain, it only brought me pleasure.

His hips started moving as he fucked my mouth. That alone was enough to wet my panties with need. I opened my eyes and glanced up at him. His eyes were shut, and his chin was resting on his chest as he let me devour him. Lines creased his forehead as he focused on what my mouth and hand were doing to him.

God, he's beautiful.

Suddenly, he pulled away. I shrieked in surprise when he grabbed me and pulled me until I was standing in front of him. His fingers found the zipper on my skirt. Without a word, he unzipped it and shoved it down my legs.

"I hope you have more of these," he mumbled before grabbing the thin scrap of lace that I was passing off for underwear.

My eyes widened as he ripped them away from my body and dropped them onto the floor. I reached back and undid the clasps on my bra. I pulled it free and dropped it on the floor next to my skirt.

"I'm going to fuck you hard," Adam said as he picked me up and dropped me onto the bed.

He opened the drawer in his nightstand and pulled out a condom. He ripped it open and slid it over his shaft.

"If I don't fuck you in the next five seconds, I'm going to lose my fucking mind." He looked down at me. "Roll onto your stomach."

I did as he'd said, conscious of the fact that he would have a perfect view of my ass. I jerked in surprise when his hands wrapped around my waist and lifted me up. He pulled me back to the end of the bed. I closed my eyes when I felt the tip of his cock touch my entrance.

"Hope you're ready for me, baby. I wanted this to last, but I can't wait any longer."

He pressed forward and entered me in one swift move. My hands balled up into fists as he filled me. While it didn't hurt as I'd feared, my body felt overly full. I felt my internal muscles stretching, desperate to accommodate his size.

He groaned and stilled, giving me time to get used to him. "You're tight, babe."

I nodded, unsure of whether he saw me or not. I didn't really care. All I wanted was for him to fuck me.

He pulled back and thrust into me again. "Fuck yes."

I closed my eyes as he began to pound into me from behind. He was rough, rougher than I'd ever experienced, but he wasn't hurting me. Instead, I felt my body come alive. As he pushed into me, I shoved my hips back, desperate for him to go deeper. I winced in pain when he went too far, but the pain sent a jolt of ecstasy through my system. The pain mixed with pleasure was almost unbearable in the sweetest way.

My breath came out in gasps as pure need took over. He increased his tempo until I felt myself moving forward on the bed. He grabbed my hips and pulled me back against him.

"You're fucking perfect," Adam said, his voice a low growl.

"Faster," I gasped out.

"Anything you want, babe."

He pumped into me, both of us moaning in unison. Sex with him was better than I could have ever imagined. My body hummed as I felt myself building. I was on the brink of orgasm when he released my hips. His fingers found my clit. He flicked it, and I shouted his name as my body shuddered. My orgasm took over, and I dropped my head onto the bed as wave after wave of pleasure engulfed me. I heard him grunt as he came. He ground his hips against my ass as he released.

When he pulled out, I almost begged him not to. I suddenly felt empty, almost hollow without him. He kissed my shoulder before moving away. I rolled onto my back and watched as he pulled the condom off and tossed it into the trash next to the bed.

He dropped down onto the bed next to me, still naked. My eyes trailed down his body. I was still unable to believe that after all these months, I'd finally had him. Unfortunately, my hopes of fucking him and forgetting him were destroyed. I knew once wouldn't be enough. Already, my body was craving him again.

"That was awesome," I said, my voice breaking the sudden silence of his bedroom.

He chuckled. "Did you expect anything else?"

I shook my head. "I had no idea."

He shoved me, his hand lingering on my hip. "Asshole."

I laughed. "I don't want to inflate your ego any more than it already is."

He rolled over so that he was facing me. "You're crushing my ego more than anything else right now."

"Somehow, I think you'll survive."

He grinned. "I had more planned, but then you started sucking me with that mouth of yours, and I couldn't hold back. I wanted a taste of you, too."

"Too bad you're a one-time deal," I said quietly.

He frowned. "What makes you think I'm a one-time-only kind of guy?"

I shrugged, pretending not to care. "I've never seen you with the same woman twice."

He paused, an almost thoughtful look on his face. "Normally, I'm not, but I'm not quite finished with you yet."

"What if I'm finished with you?" I asked.

He nuzzled my neck, his breath tickling my skin as he spoke, "Then, I'll just have to change your mind."

I sat up and rested my back against the headboard. "What do you have in mind?"

He sat up, too. "I think we could go a few more rounds tonight at least."

I grinned. "You sure you're up to that?"

"Never doubt my ability to fuck you multiple times."

"Wouldn't dream of it," I said just before he leaned over to kiss me.

Over the next few hours, he proved just how many times he could fuck me, and I loved every minute of it.

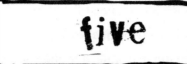

five

By the time morning rolled around, I was exhausted. Adam had proven just how insatiable he was when it came to sex.

"I need sleep," I mumbled as he pulled the covers up over us.

"Then, sleep," he said.

I glanced at the clock on the nightstand. My eyes widened when I realized it was almost seven in the morning. "I need to head back to my dorm."

"Why? You got plans?"

I shook my head. "No, but I think I've overstayed my welcome."

He wrapped his arm around me. "Shut up, and sleep, woman. I'm exhausted."

"Can't imagine why," I mumbled.

"Hush."

"You sure this is okay?"

He sighed. "What are you talking about?"

"The whole no-expectations thing. Cuddling and sleeping in together is more than just sex."

He rolled his eyes. "I usually fuck a chick and then kick her ass out my door. You spent the entire night with me, which is more than anyone gets. I doubt if sleeping for a few hours is going to cause any confusion. Now, *sleep*."

I slept.

When I opened my eyes, the clock said it was after four. I glanced out the one window in his room. It was daylight out. *Thank God.* I slowly moved Adam's arm off me and climbed from the bed. I was in desperate need of the bathroom before my bladder exploded.

I slipped from the room and walked to the bathroom. It was directly across the hall from his bedroom. After relieving myself, I washed my hands and glanced in the mirror. I barely recognized myself. My hair was sticking out everywhere. I ran my fingers through it, trying to tame it. I knew it was a lost cause. I splashed water on my face and scrubbed, trying to get rid of the black smudges of my makeup.

Once I passed for kind of presentable, I snuck back into his bedroom and picked my skirt up off the floor. I looked longingly at my destroyed underwear as I pulled my skirt over my hips. I put my bra on before hunting for my top. I spotted it on the floor a few feet away from the bed and picked it up before slipping it over my head.

When I glanced back at the bed, Adam was watching me.

"Hey," I said quietly. "Didn't mean to wake you."

He stretched, the blanket falling to his waist. "No biggie."

I shifted my weight from foot to foot. "I'm just going to go." *This is awkward as fuck.*

"All right. I'll see you later then. Thanks for last night, Amber. Best night I've had in a long time."

I gave him one last smile before walking to the front of his apartment, picking up my shoes as I went. They must have fallen off last night when he'd carried me back to his bedroom.

"Hey," Adam called from behind me.

I turned to see him standing in the hallway outside his bedroom. My eyes scanned his naked form without an ounce of regret. I'd never see him like this again. My one night of glory was up. As soon as I walked out of this apartment, I'd become a distant memory.

"Yeah?"

"How are you getting home?"

"I'm going to call Chloe to see if she can pick me up. If not, I'll walk."

"I can take you home if you need me to. Just let me get dressed."

"You don't have to do that," I mumbled, but he'd already disappeared back into his bedroom.

I sighed. Adam was nothing like I'd expected. I'd watched him for months, but it hadn't prepared me at all. I'd thought he was easy to figure out. I'd seen him act like a typical playboy, never once showing any real kindness to the women surrounding him. Being with him one-on-one was an eye-opener. While he was still rough around the edges, I'd seen a more compassionate side to him. I wasn't sure if that made my need for him worse or not.

I knew one thing. I was sad to leave him. That bothered me more than I was willing to admit. This was supposed to be simple—fuck him and leave him. It was supposed to be even easier than my deal with Alex, but it wasn't.

I sucked in a sharp breath when it hit me. I had a crush on Adam.

No, no, no, no!

Feelings weren't a part of this. They had no place here. Yet, once the realization had hit me, I knew it was true. I felt more than just lust for Adam.

"Ready?" Adam asked.

I jumped when I heard his voice. He was standing a few feet away, giving me a quizzical look. I hadn't even noticed him coming out of his bedroom or walking down the hallway.

"Yeah, sure," I said. My voice sounded almost hysterical to my ears, but if he'd noticed, he didn't say anything.

"Let's go then." Adam grabbed his keys off the hook next to the door.

I followed him out of his apartment and down to where his car was parked. We climbed in, and he shoved his keys into the ignition. I jumped again when it started, the deep rumbling causing my bones to vibrate.

Adam glanced in his mirror before pulling out. I kept my eyes straight ahead, terrified to look at him. If he knew what I was thinking, he'd stop the car and dump me out on my ass. He'd never speak to me again, and I wouldn't blame him. We had an agreement, and I wasn't following it.

No expectations. That was supposed to be a simple rule to follow. How had I fucked it up so easily? Why hadn't I realized that my interest in him was something more than I'd expected? I was so stupid. Getting attached to someone like Adam was emotional suicide. He didn't do relationships or feelings. I was sure I knew the fate of anyone who had tried since he never once mentioned ever having a girlfriend over the past few months.

"I don't think I've ever heard you this quiet," Adam mumbled as we drove through Morgantown.

I glanced over at him. "What?"

"You're quiet. That isn't normal."

"How do you know what my normal is? You don't even know me," I pointed out.

"You've been to every show since Chloe started bringing you around. I've sat at the same table as you. You talk constantly."

"I didn't even think you noticed me before last night."

"I've watched you since that first night. As soon as I walked onstage, I saw you. I couldn't seem to keep away even if I didn't talk to you." His fingers tightened around the steering wheel as if what he'd just said took a lot of physical effort on his part.

"Then, why didn't you talk to me?" I asked softly.

"Because you were off-limits. I told you before, I don't fuck my friends' friends. It always ends badly."

"It didn't end badly with us," I joked.

He shrugged. "Not yet."

"I'm not going to start acting clingy. I'm not that type of girl." I had no intention of trying to force myself onto Adam, no matter how badly I wanted him. I wasn't that pathetic.

He glanced over at me. "I realize that now. I just don't want shit to be awkward."

I laughed. "It won't be, I promise. I'm still going to hang around with you guys, but as far as I'm concerned, last night never happened. I don't want an awkward situation any more than you do."

He was quiet for a moment. "You know, I think you're damn near perfect, Amber. We might even end up being friends."

"Maybe," I said as we pulled up outside my dorm. "Well, thanks for the ride."

"Which one?" he asked, a wicked grin on his face.

"All of them," I said as I opened the car door and stepped out.

"I'll see you around," Adam said just before I shut the door.

I waved at him before turning and walking toward the entrance to my dorm. It took everything in me not to turn around to look at him one last time. Once I was inside, I caved and peeked over my shoulder. His car was still idling outside. His eyes locked with mine for a split second before he looked away and hit the gas. His tires squealed as he disappeared around the corner.

I stared out the door for a moment longer before turning and heading for my room. Once inside, I took a deep breath to settle my nerves. As I grabbed my bathroom bag and a change of clothes from my closet, I promised myself that I wouldn't spend another moment thinking about Adam. He was unattainable, and I knew that. It would do me no good to think about him. We had spent the night together, and that was the end of it. It was no different from my nights with Alex.

I could forget about Adam. I had to.

After tossing and turning for most of the night, I climbed out of bed at the ass-crack of dawn. I'd never been a morning person. The worst part was that I was up early on a weekend. That should be illegal in all fifty states.

I pulled my hair up into a messy bun and pulled on a pair of jeans and a long-sleeved T-shirt. I decided to go without makeup. For me, that was the equivalent of someone walking around in public wearing only underwear.

I debated on texting Chloe to see if she wanted to go out for breakfast, but I decided not to. It was still early, and I didn't want to bug her if she was with Logan. I frowned. Once again, I was stepping away from my friends, so they could have a relationship, and I knew it would only get worse if things continued to progress with them. I almost wished things would go back to the way they used to be. I hated myself for even thinking that way. Chloe and Logan were my best friends. They deserved happiness, especially with each other.

My stomach rumbled, pulling me from my thoughts. The only thing I'd eaten yesterday was a granola bar after I came back from Adam's apartment, and my body was demanding food. I grabbed my keys off the dresser and headed out the door. Pancakes sounded like heaven, so I headed for IHOP. It was clear across town, but it didn't matter. I had no plans for the day.

I smiled when I pulled into the parking lot. There were perks to waking up early. The lot was almost completely empty. I stifled a yawn as I opened the door and stepped inside. The hostess seated me immediately. I scanned the menu, debating on which pancakes sounded the best.

"Following me around like a stalker already? I thought we had an understanding."

I jerked my head up to see Adam standing next to my table. "Adam? What are you doing here?"

"Probably the same thing you are. I want breakfast." He slid into the booth across from me.

"Oh," I said just as a waitress stopped next to my table.

"Do you need another menu?" she asked, eyeing Adam in a way that made me want to scratch her eyeballs out.

"Nah, I know what I want," Adam said.

My gaze flickered to him. He was watching me in a way that said he wasn't talking about food. I automatically clenched my legs together, remembering our night together.

"What do you want?" the waitress asked, suddenly annoyed.

Maybe she noticed the eye-fucking going on between Adam and me.

"Regular pancakes, bacon, and scrambled eggs," Adam said, his gaze never leaving mine.

"To drink?"

"Coffee."

"And for you?" she asked me.

"The same," I said as I tore my eyes away from Adam.

"Great. I'll put your order in right away."

She grabbed my menu from my hands and walked away. I watched until she disappeared around the corner, desperate to look at anything besides Adam.

"So, why are you up so early?" Adam asked, forcing me to look up at him.

While I felt like one big ball of nerves, he was sitting across from me, completely relaxed. I wanted to kick him for being so calm and collected.

"Couldn't sleep," I mumbled. "You?"

"I have to work."

"On a Sunday?"

He nodded. "Yeah. I help my uncle run a gas station about a mile from here. Since I'm usually out late, he generally puts me on the afternoon shift. Sundays are the exception though."

"I didn't even know you had a job," I said, feeling like an idiot.

He laughed. "Well, I have to pay rent somehow. The money from our shows at Gold's helps, but it isn't enough."

"I never really thought about you having a life outside of the bar," I admitted. "Are you in school, too? I haven't seen you around campus."

He shook his head. "Nah, school isn't for me. I barely managed to graduate high school on time. I used to skip constantly. The thought of signing up for four years of hell just so I can have a piece of paper to show the world how smart I am really doesn't interest me. Besides, I don't want to end up with a shit-ton of student loan debt."

"My mom and dad pretty much told me I was going to college whether I wanted to or not. I didn't have a choice, but I think I still would've gone even if they had let me decide."

"Why?" he asked.

I gave him a tiny smile. "My parents have really nice jobs—a doctor and a lawyer. I grew up with nice things, and I really don't feel like changing my lifestyle all that much. I don't want the responsibilities they have, but I do want to be able to afford a nice house one day."

"If you aren't going to follow in their footsteps, what do you plan on doing?"

I shrugged. "Still undecided, but I'm leaning toward being a paralegal."

"Sounds fancy," he mumbled.

"Not really. I'd work at a law firm, but I wouldn't be included in all the political bullshit that my dad has to deal with."

I couldn't believe I was sitting here, telling Adam about my hopes for the future. I was even more surprised that he'd given me a few small tidbits of information about his life. For some reason, I'd never given any thought to what he did when he wasn't with the band.

"So, you said you work with your uncle?"

He nodded.

"What do your parents think about you working with him?"

I saw anger flash in his eyes, but it was gone a moment later.

"My parents couldn't care less if I was alive or dead. I doubt if it bothers them that their only son is working at a gas station."

If it hadn't been for Chloe's twisted relationship with her mother, I would've frozen in shock at his words. While I had two parents who really loved me, I'd seen the ugly side of Chloe's fucked-up life. I'd sat with her when she would come to my house beaten and bleeding. I'd listened to the things her mother said to her when she bothered to call her only child. So, no, Adam's words hadn't shocked me the way they should have. I was pretty sure I'd seen it all already. Nothing he might say about his parents would shock me.

"I don't speak from personal experience, but I've seen how screwed-up parents can be. It's too bad that yours suck."

He paused, obviously caught off guard. He probably thought I'd try to apologize for whatever they had done to him and then try to make him feel better. In situations like this, there was nothing I or anyone else could say to make things right. Sometimes, fucked-up situations stayed that way.

Finally, he gave me a small grin. "They do suck, but I'm over it. I've been on my own since I was eighteen. Well, that's not entirely true. My uncle helped me after they kicked me out on my ass with nothing more than a suitcase full of clothes and my guitar. He gave me a job and helped me find a place to live."

"How long has it been since you talked to them?"

"Three years."

"So, you're twenty-one?"

He nodded.

"Have you tried to contact them at all?"

He shook his head. "Nope. If they want to find me, all they have to do is talk to my uncle. Until then, I'm fine with how things are. I don't need them."

Our waitress appeared, her arms full of plates. We fell silent as she put everything down on the table in front of us.

"Do you need anything else?" she asked.

"We're good." I picked up my fork and dug into my pancakes.

When Adam chuckled, I looked up.

"What's so funny?"

He shook his head. "I just told you more about me than I've ever told another chick—well, except for Jade, but she doesn't count as a girl. She's a band member."

"I'm glad you told me. I would be lying if I said I wasn't curious about you."

He raised an eyebrow. "There's nothing to be curious about when it comes to me. What you see is what you get."

Somehow, I doubted that, but I kept my opinion to myself.

We finished breakfast in silence. I didn't mind though. It wasn't that awkward silence where I felt like I was drowning. Instead, it was peaceful.

"I should probably head to work," Adam said after finishing his coffee.

"I guess I'll see you later," I said as I watched him stand.

He threw a few dollars down on the table to cover his bill before walking away. I didn't dare turn around to watch him leave. I stared at the spot he'd just left, wondering what the hell had just happened between us. For a moment, it had seemed as if we were almost…friends. That thought terrified and exhilarated me all at once.

I waited another minute or two to make sure Adam was gone before throwing down a few bills on the table to cover my own meal. I grabbed my wallet and stood. I passed several customers coming in as I made my way to the door. Once outside, I walked to where I'd parked my car.

"Amber!"

I jumped when I heard someone call my name. I looked to my left and saw Adam approaching me.

"Yeah?" I asked, surprised that he hadn't left yet.

He stopped in front of me with an uneasy expression on his face. He ran his hand over his Mohawk, making me smile. He looked absolutely adorable. I'd never thought I would use the words *Adam* and *adorable* together in a sentence, but there it was.

"What are you doing tonight?"

I shrugged. "Nothing that I know of. Why? You guys playing at Gold's?"

He shook his head. "No, no show tonight. Why don't you stop by my place tonight? I get off work at six."

I couldn't hide my surprise. "You want me to come by again?"

For the first time since I'd met him, Adam looked unsure of himself.

"Yeah, I guess I do."

I paused for a moment until I could find my voice again. "All right. I'll be there."

six

I stared up at Adam's apartment building. The entire day, I'd felt nothing but excitement over seeing him again. Now that I was here, doubt started to cloud my mind. Spending more time with him was a bad idea. I knew it, and from the hesitant way he'd acted this morning, he' knew it, too.

Nothing good could come from this. I already knew it wouldn't be cut-and-dried like my relationship with Alex. I'd been attracted to Alex. With Adam, it wasn't quite that simple. Obviously, most of my feelings were derived from carnal needs, but a small part of me was attracted to Adam because of who he was.

When Chad had cheated on me, I'd made a vow to myself to never get tangled up with another man the way I had with him. It just hurt too damn much to have feelings involved. The pain I'd felt with Chad would be nothing compared to what Adam could do to me if I let him. I could tell that much already.

I reached forward and grabbed my key. I started my car, my mind made up. I was going to go back home and forget that I'd been stupid enough to get involved with someone like Adam. I put my car in drive, but I couldn't bring myself to push the gas pedal. I felt like I was being torn in two. A part of me was determined to run away from him as fast as I could, but another part was just as determined to get out of this car and climb the stairs to Adam's apartment.

I put the car back in park and shut it off. I cursed at myself as I climbed out of my car and walked to his building. I knew I'd regret this later. I just knew it. But for now, I was going to take whatever Adam had to offer and pretend I didn't give a damn.

I walked into his building and went up the stairs to the second floor. When I reached his door, I raised my hand to knock. Before I could, the door swung open. My mouth went dry when I caught sight of a shirtless Adam. My eyes dipped lower. He was wearing only a pair of shorts that rode low on his hips. I almost sighed at the sight of that perfect V disappearing into his shorts.

"I wasn't sure if you'd come up or not," Adam said.

I forced my eyes back up to his face. It was harder than I'd thought it would be. "I'm here." It wasn't the most poetic thing I'd ever said, but my mind wasn't fully functional at the moment.

"I saw you park down there about fifteen minutes ago. You almost left." His rich brown eyes stared at me intently.

"But I didn't."

He held the door open wider so that I could pass through. I walked to his couch and dropped my purse onto it. I shivered when I felt Adam step up behind me. He wasn't touching me, but I could feel the heat of his body soaking into my back. I was aware of him like no one else. I stilled as his fingers softly touched my hair. He pushed it back until my neck was visible. He stepped closer so that his body was flush against mine.

"Why didn't you run from me? You wanted to." He dropped tiny kisses along my neck. He pulled my shirt aside, and then he kissed my shoulder as well.

"Maybe I wanted something from you," I whispered.

He paused for a moment before kissing my neck again. "And what would that be?"

I turned until I was facing him. His dark eyes were clouded with desire. I reached up and cupped his face. Without saying a word, I stood on my toes and kissed him. It wasn't as heated as our previous kisses, but it was incredible in its own way. Soft, gentle kisses were just as good as fast and furious ones.

Adam pulled away, his eyes smoldering. "I don't know why I asked you here tonight."

I raised an eyebrow. "I assumed it was because you wanted more sex."

He grinned. "I do. I guess I just don't normally do repeat performances with anyone. But you..." He paused to run his fingers down the side of my face. "You're different. I can't seem to get enough of you."

"I would take that as a compliment if it weren't for the massive frown on your face."

"I don't want shit to get complicated. I know how women work." He dropped his hand.

I winced at the lack of emotion in his voice. It was like a switch had been flipped. Only seconds before, I'd seen a softer side of him. Now, it was gone.

"I'm not asking you for anything," I told him, my voice as flat as his. "I thought we had an understanding."

"We did. We do." He ran his hands through his hair. "If this goes south, Drake will kick my ass."

I rolled my eyes. "Who died and made Drake the boss?"

He grinned, but it faded quickly. "I like you, Amber. I don't want to hurt you. I was serious when I told you that I thought we could be friends."

"There's no chance that you'll hurt me," I lied. "I don't expect anything from you, except sex."

He stared at me for a moment before finally speaking, "All right then. No expectations."

He leaned forward to kiss me, but I stopped him by pressing my fingers to his lips.

"I do have one question though."

"What?" he asked against my fingers.

I pulled them away. "Is this it, or what? I mean, is this the last night we'll be together?"

"Do you want it to be?"

I bit my lip as I thought about how to answer him. "Not really. If you're not opposed to it, I'd like to continue seeing each other."

"Like I'd turn down sex with you," he teased.

"Are we exclusive?" I asked, almost afraid to hear his answer.

His playful manner disappeared, and he was back to studying me. "Exclusive would imply some kind of relationship."

"No, it wouldn't. I've had an…agreement before with someone else."

His gaze turned hard. "What do you mean?"

I swallowed roughly at the dark look in his eyes. "There was a guy I met when I started at WVU. We hooked up at a party. Neither of us wanted a relationship, but we had a good time together. We agreed not to screw around with anyone else while we were together, but we weren't dating or hanging out."

Adam took a step back as if I'd slapped him, his eyes filled with revulsion. "How often do you do shit like that?"

"What the fuck does it matter?" I asked as my temper flared.

What right did *he* have to judge me about who I'd slept with? He'd left the bar with more women than I could count.

"I never took you for a whore. That's part of the reason I thought you were different," he growled.

"Who are you to judge me, Adam? I know you've slept around. I don't look down on you for that!"

"How many?" he asked.

"How many what?"

"How many men have you slept with?" he demanded.

I was going to cry. I could feel tears of anger and embarrassment building behind my eyes. I'd never been looked at the way Adam was looking at me right now—like I was complete trash.

"That's none of your damn business!" I shouted.

I turned away from him and grabbed my purse. I shoved past him and headed for the door. This had turned into an even bigger disaster than I'd expected.

"Where the hell are you going?" he demanded as he grabbed my arm to stop me from leaving.

"I'm going home! Fuck you, Adam. Just fuck you!"

I tried to jerk my arm away from him, but he wouldn't release me.

"How many?"

It came out as nothing more than a whisper, but I stopped struggling. Instead, I looked him in the eye, throwing every ounce of rage I had into my glare.

"Three," I said quietly. "I've slept with three men. I thought I loved one, and he ripped my heart out. I walked in on him fucking someone else. Alex was just for fun because there was no way I would ever open myself up to someone again. And last but not least, you. You are, by far, the biggest mistake of all."

I jerked my arm free and stormed to the door. I didn't glance back as I threw the door open and stormed out into the hallway. Tears began to fall as I ran down the steps and outside to where I'd parked my car.

By the time I made it home, I could barely see. I sat in my car for several minutes, trying to get my tears and my breathing under control.

How dare he!

He'd had no right to judge me. I wasn't perfect, but I sure as hell wasn't a whore.

"Fuck you, Adam. *Fuck you!*" I screamed, not caring if anyone was close enough to my car to hear me.

I was done with Adam, totally and completely done. He could burn in hell for all I cared.

I spent the next two days pretending like nothing was wrong. At least, I tried. My argument with Adam kept running through my mind. Every time I thought about it, I felt angry and hurt. Of all the people in the world, Adam was the last guy I'd ever expected to treat me the way he had. I hated how much that stung.

By Wednesday, I was at my limit. I would even avoid Chloe when she tried to talk to me. I was wallowing in self-pity. I didn't have room for anyone else's problems. Considering the way Chloe had acted with Drake, I knew she was going to end up coming to me with a problem. As pissy as I was, she wouldn't want to hear my advice to her.

I almost screamed in annoyance when someone knocked on my dorm door later that night. Chloe had been called in to work. I'd heard her tell me that much before I ran off this afternoon, so at least I knew it wasn't her. My roommate wasn't around, and I doubted if it was someone looking for her. As far as I could tell, she didn't have many friends. I would feel sorry for her if she wasn't such an annoying pain in the ass.

I opened my door to glare at whoever had disturbed my sulking. My mouth dropped open in shock when I saw Adam standing in the hallway.

"What the hell are you doing here?" I blurted before I could stop myself.

He gave me a small smile, one I would have found endearing a few days before. Now, all it did was annoy me.

"I wanted to talk to you."

"I think we did enough talking the other night. How did you even find out which dorm room was mine?"

He shrugged. "I knew which building, so I came in and asked around. You weren't that hard to find."

He pushed through the door before I could stop him.

I closed the door and turned to glare at him. "I don't remember inviting you in."

"That's because you didn't." He smirked at me.

"Adam, what the fuck do you want? Just say whatever it is you came here to say, and then get out." Yeah, Bitch Amber was in full-on bitch mode tonight. He deserved nothing less.

The smirk slipped from his lips, but instead of answering me, he turned away and looked around my dorm room. I stepped away from the door so that I could watch him.

His gaze landed on my side of the room. "I'm betting this is your side." He glanced over at me.

"What gave it away?" I didn't even try to keep the sarcasm out of my voice.

"Well, the other side is decorated with rap posters, and the lamp is shaped like a unicorn. This side has Seether and Korn posters hanging up, and for some reason, I don't see you collecting unicorn shit."

I shrugged. "I like rock and heavy metal music. That should be pretty obvious, even to someone who barely knows me—like you."

He winced, understanding the double meaning. "Look, I'm sorry for what I said the other night. I had no right."

"Your apology would mean so much more if you weren't apologizing for calling me a whore."

He sighed as he dropped down onto my bed. I pretended not to care that *Adam* was on my bed.

"I knew you weren't going to make this easy."

"Why would I? You sure as hell didn't make Sunday night easy for me."

"Because I was an asshole, and I know it. Look, I don't apologize—ever. So, the fact that I'm here should count for something."

I snorted. "I don't know what you want from me, Adam. You apologized. Great. It doesn't mean anything though. Nothing you say or do can make up for it. You really hurt me."

"I didn't mean to. I was just surprised. I never took you for—"

"What? A whore?" I spit out.

He shook his head. "You're not a goddamn whore. I never thought you were. I was just angry with you, and I said stupid shit because of it. I knew you weren't completely innocent since you slept with me, but I didn't think you'd be one of those women who slept around."

"Sleeping with three guys is sleeping around now? Good to know," I muttered. "How many women have you slept with, Adam? Let's total them up, so we can decide what to classify you as. Obviously, *whore* is too weak of a word when it comes to you. We'll have to get creative."

He stood so abruptly that I took a step back. He stepped closer to me until he had me pinned against the door.

"Nothing I say is coming out right. What I said to you was inexcusable. I know that, and I'm sorry that I hurt you. For the past three days, I've thought about you constantly. It's bullshit, Amber. I can't get you out of my fucking head. I hate it. I couldn't leave things the way they were. I thought that if I came over and apologized, then maybe I'd finally be able to leave you alone. Now that I'm here with you, I know it's going to be fucking impossible. With you this close, the only thing I can think about is stripping you out of those jeans and fucking you so hard that you won't be able to stand for a week. My dick is constantly hard when you're around, and it fucking pisses me off."

My eyes widened as he finished his speech. I was pretty sure it had nearly killed him to say that to me. Admitting that he thought about me was a weakness, and Adam didn't seem like the type of guy to have weaknesses.

"What do you want me to say to that?" I finally asked.

He growled at me. He literally *growled.* "I want you to say that you forgive me. Then, I want you to tell me to fuck you until I make you scream so loud that your entire dorm hears you."

He pressed his body up against mine, and I felt just how hard he was. A whimper escaped me as my body responded to what he wanted. I cursed myself for being so damn weak around him. He'd hurt me when he called me a whore. If I had any self-respect at all, I would shove him away and demand that he leave.

All I could do was stare at him. His chest was heaving, his breath hot against my face. He was so close to me that I felt like our bodies might mesh together at any moment.

God, he was so fucking beautiful.

"Say something, damn it!" He looked me right in the eye.

"You really hurt me. I'm not a whore. I've never been one. If I didn't care about you, even a little, I never would have slept with you. I realized that as we were leaving your apartment. Yeah, I slept with Alex even though I didn't care about him at all, but that was because I was trying to protect myself from getting hurt again."

"You care about me?" He released me and took a step back.

From the look in his eyes, that was the worst thing I could have said. He had some serious commitment issues.

"Yeah, I care about you," I said once he'd moved far enough away that I could breathe again. "I'm not saying I'm in love with you or that I want you to be my boyfriend, but I do care about you."

"Like a friend?" he asked, his voice hopeful.

I closed my eyes for a moment. I needed to get my head together. Admitting to Adam that I cared about him was going too far. If I told him that I did want him, he'd run so fast that he'd leave burnout marks on my carpet.

"Yeah, like a friend—at least, someone who could potentially be a friend," I finally said as I opened my eyes.

The look of sheer relief on his face made me glad that I'd lied to him.

"I think we could be friends." He paused. "I've never had a friend who I fuck. I don't even know how that works. Should we make a schedule—lunch together on Tuesdays, fuck in public on Thursdays, bathroom sex on Saturdays?"

I laughed, unable to stop myself. "You're the biggest asshole I've ever met."

"But I'm a god in bed. That makes up for it."

"Sadly, it does." I ran my hands through my hair, not caring that I was screwing it up. "I accept your apology, but I'm not sure where we go from here."

"I say we go to your bed." He grinned. "That's the only sentence that has come out right since I walked into your room."

"I hate myself for even wanting you. I hope you know that. I think you're a total asshole most of the time."

He shrugged. "I am, but I promise that I'm a lot nicer to you than I am with most people."

"Gee, that makes me feel better."

He took a step closer to me. "I want you more than I've wanted anyone in a really long time. You know that I don't do relationships, so if that's what you're hoping for, I'll walk away now and never bother you again. But if you're okay with just fucking and being friends, then I say we keep whatever fucked-up *relationship* we have going and continue to fuck each other's brains out."

"What about other women?" I asked. "And men?"

He studied me for a moment. "I'm not the kind of guy to settle for just one woman, Amber. If I stood here and promised not to screw around with anyone else while we're doing this, I'd be a dirty liar. I'm not going to make a promise I can't keep."

"And if I feel the same way? What if I find someone else I want to fuck?" I asked, keeping my voice calm even though I was raging inside. I knew that I wouldn't want anyone else while I was with Adam. One night had been more than enough proof of that.

His jaw clenched. "I don't expect you to be with just me, especially when I'm not willing to be with only you."

"Then, we have an agreement," I said quietly. I couldn't believe that I was going to willingly sleep with him, knowing that he could be fucking other women later. Maybe I was a whore after all.

"Works for me." He took another step closer.

I reached out and ran my hands down his chest to his stomach. "I don't want anyone to know about this. If Chloe and Logan find out, they won't understand. We keep whatever this is between the two of us."

He grabbed my hands and moved them away. He shot me a grin as he picked me up and carried me over to my bed. "I can handle that. Now, are we done talking?"

I nodded as he set me down on the end of the bed. "We're done talking."

He grabbed my shirt and pulled it over my head. I'd taken my bra off once I made it back to my room after classes, so my breasts were on full display.

He hungrily stared at them, his eyes darkening. "Jesus Christ, woman. You have perfect tits."

He pushed me down onto the bed and grabbed my sweatpants. He yanked them off with only a few tugs, and then my underwear went next. Once I was completely naked, he pulled his shirt over his head. I didn't even try to hide the fact that I was staring at his perfect body. He kicked his shoes off before discarding his shorts and boxers. He pulled a condom out of the pocket of his shorts and tossed it onto the nightstand.

He knelt down in front of me and spread my legs. "I've wanted to taste you again since that night. It's all I've thought about. You're so fucking addictive." He ran his hand down my stomach to where I was already growing wet.

I jerked when he shoved two fingers inside me. He started pumping them in and out of me. My hips rose automatically.

"And so responsive," he whispered before leaning forward and running his tongue across my clit.

I jerked again when he started circling my clit with his tongue. His tongue ring was a gift from the gods. I writhed as his tongue and fingers attacked my body. Everything he did was incredible. I had no idea how I'd survived before he came along. Sex was one of my favorite things, but with Adam, it was an earth-shattering experience that left me begging for more.

Within minutes, my body shuddered as I came. His tongue continued to explore until my orgasm slowly faded. He kissed his way up my body to my breasts. He sucked my nipple into his mouth, and I gasped. I grabbed his head and pulled him closer. He released my nipple and moved to the next one. He bit down gently before releasing it as well. I shivered when he blew on it, his breath driving my wet skin mad.

"Are you ready for me to fuck you?" he asked.

I nodded, unable to speak. He grabbed the condom off the nightstand and tore the wrapper open. Within seconds, he had it on. He kissed me greedily before entering me in one hard thrust. My body tensed from the twinge of pain I felt. Even though I'd been with him only a few days before, it still took a bit for my body to adjust to his size.

He pulled back and pushed in again, gentler this time. I relaxed as I wrapped my legs around his hips to allow him to go deeper. He kissed me roughly before he slammed into me again. My breath caught as his hips pushed forward over and over. I gripped his shoulders hard enough to break skin, but neither of us cared. We became a tangle of lips and hands, both of us trying to get closer to the other. I squeezed my internal muscles, and he moaned loudly.

He stilled for a moment and stared down at me. "Do that again."

I squeezed once again, loving the way he sounded as he moaned.

"Fuckin' perfect," he muttered before finding his rhythm again.

After that, the only sounds in the room were those of our bodies coming together over and over. His breath became ragged as he fought for control. I closed my eyes as my body exploded again, my orgasm catching me by surprise. I tightened around him as I came. He cursed as he came right along with me, our bodies syncing perfectly.

After a moment, he finally pulled away. I watched as he stood and tossed the condom into the garbage can before dropping down onto the bed next to me. I closed my eyes, unable to look at him. I knew I was setting myself up for a really fucked-up ending with him, but I didn't care. Sex with Adam was worth all the heartache in the world.

"I'm glad we settled our differences. This whole friends-who-fuck thing is working out pretty damn well for me," Adam said.

I reached over and smacked his damp chest. "Fuck you."

"You just did, but I'm sure I could go again. Give me about two minutes. That pussy of yours calls to me."

I opened my eyes and grinned at him. "I feel like you're just using me for sex."

"Never, babe. I like staring at your tits, too. Sex is optional."

I raised an eyebrow.

"Okay, maybe not," he added.

"You have such a way with words. I'm a lucky girl," I mumbled before closing my eyes again. I was suddenly exhausted. All I wanted to do was sleep.

"I should probably go," Adam said.

I felt the bed move as he stood. I opened one eye to see him pulling on his boxers and pants. I finally sat up once he had his shirt on, and I watched as he laced up his shoes.

"I should probably get dressed before my roommate walks in. Shit might get awkward if I don't."

"Is she hot? If so, I'm willing to take you both on at once. This might just end up being my favorite room in all of West Virginia."

I snorted at the thought of my prissy roommate having a threesome. "You're not her type."

"I'm everyone's type." He grinned at me.

"Not everyone's. Now, get the hell out of my room. I need sleep."

He stepped closer to the bed and bent down to kiss me. I closed my eyes as his lips moved against mine. Even something as simple as a kiss made me want more from him.

I pushed him away before standing and picking my clothes up off the floor. "Go."

He held up his hands, his usual smirk on his face. "I'm out of here. Oh, just in case you need me in the middle of the night, I should give you my number. I wouldn't want you to get lonely and have no way to get a hold of me."

I rolled my eyes but grabbed my phone off my desk. He recited his number, and I added it to my phone. I sent him a text so that he'd have my number as well.

"I just texted you, so you have my number now." I tossed my phone back onto the desk and started putting my clothes on.

"All right. I'll see you later." He opened my dorm door and left.

Once he was gone, I dropped back down onto my bed. I inhaled deeply, noticing that his scent was covering my body and my bed. I had no doubt that I'd sleep soundly tonight—as long as I didn't think too hard about the agreement I'd just made with Adam or about getting my heart ripped out. Again.

seven

I didn't see Adam on Thursday.

On Friday night, I almost went to the bar to watch the band play, but I couldn't bring myself to do it. I knew what would happen if I had to watch him leave with another woman. My crazy would come out, and I'd destroy any progress I'd made with him.

I'd given a lot of thought to my agreement with Adam. I hated to admit it, but I thought that it was for the best. He didn't do relationships, and I didn't want one, but we both wanted each other. Keeping things strictly physical was the only way I could walk away without getting hurt. I just had to keep reminding myself of that.

That didn't mean I was secure enough to watch him leave Gold's with some little skank. Instead, I planned to stay in with only my iPod as company. It wouldn't be the most exciting Friday night, but it was better than the alternative.

I fell asleep shortly after lying down. I hadn't even realized how tired I was until I awoke a few hours later because my phone was ringing. I groaned as I stood and grabbed my phone off my computer desk where it was charging. I hadn't dared put it within reach, especially when I used it as an alarm. I knew I'd shut it off without really waking up, and I'd miss every morning class I had.

"Hello?" I mumbled. My eyes weren't functioning enough yet to even see who was calling.

"Amber?"

Adam's voice pulled me from my fog. I glanced at the clock on my nightstand. It was a little after ten.

"Adam? What's wrong?" I asked. "Shouldn't you be playing?"

"Our show was cut short," he said, his voice clipped with annoyance. He sounded pissed.

"Why?"

"Can I come over? I need to talk to you about something."

"Um…yeah, sure."

"I'll be there in twenty." He disconnected the call before I could reply.

Well, okay then.

I put my phone down and walked over to my bed. I climbed in and snuggled down into my pillow. If it had been any other guy, I would be rushing around to fix my hair and put makeup on. I didn't feel the need to do so with Adam. That surprised me. I'd think that I'd want to look my best when he was around, but I just didn't care. I was comfortable enough with him already that it didn't bother me in the least for him to see me with no makeup on, my hair looking like a hot mess, and all while wearing pajamas my mom had bought me. I'd been in a relationship with Chad for a year, and I had never felt this comfortable. Maybe I was mistaking lust for something more with Adam. That was the only explanation I could think of.

Twenty minutes later, Adam knocked on my door. Usually, he had a carefree expression on his face, but tonight, he looked pissed.

"Hey," I said as I studied him.

"Can I come in?" he asked.

I held the door open and took a step back. "Sure."

He stepped through and glanced over at my roommate's side of the room. "Where's your roomie?"

"She goes home on the weekends. Why?"

"I just wanted to make sure we were alone. I know you're going to blow up when I tell you what happened tonight."

"What? Was it something bad?" I closed the door and walked over to my bed. I dropped down onto the edge and expectantly stared up at him.

"Yeah, it was bad."

"Okay…" I said when he hadn't elaborated further. "Are you going to explain? Or are you going to stand there all night, watching me?"

He grinned, but it was a tiny one. "I'm debating."

"On what?"

"Whether or not to fuck you first. Once I tell you, I doubt you'll be in the mood."

My stomach dropped. "What did you do?"

He shook his head. "It wasn't me. It was…Chloe."

"What did she do?"

He sat down on the bed next to me. "She fucked up, Amber. She fucked up so hard. Logan came into the bar tonight while we were playing. He jumped up onto the stage and started fighting with Drake."

"Oh my God! Why? Logan wouldn't do something like that."

"Because Drake and Chloe have been fucking behind his back."

I froze as I tried to process what he had said. "No, she wouldn't do that to Logan."

He looked grim. "She did. Drake admitted that it happened. I guess Chloe finally told Logan, and he went after Drake. Both of the dumb fuckers care about her. If Eric and I hadn't been there, they would have killed each other. We had a hell of a time pulling them apart."

I wanted to scream. "How could she be so fucking stupid? Logan loves her so much. He has for years!"

"She loves Drake. I know it doesn't make it better, but she does. Even I could see it." He cursed. "This is why friends shouldn't get involved. Drake and Logan both pretended to be her friend. Look at how that turned out."

"I need to find Logan," I said as I stood. "I need to make sure that he's okay."

Adam grabbed my arm. "Leave him alone tonight. He is going to have to deal with this on his own."

"I need to make sure he's okay!" I said again as I tried to pull free.

"He was fine when I left them, but I know he's not going to want to be around anyone tonight, especially you."

"What? Why? I haven't done anything to him!"

"No, but you're friends with Chloe, too."

"Not anymore," I said, my body shaking with fury as I thought about what Chloe had done. "I'm not friends with someone who could do that to a person she loves."

He pulled me down onto his lap and wrapped his arms around me. "You don't know the whole story, Amber. Don't judge her until you find out what really happened."

"Bullshit. I'll judge her all I want. I knew Drake was going to be a problem. I told her before to stay away from him. But did she listen? Of course not!"

He pushed up the back of my tank top and started rubbing circles across my spine. I hated myself for it, but I started to relax instantly. His touch was so calming to me.

"Sometimes, we can't stay away even though we should," he said quietly. "Sometimes, we have no choice."

I wondered if we were still talking about Chloe. "We always have a choice."

"No, we don't. Look at the two of us, Amber. I can't seem to stay away from you for long, and we're not even together. We're just having fun. The thought of leaving you alone makes me want to break shit."

"Keep talking like that, and I'll start to wonder if you actually care about me," I said in a teasing tone.

"Friends care about each other." He leaned forward and kissed my shoulder. "I care about fucking you right now. I think it'd be a good distraction from your friends."

I shook my head. "Not tonight."

He paused, his lips still against my shoulder. "I knew I should have fucked you first."

He picked me up and sat me down next to him.

I glanced over to see him watching me. "What?"

"You going to be okay? Can I leave? Or will you go storming up to Chloe's or Logan's rooms?"

"I won't go tonight, but I am going to talk to Logan in the morning. I want to know exactly what happened. I can't believe Chloe would do something like this."

Adam stood. "Sometimes, we all do stupid shit, things we can never take back, no matter how much we wish we could."

"You sound as if you're speaking from experience."

"I am." He looked away. "I need to go. Call me tomorrow, okay?"

I nodded. "Yeah. See ya."

As soon as the door closed behind him, I wished that I'd asked him to stay.

Logan didn't answer his door the next day. I wasn't sure if it was because he wanted to be alone or if he just wasn't home.

He didn't answer the next day either.

On Monday, I finally caught him as he was walking into our dorm.

"Logan! Wait!" I yelled as I ran to catch up with him.

He stopped and turned toward me. Once I caught up, he started walking again.

"Logan—"

"Whatever you have to say, it can wait until we get to my room," he said without turning around again.

I stayed silent as we climbed the stairs to the third floor. When we entered his dorm room, he dropped his books on the bed and turned to me. It took everything in me not to run and jump into his arms. He looked like absolute hell. His normally tan skin looked pale, but it was his eyes that did me in. Logan had the most beautiful blue eyes I'd ever seen. One look at them could pull you in. Right now, his eyes looked dead, and the dark circles under them said he hadn't slept in a while.

"Oh, Logan," I whispered as I crossed the room and hugged him tightly, unable to stop myself.

He tensed in my arms. "I take it she told you."

"No, but Adam did. I'm so sorry, Logan. I never thought she'd hurt you like this." I dropped my arms and took a step back.

"Neither did I," he said as he sat down on the bed. "I love her more than anything in this world, Amber, and she completely destroyed me."

"I know. I'll never forgive her for this." I sat down next to him.

He shook his head. "This shouldn't affect your relationship with her. This is between her and me."

"Bullshit. You're my friend, and she hurt you. It's officially my business."

"No," he said sharply, "you're not picking sides. Chloe is going to need you to help her deal with this."

I stared at him, unable to believe he'd just said that. "You can't be serious. She *cheated* on you, and you want me to help *her* deal? She. Cheated. On. You."

He winced. "I know she did. But I talked to her on Saturday, and what she did is tearing her apart. No matter how bad I want to be there for her, I can't right now, so that leaves you to deal with her."

I shook my head. He was being so...Logan. Chloe had wronged him, yet he was still worried about her.

"You're ridiculous. How can you even care about how she feels after what she did to you?" I asked.

He looked away. "You wouldn't understand."

"Then, explain it to me, Logan!"

"Because I still love her. I fucking love her so much it hurts. I want to hate her, but I can't. I just can't!" he shouted. His chest heaved as he fought for control.

I reached for him, but he pushed my hand away. I dropped it back into my lap.

"Logan, I don't know what you want me to say. I want to make this better for you, but I don't know how."

"Just take care of her. That's all I ask."

"Okay," I whispered even though I knew I was lying to him.

"Can you go? I just...I don't feel like talking about this anymore." He turned away from me.

"Yeah, I'll go. If you need me, you'll call?"

"I'll call."

I hated to leave him, but I didn't want to make things worse, so I left. Once I shut his door, I leaned against it and closed my eyes. I hated how much he was hurting right now, and it was all because of Chloe. I loved her, but I couldn't even stomach the thought of her at the moment. There was no way I would comfort her like he wanted me to. I didn't even want to look at her.

Adam had said that Chloe loved Drake. If that was the case, love was the biggest motherfucker of all. Love was supposed to be the one thing in this world that was completely pure. That was a lie. I'd thought that I loved Chad. Because of that, I'd ended up broken. No, love wasn't pure. It was tainted with so much pain that it made me want to run away.

I thought about my complicated relationship with Adam. I cared for him. Of that, I was sure. But I didn't love him. I wasn't even sure I liked him some days when he acted like an ass. But I knew that with enough time, I *could* love him.

Seeing Logan in that much pain was a wake-up call for me. I would never let myself be torn to shreds like that. *Never.* I would put up an emotional wall so thick that whatever I thought I felt for Adam would never break through.

Fucking was all I'd let myself have, and I'd make sure that it was enough.

eight

Weeks went by at a snail's pace.

Logan had closed himself off from everyone, including me. I tried to talk to him a few times, but he pushed me away before I had a chance to say anything more than hello. That hurt, but I understood why he wanted to be alone. Logan had always been so contained, and now was no different.

I hadn't spoken to Chloe at all. I saw her a couple of times, but I didn't even acknowledge her existence. She deserved nothing less. I'd never been so angry with her as I was now. She'd royally screwed up, and she knew it. She could suffer alone. Maybe it would show her just how much her actions could hurt others.

Even though I was angry with her, I missed her. I could lie to everyone else, but I couldn't lie to myself.

As weeks slowly passed, I would find myself grabbing my phone to call her. I forced myself to keep my distance though. No matter how much I missed her, she'd done Logan wrong, and she needed to suffer.

I would see Drake weekly when I went to their shows. Since I'd decided to keep my distance emotionally from Adam, I made myself go to the band's shows. I needed to accept the fact that I wasn't the only woman he wanted. I'd expected him to leave with other women, but he never did. If I was around, I was the one he took home. I tried not to think too hard on why.

Drake looked as bad as Chloe and Logan. All three of them looked as if they hadn't slept in weeks. I wondered if they really hadn't. I almost felt sorry for Chloe and Drake, but when I remembered how broken

Logan had looked when he talked to me, I found it easy to push away any sympathetic feelings.

Since I wasn't hanging out with Chloe or Logan, I would find myself spending more and more time with Adam. It seemed that we were constantly together. If I wasn't at his apartment, I would be out with him. It wasn't something that either of us had planned. It just kind of happened. But through it all, I kept my resolve to keep things strictly physical. I found myself liking Adam as a person, and I even went as far as to consider him a friend. It felt weird to think of him like that, but I started to get used to it. After all, we were supposed to be friends—with benefits.

Adam and I would talk about the situation with Chloe, Drake, and Logan occasionally. We didn't agree—at all. He saw Drake's side while all I could see was Logan's.

"He's so fucked-up, Amber. I've never seen him like this," Adam said as we stared up at the ceiling of his bedroom.

I pulled the blanket up tighter around my naked body. "He should be fucked-up, Adam. He pushed his way into Chloe's life and completely screwed up everything she had with Logan."

"You don't know him the way I do. He doesn't mess around with chicks who are taken. He doesn't need to. If he didn't care about Chloe, he wouldn't have gone after her."

"Maybe, but it doesn't change anything. He's still the reason that things are the way they are."

"It wasn't just him. Chloe could've said no," Adam pointed out.

"Oh, I know. Trust me, I know. Chloe is on my shit list until they get all of this straightened out. She's just as much at fault as he is. Maybe more. The only one completely innocent in all of this is Logan, and he's the one who has suffered the most."

"She's never looked at Logan the way she looks at Drake. I knew something was going on between them, but if you want the truth, I didn't care enough to ask. You might get pissed, but I wish Drake would just man up and go talk some sense into Chloe. It's obvious to everyone that they love each other. Logan didn't stand a chance."

I sighed. "It does piss me off to hear you say that. I don't know Drake, nor do I care about him. I wanted Logan to be happy, but I don't see that happening now, especially if what you say about Chloe is true. I don't see her ever giving him another chance if she loves Drake."

Adam rolled over and pinned me to the bed. I froze in surprise.

"If any good has come out of our friends' fucked-up choices, it's the fact that they made me realize what an awesome thing we have going on here."

"What do you mean?"

He grinned down at me. "The two of us get along perfectly. There's no pesky emotions tied to what we're doing. It keeps things simple, easy, clean. We fuck whenever we want and go about our business. It's kind of perfect."

"Be still my heart. You're such a charmer," I mumbled.

He leaned down and kissed me. "What can I say? I like to fuck you. Your pussy—it calls to me."

"And here I thought you kept me around for my charming personality."

He nuzzled my neck. "That, too. But mainly because you ride my dick better than anyone else I've messed around with."

His head dipped lower, his lips closing around one of my nipples. I sighed in contentment.

Simple. Easy. Clean. No pesky feelings to ruin this moment. I could handle that.

A few days later, Logan knocked on my door. I was surprised to see him, but I was glad that he was finally ready to talk to me.

"Hey. Can I come in?" he asked.

"Sure," I said as I let him in.

As soon as I closed the door, he spoke, "I talked to Chloe last night."

I tensed. "And?"

"She said you haven't talked to her since everything happened."

"Nope, I haven't."

He ran his hand across his face in irritation. "I told you, I didn't want you in the middle of this, Amber. You weren't supposed to shun her."

"I heard what you said, but it wasn't your choice to make. I'm allowed to be angry with her if I want."

"I had a really long talk with her, and we cleared the air. I want you to do the same," Logan said, completely ignoring what I'd just said.

"You can't be serious! You're friends again after what she did?"

"I can't stand not to have her in my life. I'd rather have her as a friend than not at all."

I shook my head. "You might find it easy to forgive, but I don't."

"This isn't about you!" he shouted. "I want things to go back to the way they were. That's impossible if you continue to hold a grudge against her!"

"What do you expect me to do? Run up to her room and tell her everything is forgiven?" I shouted right back at him.

"That's exactly what I expect you to do. If not for her, then for me. She loves him. Nothing you or I do will change that. It's time to get our lives back to the way they were. If that means she ends up with him, then that's what will happen. Stop acting like a child, and let it go."

"It's not that simple," I said.

"It is that simple." He walked to the door. "Fix this shit, Amber. I don't care if you have to lie about how you feel. Just fix it—for me."

Then, he was gone.

I found myself knocking on Chloe's door two days later. It had taken me that long to accept what Logan had said. I hadn't wanted to forgive her so easily, but I wasn't doing him any favors by staying away. It would only make things worse for him. And I did miss Chloe. She was my best friend. She had been for years.

Logan was right. I needed to grow up and move on.

When Chloe opened her door, I started crying at the sight of her. I hated how much I'd missed her.

Pushing away any ill feelings toward her, I threw myself into her arms and hugged her tightly. "I...I missed you so damn much, Chloe! This has been killing me inside."

She hugged me back and laughed, but it was hollow. "I missed you, too, Amber, but I got what I deserved. What I did was wrong, and I needed to pay for it."

"I'm sorry I was such a bitch to you. I was so mad at you for what you did and for not telling me. I had to find out from Adam after the fact.

I thought you trusted me more than that!" I said, unable to hide my anger.

"I did trust you. I just couldn't put you in the middle of all this. Logan is your friend, too, and if I had told you, it would have torn you guys apart. I didn't want to do that to you." She said as she walked to her bed and sat down.

I nodded as I wiped under my eyes to get rid of any smudged mascara. "I guess I understand why, but it doesn't make me feel any better about the whole thing."

Chloe stood up and looked out her window at the campus below. "I know it's a crappy excuse, but it's all I've got. I was so confused, and I made some really bad choices, but I paid for it in the end. I nearly lost Logan, and I did lose Drake."

I hadn't expected her to be so...broken. She knew that she'd fucked up, and she knew that there was no way to repair the damage she'd caused. I couldn't help but feel a tiny bit sorry for her when I'd heard the way she said Drake's name. It was killing her to be away from him.

"Have you talked to Drake since all this happened? I've been to some of the band's shows. He seems as depressed as you are."

She turned back toward me. Her shoulders were slumped in defeat. "No, I haven't. I thought it was best to cut ties with both of them. We all need time to heal from this. I want him, but I don't even know how he feels about me now. Besides, I don't think it would be fair to Logan if I caused this and then skipped merrily off into the sunset to live my happily ever after."

I snorted. If she only knew what Logan had said to me - He *wanted* her to be with Drake if it would make things go back to normal.

"Yeah, you've been living your happily ever after all right. Do you really think Logan wants you to go on like this? He wants you to be happy, Chloe. That's all he's ever wanted."

She sighed as she started gathering up dirty clothes off the floor. "I don't know. I just know I hurt him, and I don't deserve to be happy. I'm sure Drake has moved on by now anyway."

I picked up a dirty sock and threw it at her. "Did you listen to anything I just said? Drake is as miserable as you are, and he definitely has not moved on. You have no idea how many girls I've watched him practically throw off of him at the bar. That boy is in mope mode. Trust me."

She growled as she shoved the dirty sock in the laundry basket with the rest of the clothes. "I can't, Amber. I just can't. If he rejects me, I'll never survive it."

I kept silent even though I wanted to tell her what Logan and Adam had said. I knew without a doubt that she'd end up with Drake even if she didn't realize it yet. If Logan wanted me to play nice and help Chloe, then I would. I didn't agree with what he'd said about letting her move on with Drake, but I did want Logan and Chloe both to be happy.

God help me. I was going to play matchmaker.

⸺ ⸺ ⸻ ⸺ ⸺

The next couple of weeks passed without incident.

When I'd told Adam what had happened with Logan and Chloe, he'd seemed relieved. "It's about damn time," he'd mumbled.

I started spending time with Chloe and Logan again, but things weren't like they had been before. Logan rarely smiled, and Chloe acted as if she was walking around in a daze. A few times, I'd mentioned that she should talk to Drake, but she'd shot me down.

It was now three weeks after I'd forgiven her, and nothing had changed between Chloe and Drake.

I was at the bar with Chloe's roommate, Rachel, to watch Adam and the rest of the band play. I already considered the night a win because of Adam.

The band was covering "Turn Me On" by Royal Bliss. As Drake sang the chorus, Adam stopped playing his guitar and jumped offstage. He grinned wickedly as he grabbed me out of my chair and carried me up onto the stage with him.

"This song was made for us, babe," he mumbled before going back to his guitar.

I spent the rest of the song onstage next to him, dancing and laughing.

When my phone started flashing, I saw that Chloe had texted me. I smiled when I read it. *This night was going to be epic in so many ways.*

Chloe: Off work early. Going home. See you tomorrow.

A plan instantly formed in my mind. Chloe worked at Starbucks, which was directly across the road from Gold's. Every time I'd tried to get her to come watch the band play, she had used work as an excuse. Tonight, she didn't have an excuse.

Me: At the bar. Come over.

Chloe: Can't. I'm too tired.

I frowned. There was no way I was letting her escape again. I dialed her number.

She picked up on the first ring. "Yes?"

"Don't *yes* me, Chloe Marie! Get your butt over here. They're playing a bunch of new stuff tonight, and it's a great show. If you want, you can leave before they finish. It's not like I'm asking you to have a heart-to-heart with him. Just come watch them play."

She hesitated before finally giving in. "All right. I'm across the street, so I'll be there in a minute."

That was easy, I thought to myself as I put my phone down.

Chloe appeared a few minutes later. She was out of breath as she sat down in a chair next to Rachel. Rachel and I both broke out in giggles at the sight of her. She looked like she'd just walked through a war zone.

"What happened to you?" I asked.

She pointed over her shoulder to the crowd of rowdy patrons. "It's a damn mosh pit back there. I'm lucky I made it here with all my limbs intact!"

We continued to laugh as a waitress brought her a beer. Chloe gave us a dirty look as she took a sip of her drink. Her eyes instantly darted to the stage in front of us. I looked up to see Drake staring right at her. She looked away and started chugging her beer.

Adam caught my attention and gave me a questioning look. I just shrugged. It wasn't like I could explain to him what I was doing. He wouldn't understand. Love wasn't something he'd *ever* understand.

Chloe motioned for the waitress to bring her another beer, but I shook my head.

"No way are you getting wasted and making an ass out of yourself. Just watch the band, and enjoy the music."

She groaned as she laid her head down on the table. "You're killing me, Amber—slowly and painfully. I hope you know that."

I slapped her on the back as the band finished their song. "I know. I'm thoroughly enjoying myself right now. If you won't man up and talk to him, someone has to push you into it."

She opened her mouth and gaped at me as it finally clicked. "This was a setup, wasn't it? You can forget about it, Amber. I'll be long gone by the time they finish. Actually, I think I'm going to leave now before you can try anything else on me."

She stood and turned to leave just as Drake's amplified voice filled the bar. "Thanks to everyone who came out tonight. We've got one more song for you guys before we're done. It's another new one, and we hope you'll like it."

His eyes locked on hers as she stood there, staring at him in a trance.

Finally, he spoke, "This one…well, this one is for those who have had their heart ripped out, for those who thought they had found love, only to have it viciously ripped away and without any regard to their feelings." He raised his hand above his head and shouted, "To all of us who are empty inside!"

With that, Jade slowly started into the song, and Adam and Eric followed closely behind. As Drake started singing, I watched Chloe's whole body tense. It was almost too much to watch. I glanced up at Adam to see him watching me. I swallowed roughly and forced my eyes away from his. I didn't want to think about him at the moment. I wasn't sure why, but I just didn't.

Drake started singing, and I froze as I listened to the lyrics.

I wasn't sure what it was,

What you did to me,

I felt myself change.

Something shifted when I looked into your eyes,

Engulfing me in flames,

Burning me to the core,

But it wasn't meant to be.

You see, you and I,

We're a whirlwind,

Destroying everything in our path.

But isn't that what love does?

It makes us weak, far from free.

I gave you everything, and you turned it back on me.

You turned it back on me.

He whispered the last line. Before his voice died, Chloe was running through the crowd, pushing people as she went. I jumped up and chased her through the bar. By the time I shoved my way through the crowd to the exit, she was already gone. I made it outside just in time to see her car tearing out of the parking lot.

"Son of a bitch!" I shouted as her car disappeared.

I jumped when Drake appeared next to me.

"Where is she?" he demanded.

"Gone."

"Son of a bitch!" he swore.

"That's what I said." I hesitated before speaking again. I'd never had one-on-one time with Drake, and I wasn't sure whether I'd be helping or hurting with my next words. "She loves you. If you love her, go find her."

He looked at me, and I saw actual tears in his eyes. He was hurting more than I could have ever imagined.

"I love her, too. No matter how hard I fight it, I can't. She has me by the balls, and she doesn't even know it."

I laughed. He and Adam were more alike than I'd realized. "Then, go after her."

He looked at me for a moment longer before sprinting across the lot to where his car was parked. I watched as he tore out of the parking lot.

"What are you doing?" Adam asked from behind me.

I turned to see him standing only a foot away. "What do you mean?"

"I heard what you said to him. I thought you didn't want them together."

"They love each other, and they're both miserable apart."

"So?" he asked as he stepped closer.

"So, I want her to be happy. Logan wants her to be happy. I figured I'd give Drake a push. It's time someone gets a happily ever after."

"Love isn't a happily ever after," he said after a moment of silence. "It's a death sentence."

I shrugged. "It depends on how you look at it. Some people, like them, need it. Some people, like me...well, I'm better off without it."

He stared at me with the strangest look on his face. Finally, he closed his eyes briefly before opening them again. He stepped closer and threw his arm over my shoulder. "Come back to my apartment. Let's see if we can find a few temporary happily ever afters," he said with a devious grin on his face.

"My favorite kind."

nine

Three Months Later—May

Morgantown, West Virginia

"Thanks for agreeing to have lunch with me," Chloe said as we sat down at a local restaurant.

"I'm glad you called. I was in the middle of packing. I was desperately hoping for an excuse to take a break." I looked across the table at her.

"Me, too," Logan added grumpily. He seemed about as excited as I was about packing.

Who would have thought I'd add so many clothes to my wardrobe in less than a year?

Our freshman year of college was officially over. I would be lying if I said I was sad. I was glad to have it behind us. With all the drama between Logan and Chloe, it had been one of the worst years ever. Even after three months of semi-normalcy, things were still tense from time to time.

Drake and Chloe had ended up together by the end of the night when I'd forced her to come to the bar. She'd changed almost instantly. Gone was the shell of the girl she'd been while they were apart. In her place was a woman who smiled, a woman who laughed. While I was glad that she was back to normal, I still worried about Logan.

He'd told both of us that he was happy for her, but I could see the way he'd look at her when he thought no one was paying attention. I'd almost called him out on it more than once, but I couldn't bring myself to burst the tiny bubble of happiness surrounding our friendship.

Adam and I were still...*friends*. Absolutely nothing had changed between us. I'd also never witnessed him taking another woman home. I'd asked him once or twice if he was, but he always evaded answering me. I had no idea what to think about that. While it pleased me that I seemed to be enough for him, I also worried that I'd grow soft toward him and maybe even open up my heart. I almost wished that he still acted the way he used to. It would make it easier for me to keep my heart and my vagina in their rightful places.

"I need to talk to you guys about something," Chloe said as she looked anywhere but at us.

"What?" I asked curiously.

"My mom showed up at Drake's house yesterday."

"What?" I shrieked.

I hated Chloe's mother. She'd abused her own daughter both mentally and physically her entire life. It'd been a long time since any of us had seen her, and I had hoped that she'd disappeared permanently. Nothing good ever came from her presence.

"What happened? What did she want?" Logan asked.

I glanced over to see worry in his eyes.

Chloe shrugged, but she wouldn't look at either of us. "Apparently, my aunt is dying. My mom wants me to go to Ocean City with her to see my aunt one last time."

"Holy shit," I said.

"Yeah, I know. I've never been close to my aunt, but she has always been good to me. She even helped me get home when my mom left me at her house one summer."

"Still, no one would expect you to go see her with your mom there," Logan said.

Chloe finally looked up. "I'm going."

"You can't be serious!" I exclaimed.

"I am. My mom only wants me to go because my aunt plans to leave money for both of us, but she won't if she doesn't see me for herself."

"No money is worth dealing with your mother," I said, surprised that Chloe would even want that money. It wasn't like her at all.

"I'm not going for the money. I'm going to make sure that my aunt doesn't give my mom a damn dime. She doesn't deserve it. Besides, she'll only use it on drugs. I know her."

"You're absolutely insane, woman!" I told her.

"Chloe, this is insane. You're willingly walking into the belly of the beast. Even if you change your aunt's mind, you're still going to be stuck in a house with that woman when your aunt breaks the news. I don't see that ending well," Logan said as he looked at Chloe with concern.

"I won't be there when my aunt tells her. I'm only staying long enough to convince her not to give my mom the money, and then I'll be in my car on my way to one of Drake's shows. But if things do go bad, Danny will be there to help me, and I'm sure Jordan will be, too."

Adam, Drake, and the rest of the band were leaving in two weeks to go on tour. They'd managed to book a few shows on the East Coast, mainly playing in small bars like Gold's. I hated to think about Adam leaving even if it was only for the summer. I shouldn't care though. Logan and I were leaving for Charleston in two days. Logan and his mom didn't get along well, so he was going to use Chloe's old room at my house.

Even though I knew Chloe's cousin, Danny, and his best friend, Jordan, were going to be at her aunt's house, I still didn't like the idea of her being under the same roof as her mom.

"How long are you staying?" I asked before sipping my coffee.

"Not long. Drake will be playing shows in Maryland while I'm there, so whenever I'm done at my aunt's house, I'm going to meet up with him and continue on."

"So, you'll still be gone all summer?" I pouted.

When Chloe had mentioned that she was going to stay with Drake instead of coming home with Logan and me, I'd been pissed. I'd expected this summer to be a break from all the craziness. I'd hoped things really would go back to normal between the three of us, but that obviously wasn't going to happen.

"Yes, I'm still going with Drake. You'll have Logan to keep you company. Take *him* shopping," Chloe said.

I didn't miss the glare Logan sent her way.

"Yeah, not happening. I have better things to do than walk around the mall for six hours while Amber searches for the perfect pair of shoes," he said with a visible shudder.

Chloe laughed, earning a glare from me. My two best friends liked to tease me over the amount of time I spent shopping. I couldn't help it. Clothes were my life.

"Shut up, both of you. I don't need either of you to go shopping with me. I can have fun all by myself!" I said, still glaring.

"We know you can, Amber," Chloe said as she tried to hide a smile.

"And you'd better freaking call me at least once a week while you're gone! I mean it. I can't go from spending every day with you to nothing for three months," I said.

"You know I will. I'm going to miss you guys, too, you know. This isn't all one-sided. It's been a long time since I spent any real amount of time without you two, and it's going to suck."

"Damn straight it will!" I practically pulled her from her seat to hug her.

Chloe giggled as she turned her head to look at Logan, who was watching us as if we'd lost our minds.

"Get over here, big guy. Group hug!" Chloe said.

He rolled his eyes as he leaned in and wrapped his arms around both of us. "You two are completely mental. How I'm even friends with either of you, I'll never know."

I stuck my tongue out at him. "You know you love us both, so shut up."

"Yeah, I do," Logan said as he pulled away.

He wouldn't look at Chloe. I fought to hide my frown. God, he was still hurting so much. I wasn't sure if time would be enough to fix what love had done to him.

"Is that everything?" Adam asked as he shoved another box into the back of my car.

"It'd better be. I don't have any more room." I watched him slam the trunk closed.

He chuckled. "What the fuck do you do with all these clothes?"

"Um, wear them. Duh."

He shook his head. "I will never understand women's obsession with clothes. I have, like, ten shirts and a few pairs of jeans."

I rolled my eyes. "It's different for girls. We can't just wear black T-shirts over and over."

"Whatever. So, what time are you leaving tomorrow?"

"We'll be on our way back to Charleston by nine. Logan is driving his own car back."

"He still planning on staying with you all summer?" he asked.

His tone had sounded as if he didn't care, but there was an emotion in his eyes that made me wonder if that was true. It looked like he was…jealous. I shook my head to clear away that thought. Pigs would fly before Adam started acting like a jealous boyfriend.

"Yeah. I'm glad he's staying with me. I'll be lonely since Chloe is going with you guys."

"Well, why don't we spend our last night together at my place?" he asked.

I grinned. "Like I'd ever say no to that."

He smirked. "You'd better not. Come on, you can ride with me. I'll bring you back here in the morning."

"All right." I locked my car and then followed him over to where he'd parked his.

After his Escort's engine had blown up—or rather, after he'd blown up the engine—Adam had traded his Escort in on an older model Cavalier. I'd learned from his friends that Adam would go through cars faster than he went through women.

The ride to his apartment was silent. He kept flipping between radio stations before giving up and putting a CD in.

"Radio stations suck anymore," he grumbled as The Amity Affliction's "Don't Lean on Me" started blaring.

"I love these guys," I said before humming along.

"Me, too."

When we pulled up in front of his apartment building, he shut off the car. He climbed out of the car, and I followed. The walk up to his apartment was as silent as the ride over.

Once we were inside, I dropped down onto the couch and rested my head against the back. "I'm exhausted. Packing sucks."

"Come here," Adam mumbled as he sat down on the couch with me. He pulled me onto his lap.

I was lying on my stomach with my head resting on his legs. He pushed my hair aside and started rubbing my shoulders. I relaxed further, his strong hands working the kinks and tension out of my body.

"Jesus, that feels good," I moaned.

We stayed that way for a while.

I was starting to doze off when he spoke again, "I'm going to miss you."

The words were simple enough, but coming from him, they were monumental. Besides commenting on how glad he was to have me as a friend, he'd never admitted to caring about me before. I wasn't even sure if he'd only said those words to be nice. They might have been said to remind me that we were only friends.

"You won't even have time to miss me once your tour starts. You'll be too busy traveling, playing, and banging random chicks," I said, only half-kidding.

"I'll still miss you," he said quietly.

I sat up, and he let his hands drop to his sides. I stared at him, noticing that he wouldn't look at me. I reached up and ran my fingertips along his cheek, loving the rough stubble on his chin.

111

"I'll miss you, too," I said, my own voice barely above a whisper. I cleared my throat and smiled at him. "You're an asshole, but you've started to grow on me these past few months."

"Tell me how you really feel." He cracked a smile.

I leaned forward and brushed my lips against his. The kiss was softer than any other between us. It was barely a whisper of a kiss, but it held so much emotion. When I tried to pull away, Adam grabbed the back of my head and pulled my mouth back to his. He hungrily kissed me, taking me by surprise. My lips parted, and his tongue darted inside to tangle with mine. I sucked on his tongue, and he groaned as his hold on me tightened. He finally broke away and stood.

He grabbed my arms and pulled me up with him. "Let's make tonight something to remember since it'll be our last one for a long time."

He tugged my shirt up and over my head. He tossed it to the floor as I unbuttoned my shorts and let them fall to the floor. He pulled his shirt over his head and dropped it on top of mine. His shoes and shorts disappeared next.

"Come on," he said as he led me back to his bedroom.

Once we were inside, I unfastened my bra and let it drop to the floor. I pulled my underwear off without a second thought. After so many months together, being naked around Adam didn't faze me in the least. I smiled as I remembered how self-conscious I'd been around him at first. We were well past that stage now.

Adam's boxers dropped to the floor, and he kicked them aside. My eyes slowly slid down his body, taking in every tiny detail of him, committing it to memory. Even after months of spending quality time with his naked body, I still marveled at just how beautiful he was.

Adam moved so that he was directly in front of me. I closed my eyes as he ran his fingertips from my shoulder down to my hip. He rested his hand there, squeezing lightly.

"You've wasted six months of your life hanging around me," he said suddenly.

My eyes popped open in surprise. Of all the things I'd expected him to say, that definitely wasn't one of them. "What?"

"You heard me." He hesitated. "You've wasted your time with me."

"I don't consider it wasted," I told him.

"I do. You could've found someone who would really commit to you, yet you hung around me. Why?"

I raised an eyebrow, completely confused by where he was going with this. "Maybe I wasn't looking for a commitment. I told you before that I didn't want a relationship. Where is this coming from?"

He looked away briefly before his eyes found mine again. "Nowhere. I was just thinking."

Before I could demand an answer from him, he pulled me closer and slammed his mouth down on mine. I wrapped my arms around him. I sighed when our bodies touched everywhere. He grabbed my legs and picked me up so that I could wrap them around him. The feel of his growing erection against my belly was enough to set my body on fire.

He moved until my back was pressed up against his bedroom wall. I groaned when he pulled away enough to slip his hand between us. His fingers found my clit and started slowly circling it. My entire body jerked in response. Every nerve came alive as I fought back another moan. It was always like this with him. The simplest touch from him could do more to me than sex with Alex or Chad had ever been able to do.

He increased the tempo of his fingers until I was thrusting my hips against his hand, begging him to stop torturing me and start fucking me.

"Adam, please," I gasped.

"What, baby? What do you want?"

"Fuck me. Please," I said.

His fingers stopped moving instantly. I stared up at him through hooded eyes.

"All you had to do was ask," he said as he shoved into me.

I almost cried in relief as I felt him filling me. We fit together perfectly. I rested my head against his shoulder as he began thrusting into me. The wall shook with the force of it. I clung to him as I cried out over and over again.

Everything was so primal about Adam—from his looks and the way he carried himself to the way he fucked me. He was a god of a man, and at this moment, I worshiped the ground he walked on.

Coherent thought left me as we worked together, bringing each other closer and closer to climax with every touch, every thrust. My entire body stiffened as an orgasm rocked me. My fingernails dug into Adam's shoulders as I called out his name.

"Son of a bitch!" Adam shouted as he pulled out of me.

I almost fell when he dropped me and stepped back, but I managed to catch myself at the last minute. I stared at him in shock as semen coated my stomach and started slowly sliding down my body.

"I didn't put a condom on," he said.

The pure rage in his eyes made me want to take a step back, and I would have if I wasn't already pressed against the wall.

My own eyes widened in shock. Adam was meticulous about wearing a condom. We'd been together actively, three or four times at least per week for six months, and never once had he forgotten.

"I'm sorry, Amber. I should've remembered."

"It's okay," I told him. "I forgot, too."

"No, it's not okay. It only takes once to…" He trailed off.

"Hey"—I took a step closer and rested my hand on his heaving chest—"shit happens. It's okay. I'm on the pill anyway. I won't get pregnant."

"I don't care. I *never* fuck without a condom. I don't want some bitch trying to hang me with a kid."

I winced, his words striking me almost as hard as a fist would. I dropped my hand and took a step back.

He looked down at me, and his eyes softened, obviously understanding just how badly he had fucked up. "Amber, no, I didn't mean you. I just meant—"

"I get it," I said, embarrassed when my voice cracked. "I need to take a shower. I'm sticky."

He tried but failed to smile. "I'll grab you a couple of towels."

He turned and walked out of the room, leaving me with my thoughts. I walked across the hall to the bathroom and turned on the water in his shower. Once it was warm, I climbed inside. The warm water pelted my sensitive skin, but I paid little attention to it. How could Adam think so poorly of me? He'd laced cruel words with pure venom. I winced again as I thought of the rage in his eyes when he'd realized his mistake.

When I finished with my shower, I saw that Adam had laid out a couple of towels and one of his shirts for me to wear to bed. I dried off and threw the shirt on before returning to his room. He passed by me without a word and disappeared into the bathroom for a shower of his own.

I debated on changing into a set of clothes that I'd left here for when I spent the night and going home. I wasn't comfortable being around him at the moment. But then I remembered that he was my ride back to my dorm. Somehow, I doubted that he'd feel amused if I demanded that he take me home.

Before I could make up my mind, he walked back into the room, his hair damp from the shower. He gave me a questioning look when he saw me standing in the middle of his bedroom.

"Do you want me to go home?" I blurted before I could stop myself.

He paused. "Do *you* want to go home?"

I bit my lip. "I think I should."

"Why?" He seemed genuinely confused, which only annoyed me.

"Because of…earlier."

He ran his hand through his wet hair before walking over to the bed and sitting down. "Sit down, Amber. I think we need to talk."

I cautiously crossed the room and sat down next to him. "Okay…"

"Look, I'm sorry for what I said earlier. I didn't mean to imply that you'd be a girl who would try to trap a guy by getting pregnant. I just meant it in general. I know you're not like that."

"But you were so angry," I whispered.

"I was angry with myself for forgetting. I don't forget—ever. But with you, I did. I let my guard down."

"I still don't understand though. If you don't think that I'd try to screw you over, then why did you get so pissed?"

"There's shit you don't know about me, Amber. I'd rather forget some things in my past. Let's just leave it at that." He stood and walked to his side of the bed. I watched as he pulled the sheets down. "Just know that I would never think that about you, okay? Now, let's get some sleep. I'm exhausted from carrying all your shit to your car."

"Okay." I stood and pulled the covers down on my side.

I wanted to say more, but I knew he'd never answer the questions I wanted to ask. *What on earth could have happened to make him react like that?* He'd been so angry that I'd actually been a bit afraid of him. Then, the way he'd cut me with his words…

I lay down and pulled the covers up to my chin. Adam climbed in next to me. He tugged me over and wrapped his arms around me.

"I'm sorry," was all he said.

I closed my eyes and enjoyed the feel of his body against mine. Without a doubt, I knew that it would be the last chance I had to be with him like this for a very long time.

———— ———— — ————

"Send me a text when you make it home, okay?" Adam asked the next day.

He had driven me back to my dorm, and we were standing next to my car in the parking lot.

"I will, Dad," I teased.

"I'm serious. I hate that you're driving all the way to Charleston on your own."

I rolled my eyes. "I'll be fine, but if it makes you feel better, I'll text you when I get there."

"Good. I'll be waiting."

We stood awkwardly, neither of us sure how to say good-bye. I hated to admit it, but I wasn't ready to let him go just yet. I wanted to kidnap him and bring him back to Charleston with me.

"Be careful on the road this summer," I finally said.

He grinned. "Now, who's worried?"

I smacked his chest. "I know you, and trouble seems to find you."

"I have no idea what you're talking about." He grinned down at me.

I surprised both of us when I lurched forward and wrapped my arms around him. After a moment of hesitation, he hugged me back.

"Don't forget about me," Adam said as we pulled apart.

I wasn't sure if he was joking or not.

"Like I could," I told him before standing on my toes to softly kiss his lips. "Be safe."

"I will."

I stepped back and opened my car door. "Well, I guess this is good-bye."

"I guess it is. I'll see you in a couple of months after school starts and the tour ends."

I nodded. "I know."

I climbed into my car and started the engine. I rolled my window down and gave him a small smile. He smirked at me but said nothing. I put the car in drive and pulled away from the parking lot. I watched him in my rearview mirror until I turned the corner. He hadn't moved.

I was shocked when I felt a tear sliding down my face. I was going to miss him so fucking much even though I shouldn't. Nothing about our relationship should make me miss him, but I knew I would. Already, I felt a hollow ache in my chest.

If I were a weaker woman, I would seriously wonder if I was falling in love with him. I pushed the thought aside as I wiped my tears away.

I was being ridiculous. There was no way I could fall in love with Adam.

Then, why did my tears start falling harder than before?

Two Months Later—July

June and July had been blissfully peaceful. After everything that had happened at school, I'd loved every single minute of my peaceful summer. My mom and dad had been ecstatic that I was back home. The first few days had consisted of more family time than I'd ever thought possible. They'd even taken days off of work just so we could go places and spend time together.

In true Mom and Dad fashion, they'd made Logan feel as welcome as me. He'd seemed unsure of how to handle their attention at first, but he quickly grew used to it. While we'd been best friends since our freshman year of high school, he'd never really spent one-on-one time with my parents.

His mom wasn't like Chloe's, but I knew that his mom hadn't spent a lot of time with him. Truthfully, he barely mentioned her. Even though he was in the same city as her, he never once said a word about going to see her. I didn't pry, but I was curious as to whether or not something had happened with them. When I'd asked, he'd simply shrugged and told me she hadn't even asked if or when he would come to see her. He didn't see the point in visiting when she was almost never home.

Once my parents had started back into their usual routine, Logan and I would spend most of our days by the pool. I'd even managed to get him to go to the mall with me a couple of times. He'd grumbled the entire time, but I hadn't let him ruin my good mood.

After texting Adam to let him know I'd made it home safely, I hadn't heard from Adam—at all. I had expected him to text me once in a while to let me know how the tour was going. Instead, I would find myself checking my phone daily, only to be disappointed when I didn't see anything from him. I told myself that it didn't matter. Adam and I were friends and nothing more. *But still...didn't friends text when they were apart?* I wasn't expecting a love letter, but even text saying, *Tour is going good*, or, *Hope you're well*, would have sufficed.

I tried not to think about him too much. Some days were better than others. I also had the small problem of the fact that I hadn't had sex for two months. To me, that was an eternity. I debated on if I should go out to find some random asshole to hook up with, but I couldn't bring myself to do it. Somehow, I doubted if Adam was having the same problem as me. He was playing shows constantly, surrounded by women who were more than willing to tumble around with a hot guy who played in a band. Guys in bands were fucking nirvana to most of the female population.

Every time I thought of him with someone else, I would feel a surge of jealousy.

Chloe had been almost as distant. Besides a phone call here and there, she didn't really try to stay in contact with Logan and me. When she did finally take a break from her busy life, she would barely give me any details as to what she was up to. I did know that she'd ended up staying with her aunt longer than she'd expected, but I didn't know why.

So, when she called me late one evening, I was surprised. Logan and I had just walked inside from spending a few hours by the pool when my phone rang.

"Hello?" I answered cheerfully. When she didn't respond after a few seconds, I spoke again, "Chloe? Are you there?"

"Yeah," she croaked out. I listened as she cleared her throat before continuing, "Yeah, I'm here."

Her voice didn't sound right, and I instantly went on alert.

"What's wrong?"

"It's my mom," she choked out.

"Oh hell, what did she do now? I swear to God, I'm going to punch that bitch in the face! I'm so sick of this shit!" I growled.

I knew that her mom would try something with her. That was why I hadn't wanted her to go to Ocean City in the first place.

"You don't have to worry. She's dead."

"She's...what?" I asked, unable to process what Chloe had just told me.

"She killed herself."

"I...oh God, Chloe!" I cried. "Logan! Logan, get in here!"

Logan walked into the room with a look of concern on his face. "What's wrong?"

His whole body went rigid as I told him what Chloe had just said. He lurched forward and grabbed my phone from my hand without saying a word to me.

"Chloe? Are you okay?" he asked, his voice full of concern.

"No, not really," I heard her say as I leaned close to hear the conversation.

"Where are you?" Logan asked.

"At my aunt's house. Danny and Jordan are both here with me."

"Give us a couple of hours to get packed and make the drive. What's the address?"

Logan grabbed a pen off my desk and scribbled the address on the back of an envelope. He disconnected the call without another word. He tossed the pen back down before walking toward the door. "Hurry up, and pack. We're going to Ocean City tonight."

I packed quickly.

——— ———— — ——

It was several hours later when we pulled up to a black wrought-iron gate.

"Are you sure this is the place?" I asked skeptically. I knew Chloe's aunt was loaded, but a security gate seemed a little much.

We stopped next to a guardhouse.

"Only one way to find out," Logan said as he rolled down the window.

A moment later, a man appeared at the window. "Can I help you?"

"We're Chloe's friends. Can you let us in?"

"Miss Richards?" he asked.

Logan nodded. "Yeah."

"What are your names?"

Logan gave our names and waited as the man scanned a piece of paper on a clipboard.

"I don't see either of you on the list. I'm sorry, but I can't let you in without permission."

"You can't be serious," Logan said, irritation clear in his voice. "Let me call Chloe." He grabbed his phone out of the console and dialed Chloe's number. When she answered, he spoke, "Chloe, it's Logan. We're at the gate, but the guard won't let us in."

I tried to make out what Chloe was saying, but I couldn't hear her.

Finally, Logan took the phone from his ear and handed it to the guard. "She wants to talk to you."

"Miss Richards?" The guard glanced at us as Chloe spoke to him. "Certainly. Sorry to bother you." Finally, he nodded. "Miss Richards has cleared both of you. Please pull forward when I open the gate," the guard said before disappearing from sight.

A second later, the gate swung open.

"About damn time," Logan grumbled as he pulled through.

We drove up the long driveway. Finally, an actual mansion appeared. It put my parents' home to shame. It was a three-story adobe-style home with red Spanish tiles. The driveway looped around in front of it, and a fountain sat in the center.

We parked in the front and started climbing out. Chloe threw open the front door and hurried to meet us as soon as we were out of the car. Even in the dim lighting, I could see that she looked like hell. Her clothes were wrinkled, and her hair was a mess. The only makeup on her face was eyeliner, and it was smudged around her eyes. Any other time, I would've given her hell for her disastrous look but not tonight.

Logan took off in her direction the moment he saw her. I followed closely behind. As soon as we reached her, he threw his arms around her and hugged her tightly.

"I'm so sorry I wasn't here sooner," he whispered to her.

"It's all right. Jordan and Danny have been taking care of me," Chloe said as she hugged him back.

Feeling left out, I quickly joined in on the hug. We just stood there and held each other for several minutes. I closed my eyes, emotions clogging my throat. No matter what happened, it would always be the three of us. We leaned on each other when one of us needed support. Now was no different, no matter what had changed between Logan and Chloe.

Logan pulled away first. "What happened?"

Chloe looked away. "Why don't we get your stuff inside, and then I can explain?"

He kissed her forehead and turned back to the car. "Sure, but it might take a while. Amber packed like she might never go home."

I snickered. "Of course I did. I knew you'd be around to carry it for me."

He scowled as he pulled two bags from the car. "Gee, thanks."

Chloe and I walked to the car and each grabbed a couple of bags. I couldn't help but laugh at the look on her face when she picked up one of my bags. She looked like she was about to fall over.

"Jesus, this one weighs a ton!" She groaned as she started hobbling toward the house.

Logan held the door open for us as we passed by. "That would be Amber's. The other one is mine."

"Of course it is," Chloe huffed as she set both bags down.

Two guys appeared from the living room and looked at the bags Chloe had just put down. Then, they moved their gaze to Logan and me.

"I take it that we have guests?" the first one asked.

Without a doubt, I knew that this must be her cousin, Danny. I could see the resemblance between him and Chloe. They had the same blondish hair and blue eyes, but while Chloe was pale, this guy looked like he lived at the beach, which he probably did. He stood several inches shorter and not nearly as built as the other guy. Her cousin was definitely attractive, but he wasn't my type.

I glanced at the other man, who must be Jordan, Danny's best friend. He was a big guy, probably around six feet five inches, and built like a football player. His dark hair was cut short, and he had a face with a strong jaw, dark eyes, straight nose, and full lips that made me want to stop and stare. I wanted to fan myself as I looked him over.

"Um, yeah, these are my best friends, Amber and Logan. Sorry I didn't tell you they were coming," Chloe said.

"Not a problem. While you're staying here, this house is yours, too," Danny said.

I pulled my eyes away from Jordan long enough to see Danny smiling at us.

"Guys, this is my cousin, Danny, and his friend, Jordan," Chloe said.

I smiled while Logan shook both of their hands. He seemed to be studying them.

"Nice to meet you," Jordan mumbled before looking at Chloe. "You should have told me they were coming. I would have let them in so that you could get some sleep."

"I'm fine. I really needed to see them," Chloe said as she glanced at him.

Jordan stayed silent, his gaze following Chloe's every move, as Danny crossed the room and grabbed a few of our bags. I raised an eyebrow. Obviously, Jordan had a thing for Chloe. That had to be awkward as fuck. I glanced back over at Chloe. She didn't seem to notice how he was watching her. That was my girl—blissfully unaware.

"Let's get you guys settled in." He glanced between Logan and me. "Do you each need a room? Or would you prefer one together?"

I felt my cheeks heat in embarrassment as Logan laughed. The thought of Logan and me was just so…awkward.

"Nah, she steals the covers," Logan said as he continued to laugh.

I punched him in the arm. "Shut up! We're just friends, nothing more."

Danny laughed at my embarrassment. "All right then, follow me."

Logan and Jordan split the remaining bags and carried them up the stairs with Chloe and me following closely behind.

Danny stopped at the room directly across from the one Chloe pointed out as hers and opened the door. "This one is free, and so is the one beside it. Make yourselves at home."

The boys deposited my bags inside, and Logan carried his to the other room. Chloe and I walked into my new room. I wasted no time, and I started unpacking before my clothes could wrinkle. I hadn't taken the time to fold them earlier since we were in too much of a hurry.

Chloe sat on the bed and watched me.

"Are you okay?" I asked as I hung my clothes in the closet.

"Not really, but I will be. I think I'm in shock right now more than anything. It just doesn't seem real."

I gave her a sympathetic look. "Understandable. I mean, she was horrible, but she was still your mom."

"You want to know what the last thing she said to me was? What a horrible person I am."

I walked over and threw my arms around her. "Oh, Chloe, you know that's not true."

"Yeah, but it's what she thought of me. She called me and told me that the same night she died."

I could hear the pain in her voice.

"I feel bad speaking badly about the dead, but your mom was a crazy bitch. She tried her hardest to break you, and she didn't stop until she took her final breath. But you won, Chloe. In the end, you won. You have an amazing boyfriend, friends, and family who love you more than anything, and that's something she never had."

I released her and went back to putting my clothes away. I knew Chloe, and she wasn't someone I could console with a hug.

Chloe pulled her phone out and frowned.

"Nothing I just said should make you frown," I complained.

"No, it's not that. I tried calling Drake earlier, and he never called me back. It's not like him."

"He doesn't know yet?" I asked, surprised that she'd contacted Logan and me first.

"No, that's why I was trying to call him. He still thinks I'm leaving tomorrow to meet up with him. I hope he's okay."

"I'm sure he's fine. He probably just turned his phone off or something."

She frowned. "Yeah, maybe you're right. I just really need him right now, and he's nowhere to be found."

"I hope you're not talking about me. I'm right here."

We both jumped at the sound of Logan's voice. He gave us a small smile as he entered the room and sat down next to Chloe on the bed.

"No, she can't reach Drake, and she's worried," I said as I finished putting my clothes away. I walked over to where they were sitting and dropped down on the bed next to Chloe.

"Oh," Logan said as he looked away.

"So, do you want to tell us what happened?" I asked, not wanting to talk about Drake any more than I had to around Logan.

"She killed herself," Chloe said flatly.

My mouth dropped open at the same moment Logan's eyes widened.

"I…oh, wow. I don't know what to say," I squeaked out. Of all the things I'd expected her to say, it definitely wasn't that.

Logan wrapped his arm around Chloe and pulled her close. She winced as if in pain.

His brow furrowed as he noticed her discomfort. "What's wrong?"

She sighed as she ran her hand through her disheveled hair. "I haven't told you two anything that's happened this summer."

I crossed my arms over my chest and glared at her. "Am I going to be really mad at you when you do?"

"You will be."

Chloe started speaking, her voice hollow, "You both know I only planned to stay here for a little while to make sure that my aunt didn't give my mom anything. Well, when I got here, my aunt told me that she hadn't planned to give my mom a dime. She'd simply used my mom to track me down. I told my aunt I didn't want the money, but she was…persuasive. I finally agreed to take the money and to stay until she passed to help Danny. Drake was upset that I was staying, but he understood why. He was less than thrilled to leave me with Jordan though. He tried to tell me that Jordan had feelings for me, but I laughed it off. I now know that he was right. Jordan and I…our friendship is rocky right now."

I raised an eyebrow. Maybe Chloe wasn't as blind as I'd first thought.

"Anyway, my aunt passed away. It was really hard on Danny, but Jordan and I helped him through it. An old girlfriend of Danny's, Kadi, showed up to help, too. I really liked her at first."

I didn't miss the bitterness in her voice.

"But it turns out that she was a lying bitch. She didn't care about Danny at all. She was only here to get proof that I was cheating on Drake with Jordan."

"Wait—how does this girl even know Drake?" Logan asked.

"She used to live in Morgantown. They used to hook up." She looked pissed over that little tidbit. "Anyway, she tried to break up Drake and me. Kadi had taken some photos of Jordan and me and made them look...dirty when they weren't. Jordan and I went to see Drake, and he didn't want anything to do with me. Once we cleared everything up, I drove back here to bring Jordan home. Kadi was here when we made it back. I went off and beat the ever-loving shit out of her."

I grinned and smacked Chloe on the back. "Way to go! I didn't know you had it in you."

"Neither did I," she mumbled. "Kadi's gone now, thank God."

"Sounds like you've had a crazy summer," Logan said.

"You have no idea. I haven't even told you about my mom."

"Well?" I asked when she didn't continue.

"When my aunt died, her lawyer came to the house to read the will. Danny, Jordan, my mom, and I were there. When the lawyer told her that she wasn't getting a dime, my mom threatened me and then stormed out. Apparently, she blamed me. We all thought she took off, but she didn't. Instead, she waited until that evening when I was alone in the pool. When I climbed out, she attacked me and nearly killed me. The only thing that saved me was the fact that Jordan came outside while she was trying to drown me. I ended up in the hospital, and the police started searching for my mom."

I was glaring by the time she finished. "Why didn't you call us?" I yelled.

She stared at the floor in front of her. "I didn't want to bother you guys. It's my life, and I need to deal with it on my own. Besides, I had Jordan and Danny around to help."

"Danny and Jordan are not your best friends!" I shouted.

"I know that, but you were hours away. I figured it would be easier for you if you didn't know what was happening. I was thinking of you guys."

"That's bullshit, Chloe! You always do this to us. You keep us in the dark until the last possible minute. And might I add, it always turns out so well when you do that!" I said, my gaze going to Logan.

Both of them knew exactly what I was talking about.

"That's not fair, Amber! I know what I did to Logan was wrong, and I'll regret it for the rest of my life!" she shouted back at me.

"Am I interrupting?" Jordan asked from the door. "You all right, Chloe Bear?"

She nodded. "Fine. We were just having a discussion about my poor decisions in life."

Jordan grinned as he entered the room and sat down in the chair by the desk. "I'd love to hear this."

Logan cleared his throat, looking uncomfortable. "I don't think that's such a good idea."

"Why not?" I growled. "Let someone else see how fucking stubborn Chloe is."

"Drop it, Amber. It's between Chloe and me—no one else," Logan said, emphasizing the last part.

My eyes narrowed at him. "We're all best friends, so that makes me a part of it." I turned to Jordan. "Chloe here cheated on Logan with

Drake. She kept everything to herself, just like she always does, and Logan paid the price."

Jordan didn't look surprised at all over what I'd just said. I got the feeling that he wasn't Drake's biggest fan.

"Is that true?" Jordan asked Chloe.

"Yes, I fucked everything up," Chloe said, her voice barely above a whisper.

He frowned as he looked at Logan. "Drake has a way of really screwing things up, doesn't he?"

"Enough!" Chloe shouted before Logan could respond. "You two can form an I Hate Drake club later. I have too much shit to deal with right now!"

She threw Logan's arm off of her and stormed out the door. Logan started to stand to go after her, but I laid my hand on his arm.

"Let her go. She has enough shit to deal with. I shouldn't have brought that up," I said, feeling guilty.

"No, you should've kept your mouth shut." Logan pushed my hand away and stood.

I watched as he disappeared through the door.

"Well, I sure know how to clear a room," I mumbled.

Jordan chuckled. "Almost as fast as me. I'll teach you how to do it properly one day," he said, his voice flirty.

I gave him a death stare. "Don't act flirty with me, dude. I know your rocks are hard for Chloe."

His eyes widened in surprise. "You don't fuck around, do you?"

I shook my head. "Nope. And I don't fuck guys just to help them make my friends jealous. Move along, dude."

He shrugged. "Let me know if you change your mind. It wouldn't be *just* to make Chloe jealous." He winked at me before leaving the room.

I rolled my eyes. *Men were pigs.*

eleven

Late the next day, the band's bus finally pulled up to the house.

I had started to wonder whether or not Drake was even going to show up, but Chloe had finally managed to get a hold of him earlier that afternoon.

I pretended not to care about the fact that I would be seeing Adam again after two months of absolutely no communication between the two of us. I couldn't lie to myself though. I was excited to see him again.

When Chloe had told me they were finally on their way, I'd dashed up the stairs to my room to find something to wear. I had no idea how Adam would react to seeing me, but I was determined to drive him nuts. I'd dug through the clothes I brought until I'd found an outfit I was satisfied with—a super short denim skirt and a low-cut tank top that showed off my belly.

Slutty? Yes. Effective? Hopefully.

Once I had gotten dressed, I'd taken time to apply my makeup. I'd overdone it a bit, but I didn't care. If Adam wanted to see me, then I was going to give him something to look at. If he decided to avoid me, I would try my hardest to make him squirm.

When Chloe had literally run past my door a few hours later, I'd hurried to follow her, running down the stairs and out the front door. Logan and Danny had been close behind us, but I hadn't seen Jordan.

I walked outside just as the bus pulled up in front of the house.

The bus hadn't even come to a complete stop when the doors opened, and Drake came tumbling off. He literally ran to Chloe and picked her up. He spun her around, laughing. I wanted to vomit at the cuteness. He finally lowered her back to the ground, but they kept their heads together, whispering to each other. I wondered what it would feel like to love someone that much.

My attention went back to the bus as the rest of the band climbed off. My eyes met Adam's. Pure heat shot through my body as we stared at each other. Nothing had changed during our time apart. I still wanted him just as bad as he wanted me. And I knew he wanted me. I could see it written all over his face. Without a doubt, I knew where he'd end up tonight—my room.

He looked away first, but only to pull Chloe into a hug, as did the rest of the band. She gave Adam a surprised look, obviously not expecting a hug from him.

"Don't act so surprised. You kind of grew on us," Adam said between chuckles.

Drake threw his arm around Chloe and steered her toward the house. The rest of us followed behind them, and I ended up next to Adam. Without saying a word, he took my hand and squeezed it quickly before releasing me.

"I assume you all will be staying for the next few days?" Danny asked from behind us.

Drake nodded.

"That's fine with me, but there aren't enough rooms for everyone. A couple of you will have to double up," Danny said.

"I call Chloe!" Drake joked.

"Darn," she grumbled. "I wanted Jade."

Jade laughed as she walked over and kissed Chloe on the cheek. "Just come to my room after he goes to sleep. What he doesn't know won't kill him."

I burst out in a fit of giggles as Adam, Logan, and Drake all gaped at Jade and Chloe.

"Oh, hell no! If there is girl-on-girl action, I want to watch!" Adam shouted.

I rolled my eyes as I smacked him across the chest. "I think you'll be too busy with me."

He grinned. "Right. I volunteer to room with Amber!"

"Jade can stay with me if she wants," Logan said.

We all turned to look at him, surprised. He and Jade always got along well enough, but I hadn't realized they were close enough to share a room.

"Thank you, Logan. I appreciate that. I thought I was going to get stuck with Eric, and he kicks in his sleep," Jade said.

Eric snorted. "Do not."

Logan avoided my gaze as he and Jade walked up the stairs together. Even though they kept several feet between them, I couldn't help but wonder if something was going on there. I wanted Logan to be happy, but I wasn't sure if Jade was the right girl for him. She was in a rock band, for God's sake. Logan was...gentle. I didn't want another woman to eat him alive.

"Well, *that's* surprising," Drake mumbled, mirroring my thoughts.

"All right, looks like you're getting the extra room, Eric. I'll show you where it's at," Danny said.

He followed Logan and Jade up the stairs, and Eric was right behind him.

"Yeah, Adam and I are going to go get caught up," I said with a grin.

"Hell yeah, we are. Chloe, if you and Jade decide to go all girl-on-girl, let me know. I'll be glad to help!" Adam yelled as I pulled him up the stairs.

"Seriously?" I asked when we reached the top of the stairs. I took his hand in mine and led him to my room.

"What? Girl-on-girl is hot. If you ever feel like trying something new, let me know. I'd love to watch."

I rolled my eyes. "I think I'll stick with dick, but thanks."

"I'm not going to complain about that," he said as I pulled him into my room and shut the door behind us.

He shoved me up against the wall and kissed me roughly. My fingers found his hair and threaded through the soft strands. I'd missed the feel of his lips on mine. His tongue plunged into my mouth. I bit down on it before sucking on his tongue ring. He groaned and pushed his body tighter against mine.

All the betrayal I'd felt over the past two months disappeared now that I was back in his arms. Nothing else mattered but him. It didn't matter that he hadn't tried to contact me even once. It didn't matter that he had probably slept with several other women since I last saw him. None of it mattered. All I wanted was him.

"I need you," I said, breaking the kiss.

He grunted before backing up enough to pull his shirt over his head. I did the same before dropping my skirt and slipping out of my shoes. I watched as he took his shoes and shorts off. His eyes never left mine as he slowly lowered his boxers. I stepped forward and traced the muscles in his chest. I smiled a victorious smile as he sucked in a breath, the muscles in his stomach tightening under my hands. He wanted me as much as I wanted him.

I dropped to my knees in front of him. His cock was already hard. I ran my fingertips across it before gripping it, and I leaned forward to suck him into my mouth. He groaned as he thrust his hips forward. I sucked on just the tip, loving the taste of his pre-cum on my tongue. Careful not to scrape him with my teeth, I took him deeper. I sucked hard as I slowly bobbed my head back and forth. I took him as deep as I could go before letting him slide back out.

His breathing was ragged when I finally pulled away. Without looking up at him, I ran my tongue over the tip and then blew softly. He groaned.

"Fuckin' hell, woman. That mouth of yours…" He trailed off.

I looked up at him to see him watching me. I stood and shoved on his chest, pushing him back to the bed. When he dropped down onto it, I grabbed his shorts and pulled his wallet from the pocket. I found a condom inside, and I ripped the packet open.

He watched me with hooded eyes as I stalked over to where he lay. I gave him a coy smile before grabbing his cock and squeezing. His hips came off the bed as his head fell back. He stayed still as I rolled the condom on. I stood and reached behind me to unclasp my bra. He watched with rapt attention as it fell to the floor. My thong disappeared next.

I climbed onto the bed and positioned myself above him. Slowly, I slid down onto his cock. He fisted the sheets as a groan came from deep within him.

"Goddamn," he mumbled.

I closed my eyes as I let him fill me. It'd been only a couple of months, but I still felt a twinge of discomfort as I adjusted to his size once again. I sat still until the pain disappeared. Once it was gone, I raised myself and slammed back down onto him. I bit my lip as I rode him, loving the feel of him inside me.

Every time I slammed down on him, he raised his hips to meet me. Our bodies worked together perfectly, as if they were meant for each other. The only sounds in the room were our breathing and our bodies coming together.

Just as I was about to come, Adam shocked me by grabbing my hips and flipping me on the bed. He was on me instantly. I sucked in a startled breath as he shoved back into me. While I hadn't been gentle when I was on top, he took rough to a whole new level. My head hit against the headboard as he slammed into me at a pace I could barely keep up with. I reached up and pushed against the headboard, both to protect my head and to give myself some leverage.

Sweat beaded across Adam's forehead and slid down his nose. It dripped down onto my chest, mixing with mine. Adam never slowed. He continued to ram into me until both of us were gasping for breath. I tried to keep up with him, but it was impossible.

My orgasm hit me like a tidal wave. I screamed and scratched at his arms as I came. His shout told me that he was right there with me. The orgasm lasted longer than any I'd ever had before. It kept going, and I was afraid that it would never stop. *Talk about sensory overload.*

Finally, when I was ready to cry out from too much pleasure, my orgasm finally started to subside. I kept my eyes closed as spasms and aftershocks ripped through my body. I felt Adam twitching above me, his body trying to recover right along with mine.

"That was…" I trailed off, unable to say anything else.

"Fucking nirvana," he finished for me. He leaned down and kissed me briefly before pulling away and standing.

He disappeared into the bathroom, and I heard the water turn on a second later. I stood slowly, holding on to the bed to keep myself from falling. My legs were like jelly. Once I was sure I could walk on my own, I slowly crossed the room and entered the bathroom. Adam was already in the shower. I watched his naked form as he stood in the water, his hand resting on the wall, almost as if to support himself. If his body felt like mine, I understood why.

Without a word, I opened the shower door and slipped in next to him. He opened his eyes and peered down at me. Neither of us said a word as I turned my face up toward the water cascading down around us. Once my hair was soaked, I grabbed my shampoo and started running it through my hair.

"Let me," Adam said so quietly that I almost didn't hear him.

He raised his hands and started massaging them through my hair. I closed my eyes, loving the feel of him washing my hair. It felt more intimate than anything else we'd shared.

Once he was satisfied, he dropped his hands and pulled me so that I was standing under the water. I washed the suds out of my hair. We showered side by side. It felt like we were in our own little world.

We finished and stepped out. I wrapped a towel around my body and another around my hair. I walked back into the bedroom as Adam finished toweling off. I grabbed a pair of yoga pants and a tank top with a built-in bra. After pulling on my underwear, I threw on the clothes and dropped both my towels onto the floor.

Adam came up behind me, still naked, and wrapped his arms around me. He buried his face in my wet hair. "I missed you."

"I missed you, too."

We stood like that for a few minutes before he finally pulled away. "I should get dressed."

I nodded. "Yeah, Chloe said they have a chick who cooks here. I'm sure dinner is almost ready."

"Good. I'm starved," Adam said as he walked over to the bag he'd dropped earlier.

He dug through and pulled out a pair of boxers and shorts. I frowned when he pulled out a shirt as well. It was silly, but I hated when he wore shirts.

"Why didn't you text?" I blurted out, unable to keep the question at bay any longer.

He tensed for a second before turning around to face me. "I didn't know I was supposed to."

"You weren't. I just thought that you might."

He hesitated before speaking, "I thought that we would be better off. We spent so much time together before. I assumed time apart would be good."

"For who—you or me?"

"Both of us."

I shook my head. "I thought we were friends, too, not just fuck buddies."

"We are."

"Friends talk while they're apart."

"I just..." He sighed. "I don't know what I thought."

"I do. You didn't want me to get the wrong idea. You wanted to put me in my place."

"No, that's not it!" he said, growing angry.

"It is. You wanted to remind me that we're nothing more than...whatever the fuck we are. Well, you didn't need to. I'm well aware that we're not together. You didn't need to reinforce it."

He ran his hands through his wet hair. "I'm sorry if I hurt you. I didn't mean to make you think I don't care. We *are* friends, Amber. I just thought it would be good for both of us if we didn't think about each other."

"I didn't think about you actually. I was too distracted hanging out with Logan. I'm sure you weren't worried about me either. You were too busy playing shows and fucking groupies."

He winced, but I could still see the anger in his eyes. "You're right. I was way too busy doing both."

There it was. I'd assumed that he'd fucked other women since he left, but for him to say it...I hadn't realized that it would actually hurt to hear him admit it. All summer, I'd thought about going out and finding someone else, but I couldn't bring myself to do it. He obviously hadn't had any problem moving on to the next chick.

Whatever he saw in my eyes made him take a step forward. I wanted to back up, but I stopped myself. I needed to hold my ground.

"We both knew the deal before we started fucking," he said softly. "I told you that I wouldn't make a promise I couldn't keep. I like being with you. You're amazing, but I won't limit myself to one woman."

"I know, and I told you that I wouldn't limit myself to just you. I'm not mad at you for sleeping with other girls. I'm mad because I thought you lied about us being friends," I lied.

"So, you're okay with me fucking other chicks?"

I nodded.

"Good. I thought you might…never mind. Anyway, I'm sorry that I made you feel like I didn't care about our friendship. I won't make that mistake again." He stepped closer and smiled down at me. "We good?"

"Yeah, we're good."

That was a lie, too. I felt further away from Adam in this moment than when he'd been away from me. Whether he realized it or not, he'd put me in my place—permanently.

twelve

The next few days passed in a blur.

Chloe's mother had been a piece of trash, but Chloe and Danny had insisted on giving her a proper funeral. Since the crazy woman had decided to end it all by getting run over by a train, a normal burial wasn't possible. Instead, Chloe and Danny had taken her ashes and spread them out across the ocean.

Chloe was a mess, but she tried to hide it. She spent most of her time with Drake, clinging to him as if he were her lifeline. Maybe that was why she didn't notice the changes in him. I'd noticed over dinner the first night the band spent at the house. He still acted like his usual self, but something was different. I couldn't put my finger on what it was, and it drove me nuts. After watching him for a few days, I realized that his eyes were different. They looked haunted. The fire I was used to seeing in them wasn't there. I wasn't sure what was going on with him, but I was afraid to find out. I knew it couldn't be good for him or Chloe.

Adam and I seemed to be at a standstill. We would still fuck daily, but that was it. We wouldn't talk. We'd rarely look at each other outside of my room. I knew my reasons for avoiding him, but I wasn't sure what his problem was. Maybe he'd finally decided to cut ties with me completely. Maybe he'd thought my questions that first night were proof that I cared about him more than I wanted.

I refused to consider the fact that he might be right. I knew even thinking that way would end up with him leaving me broken. I'd gone through that once. I didn't need to have it happen again, especially not with him.

Whether it was true or not, I told myself that I didn't care about him at all. I'd repeat it inside my head enough times that I actually believed myself. Still, I'd find myself watching him when he wasn't paying attention. I was drawn to him, no matter what I did.

It was the night before Adam and the rest of the band along with Chloe planned to leave to continue their tour.

Jordan and Chloe had ended up in a fight over Drake just before the band had arrived. Since then, things had been tense between them. They barely spoke. Since Chloe hadn't been giving him a speck of attention, he'd turned his advances toward me. I wasn't stupid. I knew he was only trying to use me to cause Chloe grief.

I'd brushed him off the first few times he tried to talk to me, but when I'd noticed Adam watching us closely one day, I decided that I could play the same game he'd played.

I smiled at Jordan as he approached me. He seemed shocked, but he kept walking toward me. He dropped down in the chair next to me and looked out at the pool. Chloe, Logan, Danny, Eric, Drake, and Jade were all floating on rafts, talking among themselves. Adam was sitting on the other side of the pool in a chair identical to mine. I glanced at him to see him staring at Jordan.

"Having fun?" Jordan asked.

I turned my attention back to him, giving him the biggest smile I could manage. "Yes. It's so pretty out here."

He nodded. "You been to the beach yet?"

I shook my head. "No, I haven't had a chance with everything going on. Danny said it was okay if Logan and I stayed after the band took off. I'll probably go then."

"It's nice there, but a ton of tourists are around this time of year."

I shrugged. "I'll be a tourist, too."

He grinned. "That might be, but you have one thing they don't."

"And what would that be?" I asked.

"Me. I can take you to all the good spots. Just let me know if you want me to tag along."

I leaned closer to him, knowing that Adam was watching us. I would've felt guilty for using Jordan if it wasn't for the fact that he was using me as well. I had no doubt that he was hoping Chloe would notice our exchange as well.

"What exactly do you want from me, Jordan? Just cut the shit, and tell me."

He grinned, looking unconcerned, but I saw his eyes dart to the pool where Chloe was. "Who said I wanted anything from you?"

"I told you to cut the shit. I know you're trying to get under Chloe's skin, but is that all you're trying to do? Don't play me for a fool, Jordan."

He studied me for a moment before shrugging. "Sure, it'd be nice to piss Chloe off, but that's not the only reason I'm...interested. You're hot, Amber. Plus"—his eyes drifted over to Adam—"I feel like I'm not the only one who's trying to use someone. Am I right?"

I ignored his hint about Adam. "So, you just want to fuck me to make her jealous. How sweet."

"Like I said, you're hot. Besides, Chloe made herself clear earlier when she said she was leaving with Drake tomorrow. I'm not stupid. I won't wait around for someone who doesn't give a damn about me. I'm not asking you out on a date. I just want to be buddies." He winked at me. "And I'm sure that we'd both win since Adam over there is giving me the death glare right now. That's what you wanted when you actually talked to me today, isn't it?"

"Maybe." I grinned at him. "But that doesn't mean I'm interested in your offer."

He studied me for a moment. "I think you are."

I almost laughed, but I caught myself. Without thinking, I glanced over at Adam. Sure enough, he was glaring at Jordan like he wanted to kill him.

Interesting.

My eyes flashed back to Jordan as he waited for me to speak. I could do a lot worse than Jordan. The man oozed sex. I'd noticed that the moment I laid eyes on him. I just hadn't been interested because I was too busy thinking about Adam. I hadn't wanted anyone but him. Now though, I started to wonder if Jordan was just what I needed. Adam had no problem fucking other women, so maybe I should start screwing around with other guys.

"What do you have in mind?" I finally asked.

His grinned widened, and he leaned closer. "Meet me in my room in ten minutes. You know which one is mine, right?"

I nodded. "Fine. I'll be there."

He stood and started walking back to the house. I didn't miss it when he glanced back to where Chloe was. Doubt flooded my mind. I didn't want to piss Chloe off just to get back at Adam. Friends were more important than any guys could ever be.

I stood and walked to the edge of the pool. "Hey, Chloe?" I called.

She looked up. "Yeah?"

"Come here for a second." If I was going to do this, I would make sure that it was okay with Chloe first.

She flipped off her raft and splashed into the pool before swimming over to where I was.

After she climbed out of the pool, I said, "I need to ask you something, and I want you to be completely honest with me."

"Okay…"

"If I sleep with Jordan, will you have a problem with it?"

Her mouth dropped open in shock. "Say what?"

"You heard me. I won't do it if it will cause a problem between us."

Her mouth was still hanging open. She finally closed it after a few seconds. Her eyes darted over to where Adam was still sitting. "But I thought you and Adam were together."

I laughed. "We've never been together, Chloe. We just use each other."

"Are you sure about that?" she asked, studying me carefully.

"I'm sure."

"Amber, I…" She paused. "I don't care if you and Jordan mess around, but I'm not sure you'll feel the same way once the deed is done. I don't pry into your life, but I know something is going on with you and Adam. Plus, I don't want you to regret sleeping around." I opened my mouth to speak, but she held up her hand. "I'm not saying that I'd ever judge you for your choices. I don't think you're a whore for doing what you do with Adam or anyone else. I just want you to be careful. You've been so different this past year."

"I'm not the only one," I said stiffly.

She frowned. "Point made. Just be careful, okay?"

I nodded. "I will."

She reached forward and gave me a quick hug. "I love you."

"Love you, too. Now, I'm off to have some fun." I winked at her and headed for the house.

Now that I was sure Chloe wouldn't be upset, I felt myself relax. I didn't care if what I was about to do would make me look like a whore. I was tired of playing games with Adam. If that meant moving on to someone like Jordan, then so be it. Besides, Jordan seemed like a nice enough guy. It wasn't like it would be torture to have sex with him.

I climbed the steps and walked down the hallway to where Jordan's room was. I knocked softly before pushing the door open. I stepped into the room and looked around. Jordan was lying on his bed with his hands under his head. He turned his head to look at me.

"I wasn't sure you would show," he admitted.

"I wasn't either," I said as I stepped closer.

He sat up and threw his legs off the bed. "Looks like we both need some relief then."

I grinned. "Maybe..."

He stood and walked the few feet to where I was standing. "Last chance to back out."

Instead of speaking, I grabbed his head and pulled him closer. My lips attacked his. I was desperate to feel something with him, even a margin of what I felt with Adam. I continued to kiss him, but nothing happened. It definitely felt good, but there was no spark, nothing at all.

His hands cupped my ass and pulled me closer. His erection pressed against my stomach. Heat shot through my body. This was what it was supposed to feel like when you were with someone you *didn't* care about. I felt no pull toward him besides my body's natural instincts to fuck him.

His hands slid up my body to my bikini top ties. He undid both of them, but he didn't break our kiss. I pushed him away long enough to let my bikini top fall away. I grabbed the ties on my hips and undid them as well.

I saw pure lust in Jordan's eyes as he stared at my naked body. He undid the tie on his swim trunks and let them drop to the floor. I stared at his body appreciatively. He was nothing but pure hard muscle. My eyes dropped down further and stopped on his erection. He was larger than most men, but he couldn't compare to Adam.

Shut up! Stop thinking about him! Now wasn't the time to think of Adam. I thought about him too much as it was.

I grabbed Jordan's hand and led him to the bed. I lay down with him on top of me. He kissed his way down from my cheek to my neck before finally stopping at my breasts. He sucked one of my nipples into his mouth, and I groaned. Despite the fact that I felt like something was missing, it still felt amazing. Jordan released my nipple and turned his attention to the other. After giving it the same attention, he slowly worked his way down my body.

I squirmed when I felt his breath on my skin down there. "Don't."

He raised his head to look at me. "What?"

"Don't...do that. Just fuck me," I told him. I didn't want this to be any more personal than it needed to be.

He frowned but nodded, and then he kissed his way back up my body. He rolled over and grabbed a condom from the nightstand drawer. I watched as he ripped the package open and rolled the condom on.

"You ready?" he asked as he climbed back on top of me.

"Yeah," I said as I closed my eyes.

He entered me in one smooth thrust. My head dropped back onto the pillow, enjoying the feel of him inside me.

Maybe I am a whore, I thought to myself as he began a steady rhythm. My hips rose to meet him each time. *If I weren't a whore, I wouldn't enjoy this as much as I am.*

I shook those thoughts away as I clung to Jordan. His powerful body moved on top of mine, bringing me closer and closer to orgasm. I opened my eyes to look at him. His eyes were closed as he continued to pound into me.

I glanced over his shoulder and froze. Adam was standing in the doorway, watching us. His eyes met mine, and I nearly called out his name when I saw the pain and anger in them. We stared at each other for a moment before my body betrayed me. An orgasm rocked through me. I closed my eyes as it worked its way through my system. I moaned, unable to stop myself. I felt my heart breaking as Jordan shouted his own release.

When I finally opened my eyes, Adam was gone.

Oh God, what have I done?

―――― ――――― ― ――――

Once Jordan and I finished, I dressed without a word and headed back out to the pool. Chloe gave me a questioning look when she saw me, but all I could manage was a small smile. I wasn't ready to tell her how badly I'd fucked up.

Adam never showed back up at the pool, not that I'd expected him to. The rest of us hung out around the pool until almost midnight. Finally, when exhaustion was threatening to take over, we called it a night. I glanced at the couch as I passed through the living room, debating on whether or not to sleep on it instead of going up to my room. I knew Adam was in there, and I didn't want to face him. *Yeah, I knew I was a coward.*

Chloe saw me and waited for me at the base of the stairs. I gave her another weak smile as I moved in her direction.

"Everything okay?" she asked quietly.

"Yeah, everything is fine," I lied.

"You sure about that?" She glanced up the stairs to make sure we were alone. Everyone else had already disappeared. "Did you and Jordan…"

"Yes," I said, unwilling to give her any more details.

Her eyes widened for a fraction of a second before she masked her surprise. "Oh, wow. I didn't think you two would actually do it."

I shrugged. "He's hot. What can I say?"

She studied me carefully. "I take it that it didn't go well?"

I gave her a confused look. "It went fine. Why wouldn't it?"

She frowned. "Then, why do you look like someone kicked your puppy into oncoming traffic?"

I winced at that thought. *Poor puppy.* "I have no idea what you're talking about."

I started to walk away, but she caught my arm and pulled me back. "Amber, what happened?"

I hesitated before finally caving. What would it hurt for her to know the truth? "Adam saw us."

"Oh." She didn't even try to hide her shock this time. "I take it he wasn't happy."

"He didn't say anything. He just…watched me. Then, he left."

"That explains why he didn't come back out to the pool." She sighed. "No matter what you say, I know something is going on between the two of you. I see the way you both look at each other when you guys think no one is watching. It's more than just using each other."

153

"You're wrong. We don't feel anything for each other."

She laughed, but it was cold. "Keep telling yourself that."

I pulled my arm from her grasp. "I'm going to bed. I'll see you in the morning."

I started up the steps, but I stopped when she called out my name.

"Amber?"

I looked back at her. "What?"

"We leave in the morning. It'll be a while before you see him again. Tonight is your only chance to fix this."

I didn't respond. Instead, I turned and continued up the steps. When I reached the top, cold dread settled over me. With every step I took down the hallway, the feeling grew worse. By the time I stopped in front of my bedroom, my entire body was screaming at me to run away. I had no idea how Adam would act when I walked into that room. I doubted if tonight would end well.

I took a deep breath to settle my nerves before quietly opening the door. I slipped into the dark room and closed the door behind me. The only light in the room was from the moon. It shone brightly in the sky, letting small fragments of light slip through the window. I slowly walked toward the bed, my eyes on Adam. All I could see was the outline of his body under the covers. I stopped next to the bed, my eyes never leaving his sleeping form. Now that I was closer, I could make out the shadows of his jaw and the way his hair fell over his forehead.

I closed my eyes for a moment before opening them again. This wasn't what I'd expected to find. I thought that he'd be up, waiting on me. Instead of feeling relieved, the pressure in my chest tightened. I had no idea what to think.

After a moment of standing there, watching him sleep like a creeper, I turned and opened one of the dresser drawers. I pulled out a pair of underwear and a nightshirt. After pulling my bikini off, I pulled my nightclothes on and walked back over to the bed. I slid under the sheets, careful not to wake Adam. I stared up at the ceiling for a while, listening to the deep rhythmic breaths he released, until sleep finally pulled me under.

thirteen

Something woke me. I wasn't sure what, but my whole body was tense. I slowly opened my eyes, noticing that more light was filling the room now. It was still semi-dark in the room, but I knew it would be dawn soon. I turned my head and looked over to where Adam was sleeping. My eyes widened when they landed on him. He wasn't sleeping at all. He was staring at me, no trace of sleep in his eyes, but there was something else in them. I was afraid to look too closely to know what it was.

"Morning," I croaked, my voice thick with sleep.

He didn't say anything at all. He just kept staring at me. We watched each other for another minute before I looked away.

I had no idea what to say. I couldn't tell if he was angry or hurt or if he even cared at all. Yesterday, I had been so sure that I saw pain in his eyes, but it definitely wasn't there now.

My eyes moved back to him as he moved closer. He stopped when our bodies were mere inches apart. As he looked down at me, his eyes hardened. I gulped, truly terrified of what he would say when he finally decided to speak to me.

He lowered his head, ran the tip of his nose down my cheek, and burrowed it in my neck. He exhaled sharply before pulling away.

"You smell like him—still," he said.

"What?" I asked, confused.

"You. Smell. Like. Him." His eyes narrowed. "Jordan."

"Oh."

He looked away finally, but I saw the way his hands clenched into fists against the sheets.

"Adam…" I said, but I couldn't think of anything else to say.

His gaze found mine again, his eyes still cold. "I'm not sure what pisses me off more—the fact that you fucked someone else while I watched or the fact that it actually pissed me off to see you with another man's cock inside you."

I looked away, but that didn't stop him from speaking.

"I think it's the latter. Jesus, Amber. I've never wanted to beat the fuck out of someone like I did yesterday. He was *inside you*, and he got you off. I heard you cry out when he made you come."

"I don't know what you want me to say," I said quietly.

"I want to know why you went to him instead of me if you wanted to fuck. I was right there. I saw you leave the pool to go find him." His voice was deadly calm.

I didn't dare look at him as I spoke, "He offered."

"And you felt the need to take him up on it?"

I shrugged. "Why not?"

God, he was saying so much, but at the same time, it was nothing at all. His voice, the tightness of his body, his eyes—they all told me he was angry. He cared about me. He could lie all he wanted, but he cared. If he didn't, Jordan and I being together wouldn't affect him this way.

"Why not?" he repeated. "Why the fuck not? Because I was right fucking there, Amber. If I'd known you wanted to fuck, I would've taken you up here and shoved my cock inside you. You didn't have to find some other guy to do it."

"Why does it matter to you so much, Adam? I heard you loud and clear the other day. We're not anything. We fuck, and that's it. You fuck other women, and you told me that you didn't care if I fucked other men. Those were your words, not mine. It shouldn't bother you that I was with him."

His breath caught, and I finally looked at him. His eyes held so much anger and pain in them. He looked ready to crack.

"It doesn't mean I wanted to watch you fuck him," he finally said.

"Then, you shouldn't have followed me upstairs," I shot back.

He ran his hand through his messy hair, his fingers clutching at it as if he wanted to pull it out. I wasn't sure if he was just plain pissed off or if something more was bothering him at this point.

"I can't stand to fucking lie here next to you while you smell like him!" he finally said, his voice nearly shouting.

"Wha—" My voice got caught in my throat when his mouth covered mine. I hadn't even seen him move.

His lips parted, and his tongue thrust into my mouth. I made a sound in the back of my throat as our tongues tangled together. He pressed his body down on mine, and I could feel his arousal against my stomach.

He continued to explore every crevice of my mouth, tasting me in a way he never had before.

"I'm going to erase him," he whispered as he pulled away.

I locked my fingers in his hair and pulled his lips back down to mine. I kissed him deeply, savoring the taste of him. We shouldn't be doing this. I knew that. We needed to talk, to sort out whatever the hell was happening between us, but I couldn't stop myself.

My hands slid from his hair down to the smooth skin of his back. I traced his shoulder blades with my fingers before moving them lower. He sucked in a breath as I explored him. The whole time, our mouths never separated.

159

He pulled away long enough to rip my shirt up over my head. He tossed it away before lowering himself again. My pulse quickened as I felt my nipples brush against his chest. I lived for moments like these when nothing was between us. Skin-to-skin with Adam was the only time I felt like we were truly connected.

His hands found my hips, his fingers digging into them as he tried to pull me closer. I wanted closer. I *needed* closer. I wiggled underneath him, and he groaned, his fingers tightening around my hips. In the back of my mind, I wondered if he'd leave bruises, but I didn't care.

I opened my eyes and saw that he was staring at me as he kissed me deeply. My breath froze in my chest as I stared into his dark depths. They were so full of passion, of desire. I needed him more than I'd ever admit out loud.

Adam was everything to me. I loved him. In that moment, I knew it was the truth. Despite his faults, the way he whored around, I loved him. I wanted more than just sex from him. I wanted him to be mine. Admitting that to myself was a lot harder than I had imagined, but I knew it was the truth.

He closed his eyes as he pulled his lips from mine. He kissed along my jaw, stopping briefly to suck on my earlobe. I jerked, pressing my hips against his. He hissed as he ground his hips against mine. Without a doubt, I knew that he would be inside me in a second if it weren't for my underwear and his boxers.

I ran my fingers down his sides, digging in with my nails as I went. He made a sound so deep and so primal that I almost came right then and there. He released my hips, only to catch my hands in his iron grip. He raised them above my head, pinning them there.

TAMED

Without looking at me, he lowered his head and sucked one of my nipples into his mouth. The wet warmth of his mouth was enough to make me moan, but when he gently bit down on the tip, I lost control.

My body exploded. An orgasm crashed down around me. Breath left me, and all I could concentrate on was the way his tongue circled my nipple and the heavy feel of his hard cock against my stomach. Coherent thought was nowhere to be found. The only thing I could feel was the pleasure coursing through my body.

When I finally came back down, I opened my eyes.

He released my nipple and stared at me with a look of awe on his face. "Did you just come from only that?"

I nodded, suddenly embarrassed.

He grinned, the first one I'd seen in what felt like years. "I knew I was good, but damn, I'm a fucking god."

I rolled my eyes. "Shut up."

His expression turned serious. "Oh, I'm done talking."

He kissed a trail down my stomach to the top of my underwear. His tongue slipped under the band, and I moaned. I could feel his lips turn up into a grin as he kissed my skin. He released my hands and grabbed the top of my underwear. He ripped them off, the frail strings snapping, and tossed them away.

He spread my legs and dropped his mouth to the apex of my thighs. I sucked in a sharp breath as his warm tongue ran across my clit. He sucked it into his mouth. I tried to buck my hips, but he grabbed them to hold me in place. I attempted to break his hold, but it was no use. I thrashed around before wrapping my legs around his neck to push his face deeper into me.

161

"Fuck, you smell so good, but you taste even better." He groaned before sucking on my clit again.

I exploded for the second time. A scream ripped from my throat as he worked me through my orgasm. When it passed, my entire body felt like jelly. A thin sheen of sweat covered my body. My breasts rose and fell heavily as I tried to calm my breath.

He pulled away and stood long enough to discard his boxers. Then, he was on top of me again. "You're so fucking beautiful when you come." He stared down at me.

The intensity in his eyes terrified me in the most delicious way.

"I've never seen anything like it. You just...lose yourself in it," he said.

He leaned down and kissed me softly before pushing into me. I bit down on his shoulder as I tried not to scream out in ecstasy. He filled me completely, his body fitting perfectly against mine. No one could ever compare to him.

He dropped his head to my neck. He was buried deep inside me, but he didn't move. Impatiently, I shoved my hips up. He let out a ragged breath as I continued to move against him, fucking him from underneath. He stayed still for a moment before his control finally broke. He pulled back and then plunged into me, deep and hard, his eagerness matching my own. He never slowed, thrusting into me so roughly that I felt a twinge of pain each time. I didn't care. It only brought me closer to the edge.

"So fucking sweet." He moaned as he sucked my nipple into his mouth.

I cried out as a third and final orgasm rocked my body.

"Oh God. Yes!" I shouted as I clung to him.

He called out my name as he came, buried to the hilt inside of me.

"I can't...oh God," I cried out as wave after wave of pleasure coursed through me.

His body locked up as he released inside me. His forehead dropped onto mine, his body shaking.

Every time we were together, the sex would get better. We knew each other so intimately now. We knew where to touch the other, how to move. Our bodies connected perfectly. Without a doubt, I knew that I'd never find someone like Adam again.

His body relaxed before going rigid again. He pulled out and rolled to the side, breathing heavily. "I didn't wear a condom—again. Motherfucker!"

Great, he was pissed off—again.

"It's fine. I'm on the pill," I told him, hoping that he'd let it go. I was too tired to fight with him at this point.

"It's not fine. There's always a chance—"

"Adam, *stop*. I'm not going to end up pregnant and try to tie you down with a kid. Chill the fuck out." There was a bite to my words. I didn't mean for them to come out so harshly, but I couldn't help it. Our last conversation like this ran through my mind. He didn't want to be trapped by me. *Asshole.*

He let out a deep breath. "You're right. I'm sorry. I'm so used to—"

"Covering your ass? Well, I guess I should say, covering your dick."

He smirked at me. "Funny."

I rolled away from him and stood. I didn't want to continue this conversation any longer. I walked to the dresser and pulled on a new pair of underwear and a bra. If he kept ripping my clothes off, I was going to bill him for my next shopping trip.

I found a tank top and shorts in the closet. After pulling them on, I walked to the bathroom and started running a brush through my hair. I glanced up in the mirror. The girl staring back at me looked so…lost. I felt lost. Things with Adam kept going from bad to worse.

And now I knew I loved him.

I was so fucked.

I couldn't tell him—ever. I'd seen the way he acted when I even hinted at caring about him. If I used the L word around him, he'd make an Adam-shaped hole in the nearest wall as he tried to escape me.

I pondered where to go from here as I dropped my brush on the sink and picked up my toothbrush. It didn't matter—at least, not right now. Adam would be leaving in only a few hours. The whole band would, along with Chloe. I had a little over a month until school started, and they returned home. That would give me more than enough time to sort through whatever bullshit was going through my head. Hopefully, I could pull my head out of my ass by then.

When I returned to the bedroom, Adam was up and already dressed. He sat on the end of the bed, watching as I approached. I sat down next to him, careful to keep a few inches between us. When we touched, our brains would shut off. I couldn't afford to let that happen right now. Well, I couldn't afford to let it happen again. We needed to talk before he left.

"I'm sorry for hooking up with Jordan," I told him.

He tried to smile but failed. "I overreacted. I saw you two together, and something exploded in my head. I shouldn't have said what I said."

"You shouldn't have, but I shouldn't have gone to him. We're both at fault here."

"No, you had every right to go to him. What we are, what we agreed to…I don't know what I'm trying to say here."

I smiled at him. "Were you jealous?"

"Yeah, I guess I was. I told you I was okay with you being with other guys, but I didn't think I'd actually have to see you with one of them. That sucked donkey dick."

"I'd probably react the same if I saw you with another girl," I told him. "What does that say about us?" *To me, it says that we care more than we're willing to admit.*

"That we're jealous assholes?" he teased.

"Maybe."

He sighed and ran his hand through his hair. "We still cool? If not, I get it. If you'd rather we parted ways now, I won't try to contact you when I get back to Morgantown after the tour. It'll be impossible not to see each other since Chloe and Drake are attached at the hip, but we can still be…friends if you want."

The thought of him not seeking me out made me want to cry. Even if he wasn't willing to give me what I truly wanted, I couldn't stand the thought of not having him around at all. I would take whatever he gave me. I was pathetic.

"We're fine, Adam. Relax. I like your dick too much to get rid of you."

He smiled at that, his whole body relaxing. "It *is* a really nice dick. I mean, look at it."

He stood and started to pull his shorts down, but I stopped him. I couldn't help but laugh at him.

"I've already seen it numerous times, but thanks for the offer."

He winked at me. "Anytime, babe."

I glanced at the clock on the wall. "We should probably head downstairs. You guys will be leaving soon."

He nodded before pulling me to my feet. His mouth sought mine, and he kissed me softly, so softly that it took my breath away. I didn't know he had it in him.

He pulled away without another word and walked to the door. He grabbed his bag off the floor before opening the door and disappearing through it. I sighed before following him. We walked down the stairs in silence. When we walked outside, everyone else was already standing around the bus.

I moved away from Adam and tackled Chloe from behind. She squealed as I jumped onto her back, my weight toppling us both over. I laughed as we fell to the ground.

"Jesus, Amber!" Chloe shouted, fighting not to smile.

I poked her in the ribs, and she lost it.

"Asshole," she said.

"But you love me anyway." I said as we climbed to our feet. Once we were both standing again, I pulled her into a hug. "I'm going to miss you."

"I'll miss you, too. But it's not like we'll be gone for long. I'll be back before you know it."

"I can't wait," I said.

Logan joined us. He wrapped his arms around both of us, picking us up off the ground in the biggest bear hug ever. I laughed as he put us back down. The terrible threesome would always have each other's backs. I had no doubt about it.

"I love you guys," Chloe said as we separated.

"We love you, too," I told her.

Drake walked over to us and wrapped his arms around Chloe from behind. His eyes never left Logan. My own eyes were rolled so far back into my head that I could see my brain. *Okay, maybe not but close. Jealous much?*

"You ready?" Drake asked her.

"Yeah." She gave us one last smile before walking toward the bus.

Adam brushed past me, stopping long enough to whisper into my ear, "I'll see you soon. I'll call when we get back. If you're lucky, I might even text you a few times between now and then."

I swatted his ass as he moved away from me. That had to be the most unromantic good-bye ever.

Adam glanced back at me once when he reached the bus. His eyes hardened as he looked past me. I turned to see Jordan a few feet away from me. He smirked at Adam before stepping up to me and throwing his arm around me.

"Cut it out," I mumbled as I tried to remove his arm.

"Nah. This'll give him something to think about while he's gone," Jordan mock-whispered to me.

I looked back to Adam. He was still staring at us with his fists clenched at his sides. He shook his head once before climbing onto the bus.

It's just a month. I can handle a month away from him, I thought as he disappeared.

Little did I know, it'd be much longer than a month—much, much longer.

Morgantown, West Virginia

If there was one thing I knew for certain, it was the fact that life was constantly throwing curveballs. It seemed even the most solid of plans could change in a moment, altering the future so distinctly that I could only sit there and stare at fate, wondering what the fuck had happened.

It seemed that my group of friends had more curveballs thrown at us than anyone else in the world. Fate could have at least handed us a cookie and maybe a bottle of Jager to help us as we tried to figure out what the fuck to do.

Cosmic whiplash wasn't fucking cool—at all.

Adam didn't come home at the end of the summer. None of the band did. They'd signed with a label in California only a few weeks after leaving Chloe's aunt's house. When Adam had texted me to let me know what was happening, I tried not to care that I would probably never see him again. At least he'd texted.

I did care though. I cared a whole lot.

Thankfully, I had something to distract me from my own problems—Chloe's problems. She'd left Drake less than two weeks after going on tour with them. It'd turned out that Drake had a little problem with illegal substances—mainly cocaine. That would've been hard on anyone, but add in the fact that Chloe's mother had been a drunk and an addict—well, it wasn't hard to imagine how badly it crushed her.

Once we made it back to West Virginia, Logan and I spent almost all our free time with Chloe. We even rented a place instead of staying in a dorm so that we could be around her. Neither of us wanted to leave her on her own for long. For the first few months, she was almost comatose. I'd never seen her like that before, not even when her mom had died.

Adam kept in touch—kind of. He'd text me once or twice a month. I almost wished he hadn't. Every time I saw his name appear on my cell phone screen, I'd want to throw it. I still cared about him, and being forced to read his messages was pure torture. And I was being forced. My mind would scream at me to delete them, but I couldn't. I would have to know what he wanted to tell me. If I ignored them, I'd have a constant ache in the pit of my stomach.

The band was doing well out in L.A. They were working on their album and preparing for its release and the tour that would follow. Adam was excited, as were the rest of the band members—except for Drake. He was too busy shoving powder up his nose to give a damn about anything else—Adam's words, not mine.

Just when things were starting to settle down with Chloe, Drake came back into her life. The asshole showed up on our doorstep six months after Chloe had left him. He swore he was clean and confessed his undying love.

Chloe took him back. I wanted to kick her, but when I watched them together, I knew she would've taken him back no matter what. They loved each other that much.

Personally, I would have made him suffer a little more. But what did I know about love? Absolutely nothing apparently.

It was like someone had flipped a switch on Chloe. She went from a moping, miserable creature to the happiest woman in the world. I kind of wanted to vomit a little bit when watching her practically skip around. I was happy for her though. The poor girl deserved some happiness.

With her problems no longer an issue, my own started to creep in on me. I thought about Adam more than I wanted to. I thought about him a lot—daily. It started to wear on me until I felt like I was going to explode. It had been over six months, and I still wanted him. My body craved him, practically begging for his touch some nights.

It got to be too much to handle. I hadn't been with anyone since Adam. Six months of nothing but my vibrator and a little imagination was more than I could take. I needed to get laid.

So, I did—several times by several different men that I could barely remember. I wasn't proud of what I was doing. I knew it was wrong, but I couldn't bring myself to care. When I was with someone else, I wouldn't think of Adam as much. For a few blissful hours, I could forget about Adam and the way he'd made me feel. It was only temporary though. As soon as I came back down to earth, I'd wish that I were with him.

Adam had become an addiction to me. I hadn't even realized it until he was gone. Like any other addiction, the withdrawals were horrible. And no matter how much time had passed, I still felt lost. So, I found a new addiction—sex. Only it was with anyone I could find. Sex made me feel alive.

I kept myself in check until the end of our sophomore year of college, mainly because of Chloe. Only a few days after classes had ended, Drake picked her up and moved her to L.A. where he lived— *where Adam lived*.

Adam and Chloe had both abandoned me. Without them, I felt alone. Logan was still around, but his moods would range from sad to downright evil once she'd left. She'd abandoned him, too, and he felt it.

He started spending more and more time away from the house. I wouldn't dare ask him where he went. I didn't want to know.

With no one around to hide from, I let myself go. Before, I'd only gone out once or twice a week. That wasn't enough. I started going out more and more, and then it turned into every single night. Sometimes, I would bring the men home. After Logan had caught me a few times, I started going back to the guy's places. It wasn't the smartest move on my part, but I was past caring. All I wanted was a few hours of blissful silence from my constantly churning mind. If the man wouldn't take me home, we'd find other places to go—the restroom of the bar, the backseat of a car, or even a hotel room. It didn't matter to me. As long as I got off, I was content.

I knew what I was. The other women at the bars I frequented would whisper it as I walked by.

Whore. Slut. Trash.

I didn't deny it. *Why would I?* I was doing the exact same thing I'd watched Adam do. I would sleep with anyone who looked at me.

I was living in my own personal hell, and a part of me loved it.

Naturally, things had to change on me again, and it was just when I'd started to feel comfortable with my hell. *Go figure.*

fifteen

One Year Later—August

Morgantown, West Virginia

When my phone started ringing with a number I didn't recognize flashing across the screen, the last person I'd expected it to be was Drake. I liked the guy, and he might belong to Chloe, but even I had to agree that he was hot as hell. It was just that we weren't exactly best buddies. He'd never called me before.

"Hello?" I answered cautiously, unsure of what to expect.

"Amber?"

I raised an eyebrow. "Drake?"

"Yeah, it's me."

What the fuck? "Um…hi?"

He chuckled. "I'm sure you're probably wondering why I'm calling."

"Well, yeah, a little," I mumbled as I dropped down onto my bed.

"I need your help."

"Please tell me you didn't fuck up again, Drake. I'm so not helping you if you're using again," I said, worried.

"I'm not," he said, his voice tinged with anger. "I'd never do that again. I'm not a total moron."

"That's debatable," I mumbled.

"You're…pleasant to talk to this evening," he grumbled back.

I rubbed my temples. I could already feel a headache coming on. "Sorry. What do you need, Drake?"

He hesitated. "I need your help."

"You already said that. *What* do you need my help with?" My patience was thin tonight.

He was nervous. I could tell that much, even over the phone. I was almost afraid to know what he wanted from me.

His next words came out in a rush, "I want you to plan my wedding."

"Excuse me?" I asked, sure that I'd heard him wrong.

He sighed. "Chloe and I want to get married, but she's freaking about planning it—like, completely freaking. She's terrified, and she has no clue what to do. For some reason, she thinks we need this big, elaborate wedding. She doesn't *want* something like that, but she thinks she's supposed to have one like that."

"Okay...I'm still confused. What does that have to do with me?"

"You're...girlie. You could plan a wedding, no problem. Neither of us want anything fancy, especially not Chloe. She admitted that she didn't. I don't know why she thinks we *have to* have something fancy. She's a damn lunatic. Simple is best. In fact, I have the perfect place in mind for where to have it, but I'll need your help since it's in West Virginia."

"Aw, this is so cute." I said, grinning. "Just tell me what you need me to do, and I'll do it."

He exhaled heavily, like I'd just taken the weight of the world off his shoulders. Guys were so strange.

"There's a secluded spot next to Cheat Lake. It means a lot to Chloe and me. I want to have it there. I just need you to get a few flowers, invite her cousin and Logan, and find a preacher. Can you do that for me?"

"Of course. Do you know what kind of flowers Chloe wants? Actually, why don't you let me talk to her, and we'll figure it all out?"

"No! I don't want her to know that we're planning this."

"So, you're going to surprise her...with a wedding? No way that could end badly," I mumbled.

"If I wasn't completely sure that she wanted to get married, I wouldn't do this. I promise, she'll be excited." He paused. "I think."

I groaned. "Whatever. I'll get everything ready."

"Thank you, Amber."

We spent the next few minutes going over a few tiny details. It seemed simple enough that I was sure I could handle it. Getting flowers, making a phone call to Danny, finding a preacher—I could handle that. The only thing that terrified me was the prospect of telling Logan. That would go over *real* well.

"I'll call you a few days before to make sure everything is set. Jade, Adam, and Eric don't know yet, so I'll tell them. I'm sure they'll want to be there."

"Okay," I said, suddenly desperate to get off the phone. "I gotta go. I'll talk to you later."

"Thanks again," he said.

"No problem." I disconnected the call and dropped my phone down beside me.

Adam. He was coming back to West Virginia. After an entire year, I would finally see him again.

I wasn't sure if I should laugh or cry. Maybe I should be doing both—or neither.

The thought of seeing him again had goose bumps rising all over my body. My girlie parts started singing joyfully. My heart felt like it was doing cartwheels in my chest.

But my brain told me to run like hell.

———— ———— — ——

Everything had gone according to plan, including Logan's freak-out. Still, he'd agreed to come, so I'd considered that a win.

A week after Drake's phone call, I had everything ready to go. I stood in the clearing next to Cheat Lake, waiting for everyone to arrive.

I'd taken great care when choosing my outfit. I'd told myself it was because I wanted to look good at my best friend's wedding, but really, I just wanted to look good for Adam. I was wearing a pale yellow sundress that stopped just a few inches above my knees. It hugged my curves nicely without looking trashy. Compared to the outfits I normally wore, I looked like a saint. The dress was strapless, but I had enough boobage to hold it up, thank God. I'd never live it down if I accidentally flashed everyone at the wedding. My hair was styled in loose curls, perfectly framing my face, and my makeup was light. Overall, I thought I looked pretty good—a little innocent but good. I'd take it.

Logan was with me. He looked like he wanted to bolt or kill someone. At this point, it could go either way. I prayed that he would behave himself.

"Can you at least pretend to smile?" I asked as I leaned back against his car.

He flashed his teeth at me. "There. Happy?"

I laughed. "I asked you to smile, not act like you're going to go cannibal on my ass and eat me."

He rolled his eyes at the exact same moment my phone lit up and Adelitas Way's "Criticize" started playing. My heart stopped. Only one person had that ringtone—Adam. I unlocked my phone and quickly read his text.

Adam: Almost there.

That was it. There was no *I can't wait to see you*, or *I can't wait to fuck you up against a tree*. My whole body sagged in disappointment.

"Adam, Eric, and Jade are almost here. The preacher dude is following behind them," I told Logan.

I replied to Adam, feeling a little pissy.

Me: K.

Asshole.

Logan and I both looked up as two cars pulled into the clearing. A man stepped out of the second one—the preacher I assumed—while Eric, Adam, and Jade climbed out of the first one. My breath caught when I locked eyes with Adam. God, he was beautiful. He still looked exactly the same as he had the last time we'd been together. After a year apart, I'd thought that maybe I wouldn't be so bothered by his presence. I was wrong. Seeing him caused my entire body to catch fire.

I forgot my anger, and I ran toward them. I gave a small hello to Jade and Eric before leaping into Adam's arms. He caught me, his hands instantly going to my ass. I started kissing him like I was dying, and he was my last hope. Maybe he was. Our mouths collided, and everything else was lost. He let out a low moan as he deepened the kiss. His tongue attacked mine, his tongue ring hitting against my teeth. I pressed my body against his, desperate to get closer.

He pulled away finally and set me down on the ground. I stared up at him, lost in a haze of lust and longing. My feelings hadn't changed at all. I still loved him. Time apart had done nothing to quell my feelings. This man…he was mine, whether he knew it or not.

"Damn, I've missed you," he whispered.

"Me, too."

He lowered his head so that he could whisper in my hair, "I'm fucking you tonight. I hope that's okay with you."

I smiled. It was more than okay. "We'll see."

His eyes scanned my body, causing goose bumps to rise on my arms. His eyes darkened with lust. Yeah, I affected him the same way he affected me.

Everyone looked up as another car approached. Logan whistled under his breath at the sight of the expensive Mercedes. It pulled up next to Logan, and Danny stepped out.

He shot Logan a grin. Those two had gotten along really well when we'd spent time at Danny's house last summer. "Logan, long time, buddy."

Logan surprised me when he walked over and gave Danny a quick hug as the rest of us said hello. Now that everyone was here, it was time to get them up-to-date on the wedding ceremony.

"Now that we're all here, let me explain everything," I said loud enough for everyone to hear.

Everyone turned toward me, waiting on instructions. I glanced around nervously as I realized that everyone was giving me their undivided attention.

"Okay, so…yeah, Drake said Chloe wanted a low-key wedding, which is why we are the only ones here. He wants the ceremony to take place over there"—I pointed to a spot overlooking Cheat Lake—"with Eric as best man. Obviously, I'll be Chloe's maid of honor. The rest of you just have to stand around and look pretty. Drake texted me when they landed, so they should be here any minute. Any questions?"

Everyone shook their heads.

That was easy.

As soon as everyone started talking, I turned my attention back to Adam. Damn, he looked good. He was wearing a pair of black jeans, obviously his idea of dressing up. I had to laugh at that. His white button-up shirt hugged his chest and stomach nicely, giving me a preview of what was underneath.

Before I could say a word, I heard a car approaching. My hands started sweating as Chloe and Drake pulled into the clearing.

Showtime. I just hoped that they would be happy with what I'd done.

As soon as she stepped out of the car, the confused look on her face made it obvious that she had no idea what was going on. She looked beautiful in a white sundress. Her blonde hair had been straightened, and it was hanging over her shoulders. I couldn't help but grin at the purple streaks running through it. It had taken me forever to convince her to put them in her hair. That had been over a year ago, but she'd kept adding them back.

"What's going on?" Chloe asked as she approached us.

"I thought you would have figured it out by now." Drake grinned down at her.

"I have no clue what you guys are up to."

I grabbed her bouquet of flowers off the hood of Logan's car and walked over to where she and Drake were standing.

"You're an idiot, Chloe. You're about to get married," I said as I handed her the flowers.

Chloe's mouth dropped open as she looked from me to Drake and then to where everyone else was standing. "No way."

"Way," I said matter-of-factly. "Come on, let's get started."

———— ———— – ————

The next hour was a blur of laughter, tears, and inappropriate jokes. Silent tears slid down my face as Chloe and Drake said their vows. It had taken them so long to get here. As I watched them commit to each other for eternity, I smiled through my tears. I knew without a doubt that they had finally found their happily ever after.

My eyes traveled to Adam about a million times throughout the ceremony. I couldn't help it. Each time I looked at him, he would already be watching me with a wicked grin on his face.

Once the ceremony was over, Chloe and Drake took off for their honeymoon. I had no idea what they were doing, but I knew they wouldn't be gone for long. Chloe had mentioned only a few days before that the band's U.S. tour would be starting soon.

The rest of us stood in a loose circle, making plans for the night. Danny had to head home, but the rest of us planned to stop by Gold's and have a few drinks together. Adam, Jade, and Eric had to leave the next morning, but they were going to stay at Drake's house overnight.

The moment Chloe and Drake's car disappeared, Logan broke away from the rest of us and headed for his car. His entire body was rigid.

I chased after him. "Logan, wait! Logan!"

He ignored me as he opened the door and got in his car.

"Logan, talk to me. Please."

"My head is so fucked-up right now, Amber. Just let me go. I need to be alone." He started the car.

"No, the last thing you need right now is to be alone. We're all going to Gold's for a little while. Come with us," I pleaded with him.

My heart broke as I stared at him. He looked like his world had ended. In a way, it had. He'd loved Chloe for so long, always holding out hope that maybe, just maybe, she would be his again one day. That dream was gone now, and he was forced to deal with the harsh reality of his situation.

He shook his head. "I can't. I'm going back to the house."

"Please, Logan, come with us, or all I'll do is worry about you. Come on, it'll be fun."

He exploded like a nuclear bomb. Even though I'd expected it, it still shocked the shit out of me.

"Yeah, it'll be real fucking *fun* to sit around and talk about how happy we all are that Chloe and Drake found their happily ever after. It'll be real fucking *fun* to sit there and pretend like I'm happy while I'm drowning on the inside. *Fuck off, Amber!*" By the time he finished, he was shouting.

The others were close enough that they had heard every word he just screamed at me. No one spoke a word as they all stared at Logan in shock. My lower lip trembled as I tried not to cry. Logan had never once shouted at me like that. His face crumpled in pain, but he didn't apologize. I watched as he slammed his door shut and tore out of the clearing like he was being chased by demons. He *was* being chased by demons, but they were invisible to the rest of us.

"Oh, Logan," I whispered as I wiped away a tear that had escaped.

I looked up when someone wrapped an arm around my shoulders.

Adam.

He looked down at me with a pissed off look on his face. "He had no right."

"He's hurting."

"I don't give a fuck. No one talks to you like that."

I stared up at him, hating what I was about to say. "I need to go after him. I'm sorry, but I can't go to the bar with you guys. Logan needs me more."

I wanted to spend time with Adam, but there was no way I could leave Logan alone. Adam wasn't permanent, no matter how much I wished he were. He was here one moment and then gone the next. But Logan had been there for me more times than I could count. It was my turn to take care of him.

"Fuck that. You're coming with us. Let the asshole run away. He doesn't deserve your sympathy after what he just did."

I shook my head. "He's so broken, Adam. The man you just saw isn't my best friend. Logan doesn't act like that. He's just hurting, and he lashed out at me because I was there. I have to make sure he's okay."

"No. You're coming with me."

I opened my mouth to tell him no, but Jade spoke up, "I'll take care of him. I didn't really want to go to the bar anyway."

"You don't have to. Besides, he's my best friend. No offense, but I'm not sure he'd be comfortable with you."

"You'd be surprised," she said, emotion flashing in her eyes.

"Perfect. Jade can go, and you can stay with me," Adam said.

"I need someone to drive me though. Once we find him, you can just drop me off," Jade said.

"I'll take you," I said finally.

The emotion in Jade's eyes had my brain spinning in a million different directions. Maybe Logan didn't need me right now. Maybe he needed her. Or maybe I was just too selfish to let my one night with Adam disappear.

Adam looked like he wanted to argue, but he closed his mouth when I glared at him. I shrugged out of his hold and walked to my car with Jade right behind me.

I looked back at Adam and Eric as I climbed into my car. "I'll meet you guys at Gold's this evening."

Jade was quiet for the first few minutes of the drive. I felt fifty shades of awkward. I had never really talked to Jade one-on-one before.

"Where do you think he went?" Jade finally asked, breaking the uncomfortable silence.

"I don't know. I figured we could check my house first."

She nodded. "Good idea."

Silence invaded the car again.

"He loves her so much," Jade said. "She doesn't deserve that kind of love from him, not after what she did to him."

My eyes widened in surprise. "Uh…"

She smiled at me. "I don't expect you to agree with me. They're both your best friends after all. But me? I love Chloe to pieces, but she absolutely destroyed him."

"I know," I said quietly.

"I'm going to fix him."

I wasn't sure if she was talking to me or herself, but I didn't respond. The rest of the ride was completely silent. When we pulled up to my house, Logan's car was parked outside. I breathed a sigh of relief.

Thank God he'd come home instead of going out and doing something stupid.

I started to climb out of the car with Jade, but she stopped me. "I can handle him. Go on, and spend time with Adam."

I raised an eyebrow, wondering just how close Logan and Jade were. "You sure?"

She nodded. "Yeah, I got this."

I waited until she opened my front door before pulling away. I hoped I wasn't making a mistake by leaving them alone together.

sixteen

The bar was packed. Somehow, Adam and Eric had managed to snag our old table. I'd been to Gold's a few times since they'd been gone, and it had always been taken. I guessed being a rock star had its perks.

A band was playing up on stage tonight. I couldn't help but grin at the disgusted look on Adam's face as he watched them play. Obviously, he didn't think they were as good as Breaking the Hunger. I had to agree. They weren't bad by any means, but they definitely weren't as good.

People crowded around our table the entire night. Old friends and fans of the band came over to say hello. A few of them even hung around for a while to talk. I didn't mind them at all. What I did mind were the fucking groupies who kept trying to catch the boys' attention. Eric seemed completely unaware, but Adam watched them with a smirk. Still, whenever one of the groupies approached Adam, he'd keep his distance. One girl was even forward enough to sit on his lap, but he literally pushed her onto the floor. I laughed a little too loudly over that one.

After that, Adam grabbed me out of my chair and dropped me down onto his lap. "Now they know my lap is taken for the night," he whispered in my ear.

I grinned like a moron.

It felt good to be so close to him again. It felt right. I snuggled closer to him, loving the way he wrapped his arms around me. His hands strayed to my legs a couple of times. He pulled my dress up enough so that his warm hand was resting against bare skin. I wasn't even sure if he consciously realized what he was doing. He'd never paused his conversation once.

As the night wore on, I started to grow tired from the beer and the events of the day. My mind had strayed back to Logan more than once, but I'd forced myself not to worry about him. He was with Jade. She would take care of him.

"You ready to get out of here?" Adam whispered in my ear.

I shivered as his breath tickled my skin. "Yeah."

I stood as Adam and Eric told everyone good night. Adam held my hand as we walked to the door. That earned me a few glares from some of the women in the bar, but I ignored them. I was too happy to let anything get to me.

He kept my hand in his until we reached my car. I unlocked it and started to climb in.

"Why don't we just walk over?" he asked.

"I don't want to leave my car in the bar parking lot all night," I told him, my thoughts drifting back to the women in the bar. With my luck, I'd wake up to four slashed tires.

"You're coming to Drake's though, aren't you?"

I grinned. "Yeah, I'll be there. You can ride over with me if you want."

He shook his head. "Nah, I'll walk. Wouldn't want Eric to get lost or anything."

The drive to Drake's took me less than a minute. Technically, the house was his uncle's, but I'd never met the man. He was high up in the military and never came home.

As I climbed out of my car and locked it, Eric and Adam appeared around the corner. I followed them up to the front door. After Eric unlocked it, we all stepped inside.

I didn't bother to look around as I headed for the living room. I'd only been in Drake's house once, and that was when Logan and I had helped Chloe pack her things after she'd broken up with Drake, so I knew every room in this house.

Before I reached the living room, Adam grabbed me and pulled me back to him. "Where do you think you're going?" he asked.

Eric rolled his eyes as he walked past us and into the living room. "Remember, the walls are thin. I can hear everything."

Adam laughed. "If you get too excited from listening, you can always join us."

I turned and smacked him on the chest, but Eric just laughed.

"I think I'll pass, but thanks for the offer," Eric said.

He dropped down on the couch and turned on the TV. I noticed when he turned up the volume—a lot. That brought a smile to my face.

Adam chuckled as he led me back to the bedroom. As soon as he closed the door behind us, he pulled me to him and kissed me. I moaned as I pressed my body up against his. Already, I felt the hard length of him pressing into me. The boy didn't waste any time. I pulled away far enough to reach between us and cup him through his jeans. He groaned against my lips.

"I've had a hard-on since you kissed me in the clearing. Then, you kept wiggling your ass against me in the bar. I thought I was going to lose my mind."

I grinned as I pulled away from him. "Let me see if I can help you then."

He watched as I undid the buttons on his shirt and pushed it down his arms. My fingers found the warm skin of his chest. I trailed my fingers over his tattoos before exploring lower. Adam closed his eyes as I became reacquainted with his body. I traced every bump, every crease of his tight abs before moving lower again. My hands found the button on his jeans, and I quickly popped it open. I smiled as I tugged on the zipper and then pulled his jeans and boxers over his hips. He stepped out of them as I dropped myself to my knees in front of him. After being apart for so long, I wanted to do everything I could to please him.

I grabbed his hard cock and squeezed it tight. He sucked in a sharp breath as his fingers found my hair and tangled through the curls. I leaned forward and took just the tip of him into my mouth. I sucked gently as my tongue swirled around his tip.

He groaned, his hips thrusting forward. I took him deeper and pulled back, careful not to hurt him with my teeth. He started panting as I sucked him deeper, my hand constantly squeezing and pulling.

"Fuckin' hell, woman. That mouth of yours..." He moaned as he roughly yanked on my hair.

I winced but didn't slow my pace. His hips thrust forward over and over as he fucked my mouth. I felt his body tighten before he finally released. He roared as hot cum shot into my mouth. I swallowed every drop, desperate for more.

When his body finally relaxed, I released him and stood. His chest was rising and falling quickly while he had a look of pure need in his eyes. Without a word, he reached out and tugged my dress over my head. I stood in front of him in only a thin white thong. My nipples tightened as his eyes trailed down my body. He reached out and grabbed my thong, yanking it down my legs.

Once it was gone, he grabbed my hips and pulled me to the bed. As soon as I dropped down onto it, his head was between my legs. I cried out as he sucked my clit into his mouth. His tongue attacked it, flicking over it faster and faster. My hips came up off the bed as he shoved two fingers inside me. He continued to flick his tongue as he finger-fucked me. Already turned-on, I came quickly. I wrapped my legs around his shoulders and let out a cry that I had no doubt Eric heard, even with the TV blaring. My body shook as a wave of sensation took over.

Before I could recover, Adam was on top of me. He pushed into me, groaning as I tightened around him. My breath caught as he filled me completely. No man could fill me the way he could. He wasn't gentle as he pulled back and slammed into me again. He ground his hips, causing me to suck in a sharp breath. He kept his pace hard and fast, never once slowing. He wrapped his lips around my nipple and sucked. I chanted his name over and over as I felt my next orgasm approaching faster than I would've thought possible.

"I can't...oh God, Adam. I love you," I cried out as wave after wave of pleasure coursed through me.

His body locked up as he released inside me. His forehead dropped onto mine, his body shaking. All at once, he pulled away from me and stood. I opened my eyes, awed by the sight of him. He stood several feet away from the bed, his chest rising and falling quickly. His skin was slick with sweat. I watched as a drop traveled down his stomach. He was more than beautiful to me. He was...perfect.

"Why are you over there?" I asked finally, my eyes traveling back up his body to his face.

My heart stopped when I saw his expression. A look of pure terror crossed his face, and he took a step back. Instantly, I realized what was wrong. "Oh shit, we didn't use anything," I said, my head dropping back onto the pillow. "I know you're OCD about wearing one, but I swear, I'm on the pill. You don't have to freak out."

He shook his head. "You…"

I raised an eyebrow. "What?"

"You said you loved me." His voice came out hoarse.

My entire body froze. "What? No, I didn't."

"Yes, you did." He took another step back.

"*No, I didn't,*" I repeated.

"Jesus fucking mother holy son of a bitch!" he shouted.

I didn't even bother to tell him that didn't make sense.

"Yeah, you did. When you came, you told me you loved me."

"I didn't…" I trailed off as the blood drained from my face. *Oh my God, I did.* "I…holy shit. I didn't mean it, Adam," I said, trying to keep my voice calm when I was anything but. Realizing my feelings and telling him were two very different things. I couldn't believe that I'd actually told him I loved him.

"It just slipped out in the heat of the moment. I say stupid shit when I have sex," I blabbered on.

"You've never done that before," Adam said. He looked like a caged animal, desperate to escape. "Never."

"I don't know why it slipped out. I'm sorry."

He closed his eyes for a moment. When they opened, the terror was gone, and in its place was…*determination?*

He stepped closer, his entire body rigid. When he reached the bed, he sat down next to me. "Do you?" he asked quietly.

"I…no, of course not," I said. Even I heard the shakiness of my voice.

"Don't lie to me," he said. "Do you?"

I stared up at him. If I told him the truth, he would never look at me the same again. After all this time, I wasn't sure if I cared any more. I couldn't keep playing this game with him. "Would it make a difference?"

He stilled. "No."

"Then, why are you asking me?"

"Because I need to know."

I stared at him, shocked when I realized he was blurry. Tears filled my eyes and slid down my cheeks. He didn't reach out to brush them away. He didn't do anything.

"Yes. I think I fell in love with you the moment I saw you."

He jerked as if I'd hit him. He stood and started pacing the room. "This wasn't supposed to happen! Goddamn it, Amber!"

"I'm sorry, you asshole. If I had a choice in the matter, I wouldn't. God knows I've tried to stay away from you. I've done everything I could possibly think of to make myself forget you. It didn't work. Every man I slept with, every kiss, every little thing always reminded me of you. None of them were enough to make me forget about you for long."

His nostrils flared. "How many men have you slept with?"

Wait, what? "Excuse me?"

"How many have you slept with since I've been gone?"

"Why the fuck does that matter?" I couldn't help but remember the last time we'd fought over this. He'd thought I was a whore. Back then, I hadn't been. Now, I wasn't sure.

"It just does," he said, his voice tinged with so much anger that I wanted to hide from him.

"I don't know how many," I finally said. "I've lost count. I lost count a long time ago."

Rage flashed in his eyes, but I didn't look away from him.

"Don't sit there and pretend you haven't been with other women."

His eyes narrowed. "I have."

"And that's okay, but it's not okay for me to have sex? Talk about a fucking hypocrite."

"You're different. No one can touch you."

I snorted. "That's bullshit, and you know it."

"The thought of someone else touching you and moving inside you makes me want to rip that fucker's head off. You're mine."

"I'm not *yours*," I spit out. "You made sure that I understood that. Repeatedly. The thought of me loving you sends you running across the room, yet you don't want me to be with anyone else. What the hell do you expect from me?"

"I…I don't know." He looked so broken in that moment.

I had no idea what had happened to him to cause him so much pain.

"What am I to you?" I asked finally. My voice was soft as if I was afraid my question would make him run away.

He stared at me.

A minute ticked by and then another.

"You're everything to me," he said.

Those four words stole my breath away. I couldn't speak. I couldn't move.

"But it doesn't matter. It never has, and it never will."

I felt like a weight had crushed me. "What happened to you?" I blurted out. "What could have possibly happened to make you so cold that you won't even acknowledge your own feelings?" I demanded.

I was so tired of going back and forth like this. Adam had hurt me more times than I could count, and I was tired of it. I wanted answers.

His eyes locked with mine. They were so dark that they looked almost black. "I loved someone once, and she destroyed me."

"What?" I whispered, shock filling my voice. *Adam loved someone? Was it before or after me? Who was she? What could she have done to utterly destroy him this way, to make him want nothing to do with me or any other woman?*

"I loved Hilary the moment I saw her," he said. His gaze stayed on me, but he looked like he was a million miles away. "She was everything to me."

"When was this?" I asked.

He grinned, but it held no amusement. "The first time I saw her was my junior year of high school. She was a new student. For a year, I watched her, talked to her, but I never let on how I felt. Finally, I grew a pair our senior year and told her everything. Instead of running away, she threw her arms around me and kissed me senseless. After that, we spent every day together. We did everything together."

The emotion in his voice was almost more than I could bear. I hated Hilary. He spoke of her in a way that I knew he'd never speak of me. She'd ruined him before I even had a chance to be with him.

"I wanted to marry her. I was seventeen, and I *knew* I wanted to be with her forever." He swallowed roughly. "Then, she got pregnant."

The world fell out from underneath me. *Pregnant? That means…oh God, Adam is a father. He has a child.*

"Her parents freaked, as did mine. They demanded that we get rid of it." His features turned hard. "We refused. They kicked us both out. My uncle helped us though. He gave me a job at the store and found us a place to live. It was cheap and dirty, but it was all I could afford. I worked my ass off, trying to save money before the baby came. Even though things were bad, it was probably the happiest seven months of my life."

Whoa, wait a minute. "Seven months?" Last time I checked, pregnancy took nine months.

Pure hatred flashed in his eyes. "Hilary broke down and told me the truth two months before our baby girl was due. She didn't think the baby was mine."

"What?" I gasped.

"She'd been sleeping with a guy we went to school with—Brandon. Apparently, she'd been sleeping with him a hell of a lot more than she had been with me. She was almost positive that it was his. She'd gone to him before she told me, but he hadn't wanted anything to do with the baby or her. He'd told her to stay away from him, so she came to me. She knew I would take care of her."

"Jesus," I muttered.

"I don't think she would have ever told me, except Brandon's skin tone is a bit darker than mine, so there would be no way for her to hide if it wasn't mine."

My eyes widened. "Oh."

"Yeah. I was so angry with her, but I couldn't leave her. I knew she didn't love me, but there was a chance that the child was mine, so I stayed until she had the baby." He paused, obviously lost in a thousand memories. "When Hilary went into labor, I prayed that the baby would be mine. I didn't care if Hilary wanted me or not. If that baby were mine, I wanted to keep her. I'd give her everything in the world." A tear slid down his cheek. "Abigail was the most beautiful little baby I had ever seen, but she was definitely her father's child. She had the darkest skin

I'd ever seen on an infant. It was as if God wanted me to know in that very first moment that she wasn't mine."

I clamped my hand over my mouth to keep from crying.

Adam's tears ran freely down his cheeks. "I took one look at her and saw everything that could have been. Then, I walked away. I had no future with Hilary or her baby. Even if I wanted to stay, Hilary never would have let me." He glanced at me. "Maybe it was for the best. I saw Hilary two years ago. She was out with Brandon and their little girl. Looks like me leaving had finally made him man up. They found their happily ever after."

"I don't even know what to say, Adam. I'm so sorry that she hurt you like that."

I reached out and took his hand in mine. He pulled it away as if touching me was the most revolting thing he could think of.

"It was a long time ago. It doesn't matter anymore. I learned my lesson early."

"It does matter. It still bothers you, Adam. That's why you won't let yourself feel anything for me." I took a deep breath. "I'm not her. You can't punish yourself and me for something neither of us had control over."

He glared at me. "I had control the whole time. I was the dumbass who chased her. I fell in love with her. If I hadn't, she never would've been able to hurt me the way she did. So, yeah, I had control."

I shook my head. "No, you didn't."

"I did." He shrugged as if this was a normal conversation that didn't bother him at all. "Now you know my life story. Feel honored. You're one of the few. But knowing changes nothing. No matter how much you might want me, you'll never have me. No one will."

"Adam—" I started, but he cut me off.

"You don't get it, do you? I don't care if you love me. I don't want you!" The cruelty in his voice cut through me like a knife.

"You told me I was everything to you. You wouldn't have said that if you didn't want me."

He laughed. "You are everything to me in a way. Everything I care about, you provide. You fuck me whenever I ask for it. You get down on your knees and suck me off like a good little girl. You never tell me no."

I glared at him. "You're lying. I know you are, so stop it. Just be honest with me for one damn minute."

"You want honesty? Fine. Here's what I think of you. I thought you were my friend. I thought we could fuck with no attachment. But I was wrong. You think you're in love with me, but you're not. You just want to use me like everyone else. You're a whore, Amber. You might not have been one once, but you sure as hell are now."

"Shut up!" I shouted at him.

"You wanted honesty, so there it is. I think you're a whore. But at least you're good at your job. Why do you think I keep coming back? That cunt of yours can fuck my dick like no other. I'm sure all those other guys would agree with me."

"Shut up," I whispered as I wiped tears away. "You're only trying to push me away. It won't work."

He laughed as he stood up. "Think what you want. I don't give a fuck. But I do want to be clear about one thing. This…this thing between us? It's over. I'll never stick my dick in you again. God knows what I'd catch."

I stared at him in horror. He gave me one last cruel smile before disappearing out the door. I just sat there, willing myself to calm down. It was useless. Tears continued to stream down my face, and my body shook with sobs. How could he be so cruel? He was only trying to push me away. I knew that, but it still stung like a bitch. There were so many layers to Adam, so much more than he showed the world. I'd seen parts of him that I doubted anyone else had seen.

I stood abruptly and grabbed my dress off the floor. This wasn't over. I wasn't going to just let him run away, not this time. I threw on my dress and ran from the room.

Eric looked up in surprise when I came barreling into the room.

"Where's Adam?" I demanded.

"Uh…he went out. He mentioned Gold's. He left a while ago though."

How long was I sitting in that room, crying? I wondered.

I didn't say anything else to Eric. Instead, I ran out the front door and around the block to Gold's. It was late, but the parking lot was still full. I couldn't believe it'd only been a couple of hours since I left this place. My whole world had changed.

The bouncer recognized me and grinned. "Back already?"

I nodded. "Have you seen Adam?"

"He came in a little bit ago. I haven't seen him leave."

"Thanks," I said before shoving through the crowd.

I searched every table, every face, but I didn't see Adam anywhere. I sat down on a barstool and scanned the room again. *Nothing.* If he were here, I would've noticed him. I was drawn to him like a moth to a flame. I always knew where he was. Plus, he was taller than most of the guys here. He would stick out like a sore thumb.

I sighed before standing and doing a final sweep of the tables just to make sure I hadn't missed him. Obviously, he'd slipped out without the bouncer noticing. I had no idea where Adam would be now. I'd have to go back to Drake's house and hope Adam showed up sometime soon.

I stopped by the restroom to pee before I left. As I closed the stall door, I heard a girl moan a few stalls down. Despite my crummy evening, I grinned to myself as I peed. At least someone was having a good night.

"Faster," the girl's voice begged.

I raised an eyebrow as I heard her and the dude banging against the wall. The stalls were literally shaking.

Wow...

She moaned again, and a male groan followed.

I tensed. *Holy shit.* I felt like a creeper, sitting here and peeing while listening to two strangers go at it like animals. I finished and flushed the toilet before stepping out of my stall. I walked to the sink and reached to turn on the water. Before I could, I heard the dude speak.

"Fuck yes. Your pussy is so tight, baby," he groaned.

My blood ran cold. It couldn't be. I walked to the handicap stall they were in and pushed the door open. They hadn't even bothered to lock it. I felt like I was going to vomit. Adam had the girl pushed up against the wall while he fucked her brains out. I took a step back and then another. He raised his head, my movements catching his attention. His eyes widened for a fraction of a second before he looked away. He never stopped fucking the little bitch.

I turned and ran. I ran out of the restroom and out of the bar. I didn't stop running until I made it back to Drake's house. I ran inside and grabbed my keys off the table next to the door. Eric was nowhere to be seen, thank God. I turned and walked right back outside to where I'd parked my car. With shaking hands, I unlocked my car and climbed in.

I didn't move. I didn't start my car. I just sat there.

He'd been with that woman less than an hour after he'd been with me. Bile rose in my throat. I threw my car door open and vomited in the grass. When nothing but an empty feeling remained in my stomach, I sat back up.

This hurts so fucking bad. How could he?

I knew he was angry and hurting from what he'd told me about Hilary, but he should've stayed with me. I would've been there for him. Instead, he had gone out and found the first girl who would fuck him. It hadn't taken him long at all either.

All this time, I'd sworn that I was over him. It'd been a fucking year since we last saw each other. That should've been more than enough time to move on and forget about him. But I hadn't. Instead, my pulse had sped up the moment I saw him. He had been all I could see, and I'd instantly lost myself in him. He obviously hadn't felt the same way.

I took a deep breath. My head felt like it was going to crack in two. I rested it against my car seat and closed my eyes. This was it. This moment was the one that would change everything. There was no going back now, not after what he'd said to me earlier. Then, I'd watched him with someone else. My heart couldn't take it anymore. *I* couldn't take it anymore.

He'd won. He'd broken me. I'd fallen in love with a man who didn't give a damn about me, and now, I was paying the price. I felt like my life was over.

"No," I whispered to myself. "It isn't over. I just have to start over."

I promised myself that I would never let Adam touch me again. I wouldn't let him near me.

This chapter of my life was finished. I had to start over—without Adam.

seventeen

Two Years Later—August

Morgantown, West Virginia

People come and go in life. It happens. But there are those who I thought I'd have forever.

God, I was so naive.

Chloe had left me first. She'd moved to California long ago. She'd live in L.A. when Drake wasn't on tour, and when he was on tour, she'd follow him across the country and then the world. She was living the married life with her rock god of a husband.

Her leaving had stung, but it'd been bearable since I'd still had Logan. Our terrible threesome had been dropped down to a duo, and it'd sucked, but I could handle it.

Then, Logan had left. He'd been gone for almost a year now. I still couldn't believe it. Logan had always been so in love with Chloe that I was sure no other woman would ever catch his attention. I had been wrong. He'd fallen for Jade, and after several months of fighting with her and himself, he'd finally pulled his head out of his ass and gone after her, so he was in L.A. now, too.

And I was completely alone.

I hadn't seen Logan since he left, and it'd been even longer since I'd been face-to-face with Chloe. I would still talk to both of them on the phone, but it wasn't the same.

I felt abandoned and lost. The house we'd rented had felt empty without their bickering and laughter. Once, I'd thought it was too small, but after they'd left, it'd felt huge. As soon as my lease had been up, I'd moved into a smaller apartment only a few blocks away. I hated it, too. It was so quiet. I didn't do well with quiet.

I'd graduated from college a year ago. Shortly after, I'd found a job at a local law firm, working as a paralegal. It wasn't the most glamorous job, but it paid decent, and I was content with it. I'd made nice with a few of the other girls I worked with, but I didn't feel close to any of them. It wasn't their fault. They'd welcomed me with open arms. No, it was all on me. I wouldn't dare get close to anyone, too afraid that they'd leave me like everyone else.

I hadn't spoken to Adam since *that night*. I'd seen him several times, just not in person.

Breaking the Hunger had exploded in the last two years. They were constantly on the radio, online, and on the television rock channels. I couldn't escape them even if I tried, but I didn't. I hated myself every single time I'd search for the band's name online. I'd watch their music videos over and over, my eyes glued to Adam the entire time.

I hated myself for it. I hated Adam, too. He'd broken me and left, not once looking back. For all he knew, I could be dead. No, that wasn't true. Chloe would've told him that, I was sure, but I doubted if he'd even care.

I hated men in general. I would still go out from time to time when I had an itch that needed to be scratched, but it wasn't often. I didn't crave sex the way I used to. Adam had ruined even that for me. Yeah, I was a little bit bitter.

Add in the fact that my two best friends had abandoned me, and it didn't take me long to sink into depression.

I had no idea why I'd chosen this bar tonight. I stared around Gold's as I took a sip of my cranberry vodka, my favorite drink. There were so many memories here, haunting me with every sip I took. I should've gone to another bar, any other bar, but I'd come here. I knew why. I didn't want to be alone, and the memories here were as close as I could get to my friends and...*him.*

I also had an itch that needed to be scratched. It'd been almost two months since I had sex, and my body was constantly reminding me of that. Even my body had been plotting against me lately.

As soon as I'd come home after work today, I'd all but ripped off my dress slacks and white button-up shirt. I'd gone to my closet to find the dress to end all dresses. I'd found it quickly—a bright red dress with no back. It was low-cut, showing almost too much cleavage, and it barely covered my ass, but it was perfect for what I wanted—male attention.

And I garnered lots of attention tonight, but none of the men who had approached me sparked my interest. I finished off my drink and put the glass on the bar. This night had been a disaster. Despite the craving my body had, I wasn't in the mood to deal with some scumbag's pick-up lines tonight. I grabbed my purse and stood to leave.

Before I could move, someone called out my name behind me. "Amber?"

I turned to see a man standing a few feet behind me. I squinted at him, trying to figure out who he was. Finally, it clicked. "Alex?"

He grinned as he walked over to me. "Yeah. Damn, it's been a while since I've seen you."

"Yeah, it has," I said as I studied him.

It felt like decades had passed since I'd hooked up with him my freshman year. He'd been the start of my decline, whether he'd realized it or not.

He sat down next to me. "How have you been?"

I settled back down onto my barstool. "Not too bad. I'm working as a paralegal at a local law firm."

He nodded, giving me a small smile. "You look good."

My eyes traveled down his body. "You do, too."

He'd obviously changed a little over the years but not much. He was no longer the teenager I'd hooked up with at a frat party. His blond hair was cut shorter now. His blue eyes were still gorgeous. He'd beefed up over the years. His tight black shirt clung to his body, showing off the muscles in his arms, chest, and stomach.

He grinned. "Can I buy you a drink? I'd love to catch up with you."

I shrugged. "Sure."

He motioned for the bartender to come over. I asked for another cranberry vodka before turning my attention back to Alex.

"So, what have you been up to?" I asked.

He shrugged. "I graduated with a degree in engineering. I've been working for the power company for about six months. I work a lot, but I like it so far."

"That's...impressive," I told him. And it was. It took far more brainpower than I was capable of to get an engineering degree.

He smiled. I turned my attention to the drink the bartender had just set down in front of me. I took a sip of it before turning back to Alex. I glanced down his body again. We'd had fun together before, but I'd grown bored with him quickly. I couldn't help but wonder if that would still apply. He was definitely attractive. He was also the first man I felt interested in all evening.

He leaned closer to me. "Keep looking at me like that, and our chat will end earlier than expected. I'm more than willing to do more than talk with you."

I raised an eyebrow. "I see you're still as forward as ever."

He shrugged. "I just remember how good you are in bed."

I glanced down, and something caught my eye. I froze when I saw a gold band wrapped around his finger. Anger rushed through my body. The fucker was married.

"So, anything else interesting happen to you in the past few years?" I asked, fighting to keep my voice calm.

"Not really."

"You sure about that?"

He gave me a questioning look. "Um…yeah. Why?"

"I don't know. I would think getting married is a big deal." I pointed at his ring.

He swallowed roughly before looking away. "Yeah, I suppose it is."

"You're an asshole," I told him. "What the fuck are you doing in a bar, flirting with me, if you're married?"

He looked back up at me, his eyes blazing. "I didn't come here to pick a girl up, if that's what you're thinking. Believe it or not, that wasn't my intention when I saw you either. I just wanted to say hi. But then…I got distracted."

I snorted. "Again, you're an asshole."

His nostrils flared. "Well, my wife's a bitch, so I guess that makes us a good pair."

"I guess it does." I grabbed my purse and started to stand. "Nice chatting with you."

He grabbed my wrist before I could leave. "I've been married for two years now. I've hated every minute of it. I think she has, too."

"Then, why don't you just leave her?"

"It's not that simple." He glanced down to where he was holding my wrist.

He ran his thumb across my skin, and I couldn't stop the shiver that ran through my body. If he weren't married, I would offer to let him come back to my apartment.

"It is that simple. If you love her, stay faithful. If you don't, then leave. End of story," I told him.

"It's not that easy if your father-in-law is also your boss," he grumbled. "Trust me, if I thought I could leave, I would, but I like my job. There aren't a lot of openings in the area for someone with my degree, and I want to stick around Morgantown."

I studied him for a moment. "What do you want me to say here, Alex?"

He shrugged as he released my arm. For some stupid reason, I settled back down onto the barstool.

"There's really nothing you can say. It did feel good to get that off my chest though."

"I can't believe you got married in college. From what I remember, you were all about *not* settling down."

He grinned, but it faded quickly. "I was. Then, I met Joanne, and…yeah, I thought I loved her. When she pushed me to get married, I didn't want to, but she wore me down. Then, once we were married, she started to change. The sweet, kind girl I fell for disappeared. In her place

206

was a stuck-up, controlling, *mean* woman who lived to piss me off. It's only gone downhill from there."

"Have you tried counseling?" I winced. Why the fuck was I trying to give out relationship advice? I was the last person who should be doing that.

"No. She wouldn't go anyway. She'd be afraid someone might find out that our lives aren't perfect."

I stared at him. God, he looked so…defeated and just plain old sad. "Alex, you shouldn't waste your time on someone who makes you this miserable."

"I'm trapped. There's no way I'm going to throw away my career and home just to escape her. I'll deal."

I finished off my drink and motioned for another one. It looked like I wasn't going to drive myself home tonight.

"Love sucks," I mumbled as the bartender put another drink in front of me.

I picked it up and took a drink and then another. Listening to Alex talk about his problems was reminding me of my own.

"Yeah, it does. The worst part is that I doubt if she even loves me. She just likes the fact that I'm hot, and I bring home a nice paycheck."

I grinned. "You are kinda hot."

He chuckled. "I know."

We sat in silence for a few minutes as I drank my concoction, and he sipped his beer.

"I think she's cheating on me."

I almost choked on my drink. "Why do you think that?"

"She's been…distant lately, more than normal, and she's never home. She tells me that she's out with her friends, but I don't buy it. She was supposed to be out with her friend Samantha one night, but then I saw Samantha at the gas station without her. I know Joanne is lying, but I can't catch her. I'm not even sure if I want to."

"Damn," I mumbled.

"Yeah. So, as you can see, my life is pretty fucked-up right now."

"Just a little," I mumbled.

He grinned. "You still hate me for hitting on you?"

"A little. I've decided not to punch you in your junk though. Consider that a win."

"My junk thanks you."

I laughed. I realized the alcohol was starting to hit me as the room spun a little, and I had to grab the bar.

"Whoa, you okay?" Alex asked, his voice full of concern.

"I'm fine,"

"You don't look fine."

I glared at him. "The vodka is catching up with me, that's all. I think I need to head home."

"You're not driving," he said.

I rolled my eyes. "Wasn't planning on it. I'll call a cab."

"Let me take you home."

I shook my head.

"Come on, I won't bite."

I pointed to the beer in his hand. "You've been drinking, too."

"This is my first beer, and it's still half full. I'm fine."

I shook my head again. "Thanks, but no thanks."

He grabbed my arm and pulled me a little closer. "Let me take you home. I have nowhere else to be. It's not like we haven't been alone before. I promise to be good."

I studied him for a moment before sighing. "Fine. Come on."

He grinned as he helped me stand. He kept his arm around my waist as we walked through the bar. I tried to shove it away, but he wasn't having it.

"If I let you go, you might fall. I'm only watching out for you."

"Sure you are," I muttered as we stepped outside.

I took a deep breath. The night air seemed to clear my head a little. Alex led me over to where a brand-new Dodge Charger was parked.

I whistled. "Nice ride."

"Thanks. I just bought it a few months ago. I've wanted one of these suckers since I could walk."

He helped me into the car and then walked around the front to the driver's side. Once he was settled in, he started the car and pulled away from the lot. I gave him directions to my place before leaning back against the seat and closing my eyes.

The first thing I noticed was how good his car smelled. It was a mix of leather and something distinctly masculine, maybe his cologne. I breathed deeply, enjoying the smell. I felt myself drifting off as the movement of the car relaxed me.

Alex didn't speak until the car stopped. He nudged me gently until I opened my eyes. "We're here."

I mumbled, "Thanks," as I fought to find the door handle. Once my fingers wrapped around it, I forced the door open. It felt like it weighed a million pounds.

"Need some help?" Alex asked as he opened the door further.

I hadn't even noticed him getting out of the car.

He grabbed my arm and helped me stand. I leaned into him as he shut the door, and then he walked me to my apartment building.

"What floor are you on?" he asked.

"Second," I mumbled. Somewhere in the back of my brain, I cursed the fact that my building didn't have an elevator. Stairs weren't going to be my friends tonight.

"I'll help you up. Come on."

We stumbled into the building.

I groaned as I looked at the stairs. "This is going to suck."

He chuckled. "I got ya."

Before I could say anything, he scooped me up into his arms and started up the steps. My protests fell on deaf ears as I tried to get him to put me down.

"Which apartment?"

"First door on the left."

"Keys?"

I dug through my purse until I found them. He continued to hold me as I unlocked the door. It only took three tries or maybe four. I wasn't sure. Once we were inside, he flipped on the light switch by the door.

"Want me to dump you on the couch or take you to your bedroom?"

"Bed. Down the hall, second door." I rested my head against his chest. God, he felt good.

He carried me to my room and gently laid me down on the bed. He pulled off my shoes and dropped them on the floor.

"Thanks," I mumbled as I opened my eyes. The ceiling was spinning.

"You're welcome. You need anything else?"

I opened my mouth to tell him no, but I stopped myself. In my drunken state, that question went deeper than it should have. Did I need anything? Yeah, I fucking did. I needed Chloe and Logan back. I needed

Adam to tell me he was sorry and to hold me in his arms. I needed a friend. I needed someone to make me feel something again. I was tired of being so lonely.

"Amber?" Alex asked when I didn't answer.

"What?"

"You need anything?"

I swallowed roughly, fighting back tears. "Yeah, I do," I whispered. "Stay with me tonight."

His eyes widened. "Uh…are you sure? I happen to remember you saying earlier that you wanted to hurt my man parts."

"I'm sure."

He studied me for a moment before nodding. "All right."

I watched as he kicked off his shoes. He walked to the other side of the bed and dropped down next to me. I closed my eyes when his hand closed over mine.

"You okay?"

I felt a tear slip down my cheek. "Not at all."

⸻

I groaned as I tried to roll over, but something was in my way. I reached out to push whatever it was away, and my hand touched smooth skin. *What the fuck?* My head was pounding, but I forced my eyes open.

"Oh, hell," I whispered.

A man was in my bed. Suddenly, the events of the night before came back to me.

Alex. Oh God. I let him bring me home. I swallowed roughly. *I asked him to stay with me.*

Everything after that was a blur. Tentatively, I grabbed the sheet and lifted it to peek underneath. My eyes widened. I was naked, and what I could see of Alex was naked.

"Fuck!"

Alex mumbled something before rolling over. His eyes opened and slowly focused on me. They widened when he realized who he was looking at. The corner of his mouth tilted up into a smile as he reached out and brushed my hair away from my face.

"Hey," he whispered.

I swallowed again. "I take it we…"

He smiled wider as he sat up. "Yeah, we did."

This wasn't good—at all. "Shit."

His smile disappeared. "Hey, it's not a big deal."

"Yeah, it kind of is." I sat up, keeping the covers tucked tightly around me. "You're married, Alex."

"I am, but I told you about my shitty marriage. It's not like you are trying to break it up."

"Close enough. I might not be a saint, but even I have morals." I ran one of my hands through my hair. "You need to go."

He stared at me for a moment before finally nodding. Without a word, he stood and started gathering his clothes off the floor. I kept my eyes on the far wall, not daring to look at his naked body as he dressed. I'd already fucked up enough.

Once he was dressed, he turned back to me. "Hey."

I looked over at him, surprised to see such a calm expression on his face. If I were in his position, I would be freaking the fuck out.

He grabbed a pen and a piece of paper off the dresser. Then, he scribbled something on it before walking over to me. He put the paper in my hands and gave me a small smile. "You have nothing to feel guilty about, Amber. In fact, last night was one of the best nights I've had in a long time." He hesitated. "If you want to meet up again, call me."

Then, he was gone.

I looked down at the paper in my hands. His phone number was written on it. I sighed before shoving the paper into my nightstand drawer. This was all kinds of screwed-up. I'd been drunk and vulnerable last night. I'd wanted someone to comfort me, and Alex had been there, so I'd let him. From what I could remember now that the fog was starting to clear, I'd let him comfort me several times.

"Fuck!" I shouted into the empty room.

My life was so screwed-up anymore. I'd slept with a married man, knowing that he belonged to someone else. That was low, even for me. It didn't matter that he was on shaky ground with his wife. It still wasn't right.

I sighed. I was pretty sure things couldn't get much worse for me.

eighteen

"Hey, you okay?"

I looked up at the sound of Denise's voice. She stared down at me with a concerned look crossing her face. She was one of my coworkers at the law firm. Our cubicles were side by side, and we chatted daily. Denise was probably the closest thing I had to a friend anymore.

"Peachy," I said before I broke out into a rattling cough. God, I hated being sick.

"You don't sound or look okay," she said. "You've been like this for three days. Have you gone to the doctor?"

I shook my head. "No. I didn't want to miss work."

She frowned. "You need to go to the doctor. No offense, but you look like hell, and I don't really want your germs."

I considered this sickness a punishment for sleeping with Alex. I deserved nothing less.

"I don't want to miss work," I told her again. I shivered and wrapped my sweater around me tighter.

"You have sick and vacation days, Amber. Go to the doctor. I'm not kidding. If you don't leave, I'm going to sick Nancy on your ass."

Nancy was our boss. She was a nice woman, but she didn't fuck around.

I glared at Denise, but it didn't seem to bother her at all.

I finally sighed and gave in. "Fine. Will you let Nancy know I'm leaving?"

She nodded. "Yeah. Feel better, Amber."

"Thanks," I mumbled as I gathered my things and walked to the elevator. Today sucked.

Three hours later, I was back home with a prescription for an antibiotic and strict instructions to rest. I sighed as I popped one of the antibiotics in my mouth. I wouldn't be allowed back to work for at least a week. I had enough money saved that bills wouldn't be an issue, but I hated the thought of staying home all alone. When I wasn't busy or around other people, my mind would go south fast.

After a quick call to work to let them know I wouldn't be in for the rest of the week, I heated a can of chicken noodle soup. I wasn't the best cook out there, but surely, even I couldn't screw up soup too badly. Once it was done, I sat down at my kitchen table and sipped it. It felt good against my sore throat.

I tossed my empty bowl in the sink after I finished, and I grabbed the bottle of medicine that was supposed to make me feel better and knock me out. I drank more of it than I should have, and for extra measure, I took a shot of whiskey, hoping it would help me sleep, too.

I took a quick shower before climbing into bed and snuggling down into the covers.

Within minutes, I was out.

I was miserable and tired of shivering all the time. I was surviving on soup and Gatorade, too exhausted to make anything else. Just as I'd feared, my mind wandered to things I didn't want to think about. I hated that. I was thinking more about Adam than I had in a long time.

Thankfully, my fever broke on the second day, but it took until the third day for me to feel human again. I still wasn't one hundred percent, but it was a start.

Once I was up and moving again, I washed my sweat-soaked sheets and cleaned up my apartment. I was itching to get back to work, but I knew Nancy would tell me to stay home until my doctor cleared me.

In my boredom, I was stupid enough to go on another Internet search. As soon as the image results pulled up, I wanted to toss my phone across the room. Adam was still the same Adam he'd always been. Page after page showed images of him out with women—lots and lots of women. I felt tears slide down my cheeks as I looked through them. I shook my head before dropping my phone down onto the bed. There was no use in missing someone I'd never really had.

The following day, Chloe called me. I hadn't heard from her in a couple of weeks.

"Hello?"

"Hey! What are you up to?" she asked cheerfully.

"Sick. I've been home most of the week," I grumbled.

"Ah, that sucks. I was just calling to check in with you."

I nodded even though I knew she couldn't see me. "Yeah. I'm just glad I feel good enough to shower. Trust me, going three days without a shower isn't advised. I'm pretty sure I smelled like ass."

She chuckled. "Well, you sound like you feel better at least. When do you go back to work?"

"Not until next week. I'm about to go nuts from sitting in my apartment. I have three more days of this shit."

She made a sympathetic noise. "I wish I were there to keep you company."

"Me, too." I sighed. I wished more than anything that Logan and Chloe were around.

"You could always come out here and visit me," she said.

I laughed. "Uh, thanks, but no thanks. By the time I fly out and then back, I'd only have a day with you. I love you, but there's no point."

"Call work and ask for a few days off. You told me a while back that you had, like, three weeks of vacation time saved up. Use them to come out here."

"I can't," I told her.

"Why not? It's not like you have plans."

I bit my lip. "I just...can't."

Chloe had lived in L.A. for over two years. She'd been back to Morgantown a couple of times since then, but I'd never made the trip out to visit her. I knew why. I didn't want to take a chance of seeing *him.*

Chloe sighed. "Amber, it's been a long time. Surely, you're not still thinking about—"

"No!" I cut her off. "It has nothing to do with him."

Chloe knew very little about what had happened with Adam. No one really knew anything, except that we'd parted on...unhappy terms. That was, unless Adam had run his mouth. I wouldn't put it past him to run my name into the dirt.

"Then, what's stopping you?" she asked softly.

"I..." I sighed again. I was being stupid. There was no reason for me not to visit her. I probably wouldn't see Adam anyway. I was letting him control my life even now, and it was ridiculous. "Where would I stay?"

"I have room. You can stay with Drake and me."

I could already hear the excitement in her voice.

"Please, Amber. I really want to see you even if it's only for a few days."

I groaned. "Fine. But I'm still sick, so plan on babying me."

"Deal!"

———— ———— — ——

Less than twenty-four hours later, I found myself pushing through a crowd of people in LAX, searching for Chloe's blonde head. I spotted her just before I heard her shrill shriek. She rushed over to me and threw her arms around me.

"Oh my God! Ah! I've missed you so much!" she shouted as she squeezed me tightly.

I laughed. "I missed you, too."

She pulled away and looked me over. "You look good."

"Thanks. You do, too."

Chloe did look good. Obviously, California agreed with her. Or maybe it was the married life.

I picked up my luggage and followed her out of the airport and to the parking lot. She shoved my bags into the back of her car. Once we were inside, she started the car and pulled from the lot. I stared out my window, taking in the sights. L.A. was so different from Morgantown. Comparing the two was laughable. Where Morgantown was almost nothing but farmland, hills, woods, and fall weather, L.A. was all concrete, congested roads, palm trees, and heat.

I watched as Chloe moved in and out of the congested traffic like a pro. I would be shitting myself if I had to drive in traffic like this.

"Are you feeling better?" she asked.

"Much. I still feel a little weak, but it's nothing unbearable. Those antibiotics kicked my bug's ass."

She nodded. "Good. Now I know that I don't have to baby you."

I stuck my tongue out at her. "Skank."

"Ho," She shot back.

I laughed. It was like no time at all had passed between the two of us.

"Drake and the rest of the band are in the studio today. I thought we could meet up with Logan for lunch. Just the three of us like we used to do. Is that okay?" she asked.

"Sure. It'll be just like old times."

Chloe took us to a place she said was only a few miles away from her house and Logan's apartment. It was far enough away from the main part of L.A. that the traffic wasn't as bad. When we arrived at the small diner, Logan was already waiting on us, sitting at a table outside. When he saw us, he grinned and stood. I all but jumped into his arms and hugged him tightly. I'd missed these two so much.

He finally pulled away and smiled down at me. "It's about time you decided to come visit us."

"Yeah, yeah," I mumbled, still smiling.

Logan dropped back down into his chair. Chloe and I took our seats as well. About two seconds later, a waitress appeared beside me. At least the service was good around here. Chloe and Logan ordered the same thing, so I did, too, without bothering to look at the menu.

"How long can you stay?" Logan asked.

I shrugged. "Work told me I could have next week off, too, so I'll probably stay until next weekend, if that's okay with Chloe."

She rolled her eyes. "Of course it's okay. I'm so excited to have you here. It's been too long since the three of us were together."

"Agreed." Logan grinned at me.

He looked so much happier now, compared to when he'd left West Virginia to go after Jade. There was a peaceful look in his eyes that I hadn't seen in such a long time.

"So, what do you guys do for fun around here?" I asked.

"There are tons of things to do. We can go clubbing, hang out on the beach, or go shopping."

She cringed on that last one. Chloe hated to shop. Unfortunately for her, I loved shopping.

"Whatever you want to do," Chloe added.

"Sounds like we're going to have a busy week. I can't wait to check out all the stores," I teased her.

"Ugh," she grumbled, causing both Logan and me to laugh.

"I'm free most of this week, too, so I can hang out with you two," Logan said. "Except when you go shopping. I'm busy those days."

I stuck my tongue out at him. "Your loss."

Our food arrived shortly after. We spent a couple of hours catching up at the diner before finally heading back to Chloe's house. I asked Logan to come with us, but he declined. Apparently, he had plans with Jade. I wanted to hurl when he wiggled his eyebrows at me. It didn't take a genius to figure out what kind of plans they had.

When we arrived at Chloe's house, I was surprised. I'd expected something…more. Drake was a rock star after all. I'd assumed that they lived in a decked-out mansion. That definitely wasn't the case. While the house was large, it was simple. There was nothing flashy about it. It looked like every other house on this street. It was a two-story white house with a black roof and a small front porch. The only hint that someone famous lived here was the keypad on the gate and the huge privacy fence that extended all the way around the house.

"Your house is…nice," I said as we climbed out of the car.

Chloe laughed. "Not what you were expecting?"

"Not really. I thought you'd live on the beach in a huge mansion or something."

"Nah, we like it here. No one would think to check the L.A. suburbs for Drake. Jade and Logan live in an apartment not far from here. Eric, too. Adam's the only one who lives on the beach. He's got a full bachelor pad set up there."

As soon as the words were out of her mouth, she realized her mistake. She opened her mouth to say something, but I shook my head. She frowned, but she kept quiet as we grabbed my bags from the back of her car.

Chloe unlocked her door and disabled the security alarm. Once we were inside, she locked the door and rearmed the system. I raised an eyebrow, but she just shrugged.

"We're not in West Virginia anymore."

"Obviously," I mumbled.

I glanced around the foyer, taking everything in. The walls were painted a dark red. The color was warm and welcoming. The floors were a dark hardwood. A staircase sat only a few feet away from the front door, and we carried my bags upstairs.

"Is this one okay?" she asked as she opened the second door in the hallway.

We walked into the room. It was much larger than the one I had back in West Virginia. The walls and carpet were a cream color. A queen-sized bed sat against the far wall. Other than that and a closet, the room was completely empty.

"It's perfect. Thank you for letting me stay with you."

"Of course. I'm just excited to have you here. I miss spending time with you."

"Me, too," I said as I dropped my bag down onto the bed.

"I'll leave you alone to get unpacked. Just come downstairs when you're finished."

I nodded, and she left, closing the door behind her. It took me a while to unpack everything even though I'd tried to pack light. I snorted. That wasn't possible for me.

Once everything was put away, I headed back downstairs to find Chloe. At the bottom of the stairs, I made a right and entered a living room. I stopped when I saw Chloe and Drake cuddled up on the couch. Drake held her tightly as he whispered something in her ear. She smiled before dropping her head back onto his shoulder.

They looked so...happy. They were so deep into their own little world that they didn't even see me standing in the doorway. I swallowed as I watched them. The way Drake was holding Chloe was like she was his everything. I wanted that. I wanted it so much that it hurt. I thought I'd never want a real relationship again, but Adam had changed that for me. Then, he'd destroyed any hope I had of finding happiness again. Every man I met, I would compare to him, and they never measured up.

I took a few steps backward until I was back in the foyer. Without a word, I turned and walked back up the stairs to my room, unwilling to ruin their moment together. Or maybe I just couldn't handle being around anyone right now. I wasn't sure which it was. All I knew was that I felt hollow inside.

I sent a silent prayer up that I wouldn't have to see Adam while I was here. I didn't think I would be able to handle it.

nineteen

Los Angeles, California

I loved L.A. Back home, Morgantown was considered a big city. Compared to L.A., it was barely a speck on the radar. L.A. had everything a girl could want. Plus, there was no humidity. My hair loved that.

I spent every waking moment with Chloe. True to his word, Logan would hang out with us when we weren't shopping. We had gone to the beach and hit up every Starbucks in sight. We'd even gone clubbing one night. Chloe and Logan were known by a few of Breaking the Hunger's obsessive fans, but it wasn't so much that they couldn't go out in public. I hadn't expected that. Still, I didn't complain over the fact that we could go anywhere I wanted.

The shopping had been incredible. I'd spent two days just shopping. Chloe had groaned the whole time, but I'd ignored her. It was just like old times. I just hoped I would be able to fit all my new clothes into my luggage. It wasn't like I'd had a lot of room to begin with.

I hadn't seen any of the band members, except for Drake, and he hadn't been around very much. Apparently, they were working on a new album and spending hours in the studio. I counted my blessings. I couldn't have come out here at a better time. I didn't have to share Chloe and Logan with Drake and Jade. Plus, I didn't have to worry about running into Adam. Talk about a win.

Naturally, my luck turned to shit.

Two days before I had to leave, we were sitting at Starbucks when Chloe's phone rang. Based off of her goofy grin, I knew it was Drake.

"Hello?" she asked.

Her smile faded a bit, and she glanced over at me. "Um...I don't know."

I raised an eyebrow as Drake spoke again.

"I'll see, but I doubt it. I'll call you back in a few, okay?"

When she ended the call, she looked anywhere but at me.

"What's wrong?" I asked.

"Uh...nothing," she said, still not looking at me.

Some things never changed.

"When you stare at your feet like that, I know you're hiding something. Come on, what's up?"

She sighed. "That was Drake. He wanted to know if we wanted to come to a beach party tonight. A few other bands from their label will be there, too."

"Oh, sounds fun! Is Avenged Sevenfold going to be there by any chance? If so, we need to start plotting ways to make M. Shadows fall in love with me. Maybe I can kidnap him and force him to be my love slave."

She grinned. "I don't think he'll be there, but if he is, Drake is shit out of luck. I'll help you kidnap him."

We giggled like idiots, both of us gushing about the hotness of M. Seriously, he had to be the sexiest man on earth. Even Adam and Drake didn't stand a chance against him.

"I'd love to go," I finally said once we stopped plotting our imaginary illegal activities.

"There's only one problem," Chloe said, the smile slipping away from her face.

"What?" I asked.

She bit her lip. "Um...Adam will be there. The party is at his house."

"Oh." That stopped me in my tracks. I hadn't seen him once, and I wanted to keep it that way.

"Yeah. I told Drake I'd check with you. I understand if you don't want to go. The three of us can just hang out at the house tonight."

"The three of us?" I asked, wondering if Logan would hang out with us or go to the party with Jade.

"Yeah. You, me, and Drake. He said he didn't want to go without me."

Shit. Sitting around and watching Chloe and Drake make dopey eyes at each other wasn't exactly on my to-do list.

"You can go without me," I said, forcing a smile. "I can hang out by myself for one night."

She shook her head. "No way. You came out here to spend time with me. There's no way I'm ditching you for a party. I'll just call Drake back and tell him to come home after they finish at the studio."

She picked up her phone to call Drake, but I stopped her. "Wait."

She looked up. "What?"

It was ridiculous that I was going to screw up her plans just because I didn't want to see the biggest douche bag to ever live. I needed to grow a pair of lady balls and suck it up. "We can go."

She shook her head. "I'm not going to make you go when I know you don't want to."

"It's not a big deal—for real. Adam and I parted ways a long time ago. I need to grow up and move on."

"Amber—"

"No. We're going, Chloe. I'm not passing up the chance to see a bunch of hot rocker dudes, shirtless and wet."

She grinned. "Well, when you put it like that, how can we *not* go?"

It was dusk by the time we made it to Adam's house. My eyes widened when we parked outside. *This* was what I expected a rock star's house to look like. It was tucked away at the very end of a gated community. The beach house was huge. It looked like it was literally made of glass with only a few steel beams here and there for support. The combination was striking. I had no doubt that, despite the glass walls, Adam had all the privacy he needed, thanks to the tight security we'd just passed through and the long blinds I saw in a few of the windows.

Several palm trees sat in front of his house. We climbed out of the car and walked to the back of the house. My eyes widened as I stared at the massive pool. The asshole even had a tennis court. The thought of him playing tennis was laughable.

"We have to walk down that hill, and then the beach is right there," Chloe said as we moved past the pool.

As soon as we reached the top of the path, the beach came into view. I whistled as I looked down. It was one hell of a view. I could see several people moving around on the beach. A massive fire had been built as well. Music was blaring.

As we reached the bottom of the path, I grinned. Rock stars obviously knew how to party. There had to be at least twenty people.

Several of them were guys, probably members of the bands, but the women outnumbered the men. I looked down at the white bikini I was wearing, suddenly feeling very overdressed next to some of these girls. Their bikini bottoms were nothing more than strings, and the tops weren't much better.

"I feel the need to go on a diet and have plastic surgery," I told Chloe. I didn't have low self-esteem by any means, but next to these girls, I felt plain.

She grinned and grabbed my hand, tugging me closer to the fire. "Ignore those girls. The guys only keep them around for one reason."

"Can't imagine what it would be," I deadpanned.

I looked up when we stopped next to the fire.

Drake stood and pulled Chloe into a hug. He nodded at me. "Glad you two could finally make it. I was starting to wonder if you were going to bail on me."

"I'm sure you would've been entertained even without us around," Chloe said, motioning to two girls with butt-floss bikinis walking by us.

He rolled his eyes. "Like I'd touch that with a ten-foot pole."

He sat back down on the sand, pulling Chloe down with him. I looked around, suddenly in need of some alcohol. I spotted a temporary bar set up a little ways down the beach.

"I'm going to grab a drink. You guys want anything?" I asked.

Drake held up his beer. "I'm good."

"Get me whatever you're getting," Chloe said.

I walked down the beach toward the bar, glancing around as I went. *Holy hot-rock-god overload.* Everywhere I looked, I saw dudes without their shirts. In true rock-star fashion, most of their bare skin was covered in ink. I unashamedly eyed ink and six-packs. After all, I only lived once.

When I reached the bar, a pretty girl in cutoff jeans and a neon pink bikini top smiled at me.

"Can I get two cranberry vodkas?" I asked.

"Sure," she said as she grabbed two glasses and quickly made the drinks. She handed them over. "Here you go."

"Thanks." I turned and walked back to where Chloe and Drake were sitting.

I handed one of the drinks to Chloe before dropping down next to her. My gaze drifted over to where a couple of guys were tossing a football back and forth. I watched with rapt attention, taking in every inch of them. I was becoming a groupie. I needed to get laid.

Thankfully, I didn't see the *one* rocker I had no desire to see. I found that strange since it was technically *his* party.

"So, what do you think?" Chloe asked.

"About what?" I said, forcing my eyes away from the two guys.

"About the party."

"I like it. I'm in love with the view." I glanced around at some of the guys sitting around us. "Definitely loving the view. I think if I sat here long enough, I could orgasm off of it."

She laughed.

Drake wrinkled his nose. "Let's add that to the list of things I don't need to know about you, Amber. Keep your orgasms to yourself."

"Who's orgasming?" a voice asked from behind me.

My entire body locked up, but I didn't dare turn around. I knew that voice anywhere. It had haunted me for years.

"I am. All these hot guys are sending my ovaries into overdrive," Chloe said.

I glanced at her. Her eyes were on me, and I hated the pity I saw in them.

Unable to sit still any longer, I slowly turned around. My breath caught in my throat as I stared at him. *God, he was beautiful.* I hated that I still thought so. I wished that I could think of him as unattractive. His skin was deeply tanned from hours out in the sun. His dark brown hair was no longer dyed the electric blue I was used to seeing, but he still had his trademark Mohawk. His eyebrows were both still pierced twice, and he still had a set of snakebites. My eyes drifted lower, taking in every ripple of his stomach. The boy was ripped. I wished he were fat. That would've made this a little easier.

The moment our eyes met, his widened in shock. The cheerful look on his face disappeared and was replaced by a scowl.

"What the fuck is she doing here?" he asked as he sent a glare my way. He obviously couldn't stand the sight of me, even after all this time.

The feeling is mutual, buddy.

No, that wasn't true. Despite all the shit that had happened between us, my body still wanted him. My stupid heart did, too.

"I invited her. Is that going to be a problem?" Drake said.

I was surprised by the coldness in his voice. I glanced over at him to see him giving Adam a glare of his own.

Damn. With that look alone, Drake had just gained about fifty brownie points.

"No," Adam bit out, "no problem at all. Just keep the whore away from me."

"Hey!" Chloe yelled at him. "Stop being a fucking asshole."

Adam ignored her as he turned and walked away from us. I let out a breath I hadn't realized I'd been holding.

"You okay?" Chloe asked, scooting closer to me.

"I'm fine," I told her.

"He had no right to say that to you," she said angrily.

I forced a smile onto my face. "I couldn't care less what he thinks of me."

"I've never seen him so...mean before. Adam's always so easygoing. I wouldn't have brought you here if I knew he'd say something like that." She hesitated. "What happened between the two of you that made you hate each other that much?"

I shrugged, very much aware of the fact that Drake was listening to our every word. "It's in the past. It doesn't matter." I finished off my drink. "I'm going to get another drink."

"I'll go get it. You just...stay here with Drake," Chloe said as she stood.

"Um...okay."

"I don't want you to be alone tonight."

I rolled my eyes. "I'm a big girl. I can handle being called a whore a few times without breaking out into tears or curling up into a ball."

"Stay." She shot me a look before walking away.

Once she was standing at the bar, Drake spoke, "You want to talk about it?"

I snorted. "Really? You want to sit around the fire and talk boys with me, Drake? Why don't we paint each other's toenails while we're at it?"

"We can if you want. I prefer purple over any other color though."

I grinned at him. "Smart-ass."

He stared at me for a moment, making me squirm. Drake had never looked at me like he was now. I felt like I was under a microscope.

"I think I know what happened between the two of you," he said.

"And I'm sure whatever you're thinking is wrong."

He shrugged. "Maybe, but I doubt it. You started to care about him, didn't you? And when you told him, he freaked."

I raised an eyebrow, surprised. Maybe Drake paid attention more than I'd realized.

"You two were together a lot, and then you fucked it up with feelings. Am I right?"

"Nope, not even close," I lied.

"Did you ever think that he freaked because he felt the same way?" Drake asked, pretending not to hear my denial.

"Here you go," Chloe said as she appeared with two drinks, effectively ending my conversation with Drake.

Unfortunately, his words continued to play over and over in my head.

Chloe handed me one and dropped back down onto the sand. "And look who I found."

I looked up as Jade and Logan sat down on Drake's other side. Logan gave me a small smile before turning his attention to Jade. He wrapped his arms around her and pulled her into his lap.

Great. I'm the odd one out—as usual, I thought to myself as I stared at the two couples.

I lifted my new drink and took a healthy swig of it. The vodka burned my throat, but I ignored it. At least the bartender had made it strong. I had a feeling I was going to need a lot of strong drinks to get through this night.

Dusk turned to darkness quickly. I watched my friends and the people around me. Almost everyone was drunk, including myself. My eyes kept darting around, searching for Adam. I caught sight of him a few times, but he never ventured near our little group. Every time I saw him, he had his arm around a different girl. I pretended that it didn't bother me.

Eric joined our group just as I walked back from getting my fifth drink. Or maybe it was the sixth. I'd lost count. He nodded hello at me, and I gave him a small smile. I didn't know Eric at all. He was the quiet one of the group, but whenever he spoke, everyone would listen.

I watched the fire crackle and pop until I was lost inside the flames. I felt my eyelids drooping, the vodka hitting me hard. I was a sleepy drunk. Go figure.

"Hey! Wake up!" Chloe shouted at me as she shoved my arm.

I opened my eyes and flipped her off. "I wasn't sleeping."

"Sure…" she slurred as she leaned further into Drake.

I grinned when she turned her head and grabbed his face, pulling him in for a kiss. She was obviously drunk, and she fought to turn in his lap. Once she managed to straddle him, I looked away. I did *not* need to see them banging on the beach.

"I gotta pee," I mumbled as I tried to stand. I laughed ridiculously loud as I fell back down. "Fuckin' beach keeps moving."

Logan laughed at me. "I'm sure it's the beach."

I flipped him off, too, before trying to stand again. "Hush."

I wobbled away from the fire, tripping as I went. The only thing that kept me going was the fact that I was about to piss myself. A toilet would be nice, but that would require me to go into Adam's house. That *so* wasn't going to happen.

I moved farther down the beach until the party was nothing more than background noise. The moon was barely more than a sliver, giving me almost no light to see with. That was fine with me. If I couldn't see, no one could see me.

After relieving myself, I slowly walked back toward the party. I'd made it no farther than thirty feet when someone stepped right in front of me. I bumped into a hard body and staggered.

"Whoa, sorry," I mumbled as I tried to move past the person still blocking my path. My temper flared. I was having a hard enough time trying to walk as it was. I didn't need another obstacle to go around.

"Excuse me," I said. I tried to move, but the person blocked me again. "What the fuck, asshole?" I glared up at the person in front of me. I sucked in a shocked breath when I finally saw who it was. Even with almost no light, I recognized him.

"What the fuck are you doing in California?" Adam demanded. His speech was slurred, telling me he was just as drunk as I was.

"Move." I tried to push past him.

He grabbed my wrist and pulled me back. "You don't belong here. No one wants you here."

"Back the fuck off of me!" I jerked my arm free. "I'm here with my friends. Seeing you was just an unfortunate accident."

"Bullshit. You're at my party. I don't want you here."

"And I don't give a fuck what you want." I shoved at his chest.

It felt so good to push him that I did it again. Then, I hit his chest with my fist. I reared back to hit him again, but I lost my balance and fell on my ass. It was not my finest moment.

His legs came into view though, so I did the only thing that would make me feel better. I kicked him. He cursed as he toppled over next to me.

"Fuckin' bitch," he snarled at me.

235

I kicked him again just because I felt like it. "And proud of it."

He glared at me. I glared at him. Epic drunk-glaring ensued, neither of us backing down.

Then, the fucker did something I never thought he'd do again. He kissed me. In one swift move, his body covered me as his lips sought mine. I fought him at first, but that didn't last long. As soon as I felt his erection pressed against my stomach, I caved. I blamed the alcohol.

He kissed me deeply, his tongue diving into my mouth. I bit down on it, and he moaned as he thrust his hips against me. I went from pissed to unbearably turned-on in two seconds flat. I let out the most desperate moaning sound I'd ever heard as I reached up and dug my fingers into his back.

He shoved my bikini top aside and sucked one of my nipples into his mouth. I moaned as the wet heat of his mouth overloaded my senses. He swirled his tongue around my nipple before biting down on it.

"I hate you," I mumbled when he released it.

"The feeling's mutual," he said as he undid the ties on my bikini bottom.

Once they were free, he tossed it aside and jerked his swim trunks down his hips. In one swift move, he entered me. I groaned again, my nails digging deeper into his skin. He thrust his hips forward hard enough that my body moved up the beach a few inches. He cursed as he grabbed my hips to hold me in place. I wrapped my legs around his waist and tilted my hips so that he could penetrate deeper.

"Goddamn," he said through gritted teeth as he fucked me harder. "I've waited for this for so fucking long."

His breathing was ragged as he fought for control. Far too soon for my liking, I felt him explode inside me. He never stopped though. He continued to thrust into me as his fingers found my clit. I cried out as I came, his touch breaking my control.

Once we both finished, he pulled out of me and rolled onto his back. His eyes shut, and within seconds, he was passed out. I sat up and adjusted my top. I spotted my bottoms a few feet away and snatched them up. I fought to tie the strings. Once they were in place, I moved over to him and pulled his trunks back up, giggling as I fought them. I'd never thought I'd see the day when I was actually trying to dress Adam.

I dropped down next to him and curled up with my head on his shoulder. Then, I passed out.

When I woke up, I was very much aware of four things—besides the fact that my head felt like it was going to split open. I could feel sand biting into my cheek, the sun beating down on me, an arm wrapped around me, and last but definitely not least, a very thick erection pressed against my ass.

I slowly forced my body to turn over to see who was behind me. Despite being drunk off my ass last night, I already knew, but I needed to see it with my own eyes. As I turned, Adam let out a low moan. My stomach clenched when I saw that it really was him. I'd almost thought that last night was a dream.

I watched him, taking in every inch of him. It hurt to be this close to him, knowing how much he hated me, but I couldn't bring myself to move away. Instead, I watched him as he slept.

After a few minutes, his eyes slid open. He stared at me, a faint smile curving his lips. I held my breath as I watched him. Did I dare hope that smile meant more?

Of course it didn't. In a split second, the smile disappeared as he ripped his body away from mine. I closed my eyes briefly, willing myself strength. I knew I'd need it.

"What the fuck?" he shouted. He was now standing, glaring down at me.

I groaned. "Will you shut up or at least talk quieter? I have a headache from hell."

"I told you to stay away from me, not sneak up on me for a cuddle when I passed out," he said angrily, lowering his voice.

"Um, excuse me?" I sat up angrily. My head and stomach didn't appreciate that at all, but I gritted my teeth and stood up. I stepped closer to him and poked my finger into his hard chest. "*You* were the one who hunted me down when I went to take a piss break!"

"Bullshit!" he said, but he didn't sound as angry.

"Believe what you want. You were the one who cornered me and—"

His face hardened. "And what?"

I gave him the cruelest smile I could manage. "And fucked me like the whore I am."

He opened his mouth to say something as an emotion, maybe regret, covered his features, but a voice calling my name in the distance cut him off. I looked over to see Chloe and Drake approaching us.

"Last night was a fucking mistake. As far as I'm concerned, it never happened," Adam growled just before they reached us.

"There you are. We woke up, and you were gone." Chloe glanced at Adam. "Um...are you guys okay?"

I forced a smile onto my face. "We're fine. Just catching up on how much we hate each other." I looped my arm through Chloe's and started dragging her away from Adam. "Are we heading back to your place?"

"Yeah." She glanced back to Adam.

I looked back, too, and saw him in deep conversation. Whatever Drake was saying to him had Adam waving his arms in the air like a lunatic. All he needed to do was stomp his foot, and he'd look like an overdramatic chick in the middle of a temper tantrum.

"Are you really okay?" Chloe asked once we were back in her car.

I stared out the window. "Yeah."

"Amber, talk to me, please. I want to help you."

Something broke inside of me. Suddenly, I found myself sobbing and clutching on to her hand like it was a lifeline.

"I fucked everything up," I gasped.

Chloe found a place to pull over. After stopping the car, she pulled me into her arms. "What happened?"

I told her everything—my agreement with Alex that had started my downward spiral, every horrible and wonderful detail of my relationship with Adam, the men I'd slept with, how alone I'd felt in West Virginia, and finally, what had happened the night of her wedding and last night. The only thing I left out was what Adam had told me about Hilary. That wasn't my secret to tell.

She just held me and listened as I poured my soul out to her. "Oh, honey, I'm so sorry I wasn't there for you," she whispered.

"I fell in love with him. How could I have been so stupid? He doesn't care about me. He never has."

"I wouldn't say that," she said as I pulled away. "It sounds to me like he pushed you away because he did care about you. Adam is a bit of a wild child, but he's a good guy. I think something happened to him before he met you. He's scared to commit even if he won't admit to it. There has to be a reason why. Maybe if you both calmed down and tried to talk it out—"

"He hates me, Chloe. We're past talking," I said quietly. "Can we just…I want to go home."

"Of course." She shifted the car into drive and pulled back out into traffic.

Neither of us spoke again until we were back at her house.

I started up the stairs, but I stopped and turned to face her. "I can't stay here any longer, Chloe. I'm sorry. I have to go home."

She nodded. "I understand. I don't want you to go, but I understand why you have to."

"Thank you for everything," I whispered before turning away.

As I packed, I cried. I tried not to, but with no one around to see me, I let my tears flow freely.

I slept most of the flight home. I didn't think I'd be able to, but my exhaustion won out against my mind.

Once we touched down, I gathered my things and walked swiftly through the airport to my car. I debated on staying at a hotel in Pittsburgh instead of driving back to Morgantown in the middle of the night, but I decided against it. All I wanted to do was go home and crawl into my own bed. Maybe if I were lucky, I'd sleep my life away.

My tears reappeared as I drove. I'd fought so hard to forget about Adam. Going to L.A. and then his house had been stupid. I'd known all along that there was a good chance I'd see him even though I pretended there wasn't. A sick part of me had craved the sight of him. I was so stupid.

Seeing Adam had ripped my heart out all over again. I knew he hated the fact that we'd been together on the beach, but I couldn't bring myself to regret it. I wanted all of him, but I'd take whatever bits and pieces I could get. I was so lost in him that I didn't know what to do.

My tears started falling faster as Nothing More's "I'll Be Okay" started playing in the car. That song seemed to completely sum up the last few years of my life. By the time I made it to my apartment, I was hiccupping from crying so hard.

I left my bags in the car. They would have to wait for another day. I walked straight to my apartment and then my bedroom. I dropped down onto my bed and curled up into a ball. I wiped my eyes as I tried to force the floodgates to close. I hated acting like this. Adam didn't give a damn about me, and here I was, sobbing uncontrollably over him. If he could see me now, he'd outright laugh.

That thought turned some of my pain to anger. He had no right to treat me the way he had. I'd done absolutely nothing to him, except be his friend. He had so much animosity against me just because I cared. I couldn't have found a more fucked-up guy to fall for if I tried.

"Fuck him," I whispered, wincing at the roughness of my voice.

I sat up and ran my hands through my hair, letting my anger grow. Being angry was so much better than feeling broken.

I opened my nightstand drawer to pull out a bottle of pain meds for my head when I noticed a folded piece of paper lying on top of the bottle. I picked it up and opened it to see Alex's number. I frowned. I'd never been more tempted to do something in my life. Alex wanted me, which was more than I could say about Adam. But Alex was married, and no good could come from that.

He hates her, and she's cheating on him, a voice in the back of my mind said, egging me on, hoping that I'd do something stupid.

I stared at the paper for a minute before finally making up my mind. I grabbed my phone and dialed Alex's number.

"Hello?" He sounded half-asleep.

"Alex?" I asked.

He paused for a moment. "Amber?"

"Yeah, it's me. I was wondering if you wanted to come over tonight," I said, unwilling to let myself think about what I was doing.

"Yeah, I'll be there in twenty," Alex said, surprise filling his voice.

"I'll see you then," I whispered before ending the call.

Tonight, I wanted to forget, and I knew the best way to do that.

twenty

Six Weeks Later—October

Morgantown, West Virginia

I hated the word *whore*. It sounded so…filthy. I'd been called a hundred different names before—slut, skank, ho, bitch, just to name a few—but when someone called me a whore, it would set my blood on fire.

As I stared down at my fate, I realized that they'd all been right. I was a whore.

There was no coming back from this.

I closed my eyes and willed myself not to cry. I'd done this to myself. This was what I deserved.

I hadn't always been this way. Once, a really long time ago, I'd been innocent. I'd worn my heart on my sleeve. I'd looked at every day like it was a gift instead of the plague that it really was.

Life was so damn hard. I hated it. I'd hated it for years. More than once, I'd wished that I hadn't had to deal with it, that I hadn't had to deal with *him*. But fate had laughed at me, repeatedly throwing him in my face just when I thought I'd healed.

How could I tell him this when he seemed to hate me more and more every time we saw each other? How could I tell him this after what she'd done? I was no better than her.

What was once innocent love and attraction had morphed into something…volatile and ugly. By now, it was almost unrecognizable.

Who am I kidding?

It had never been innocent. We'd seemed to be incapable of innocence, especially him.

I would never survive this. The moment I'd seen him, even though I hadn't wanted to admit it, I'd known that I would never survive *him*.

Tears fell down my cheeks, but I brushed them away as I stood and walked out of the room. When I reached my bedroom, I picked up my cell phone and dialed the only person I knew I could trust, the only person who knew every secret of mine—my best friend.

"Hey, Amber. What's up?"

"Chloe, I need you," I whispered.

"What's wrong?" she asked anxiously.

"I screwed up. I screwed up so bad," I said as my tears came faster now. "I've ruined everything."

"Amber, calm down. You haven't ruined anything. Tell me what's wrong."

"I'm pregnant." I stared down at the pregnancy test in my hand. It was the third one I'd taken. Every single one of them had had the same result—positive.

It had taken me almost three weeks to realize how late my period was. Then, it had taken me almost another week to find enough courage to buy a test. I'd hoped that if I waited long enough to buy one, my period would magically appear, but I'd had no such luck.

She sucked in a sharp breath. "Oh my God. I…I don't know what to say. Have you…have you told Adam?"

"I don't even know if it's his. It could be Alex's."

"Alex?" Her tone grew frantic.

I rubbed my temples. It was time I told her the rest. When I'd had my breakdown in L.A., I'd left out my idiocy with Alex because I'd thought it was a one-time deal. Plus, I had felt ashamed.

"I've been sleeping with him for the last few weeks." I hesitated. "We didn't tell anyone because he's married."

I heard the longest string of curse words that had ever left Chloe's mouth. Under any other circumstances, I would've laughed at her.

"You slept with a *married* man?" she shouted. "How could you do something so dumb?"

"I know it was dumb, and I know what you're thinking right now. I'm a whore. And you're right."

She sighed. "I don't think you're a whore. I think you're an idiot, but you're not a whore."

"Thanks," I whispered, and I meant it.

"So, it could be Alex's or Adam's. Is there…anyone else?"

"No," I whispered. "No one else."

"What are you going to do?" she asked.

"I don't know. I don't even understand how this happened!" I said angrily. "I'm on the pill. I take them religiously."

"Accidents happen. There's no—wait, I think I know what happened. You were sick, and the doctor put you on antibiotics, right?"

My mouth dropped open. "Holy fuck. Antibiotics screw with birth control. I *knew* that. How could I have been so stupid? Everything is ruined now. Goddamn it!"

"Calm down, Amber. Please. You need to sit down and figure out what you're going to do. You need to tell them—both of them."

"I can't. Adam hates me, and Alex is married. There's no way I can tell either of them the truth."

"You don't have a choice, Amber. One of them is the father, and he deserves to know."

"I *can't*, Chloe!" I shouted at her.

I couldn't tell them. It would ruin everything. If Alex were the father, it would destroy his marriage. If it were Adam's—well, I wasn't even going to go there.

"If you don't, I will—at least, with Adam. I mean it," Chloe said.

"Why would you do that to me? I called you because I needed someone, and you're turning your back on me!"

"No, I'm not. I'm helping you. Now, are you going to tell them, or do I have to?"

"I hate you right now," I told her.

"I know, but you won't hate me forever. Now, choose."

"Let me tell Alex first," I finally said after a brief pause.

"All right. And, Amber?"

"Yeah?"

"I'm booking you a flight back out here next week. You need to tell Adam face-to-face. This isn't something you can say over the phone."

I closed my eyes, fighting back a scream of anger...or defeat. I wasn't sure which. "Okay. Work is going to love me for this."

"They'll deal. When are you going to tell Alex?"

"Soon."

"Amber..." Her voice was full of warning.

"I'll tell him this week. I promise."

"Call me after, okay?"

"I will. I need to go."

"Okay. I love you. I hope you know that."

"I love you, too."

⸻

"Hey, I got your message," Alex said as I let him into my apartment.

It had taken me three days and several more tests to finally accept that I was pregnant. I didn't know how to feel about it. I didn't want to be pregnant. The thought of a baby growing inside me turned my stomach. If my life were different, I might have felt excitement. But no, my life was too fucked-up to welcome a child into it.

"Thanks for coming," I said as we walked over to the couch and sat down.

"You said you wanted to talk? What's up?" he asked before leaning forward to kiss me.

I softly kissed him back, wishing that things were different between us. Even if the baby belonged to him, I knew I could never love him.

"I'm pregnant!" I blurted out when he pulled away.

He froze, his eyes widening in shock. "What?"

"I'm pregnant."

"You're...no, you can't be!" he said angrily. "You said you were on the pill. Women on the pill don't get pregnant!"

"I'm sorry," I whispered. "I got sick and had to take antibiotics. They messed with my birth control. If I had known—"

"If you had known?" He laughed. "Are you fucking kidding me, Amber? I'm fucking *married*, and you're telling me you're pregnant with my child." He moved away from me, a look of pure rage on his face.

"There's more," I said quietly.

247

"More? What else could you possibly have to say after dropping that fucking bomb?"

"I don't know if it's yours. I slept with someone else, too, but it was only once. You and I have been together a lot these past few weeks, so there's a pretty good chance that it's yours."

"You..." He closed his eyes, obviously fighting to keep control.

When he opened his eyes, I wanted to run. They looked so cold, so empty.

"The kid isn't mine."

"What? You don't know that. We won't know until it's born."

"It. Isn't. Mine. Do you understand me? I'm not about to lose everything over a slut like you." He stormed to the door. "Don't contact me again. I want nothing to do with you or your *baby*," he spit out the last word like it was dirty.

"Alex, wait!" I cried as I stood and ran to the door. I grabbed his arm just before his hand touched the knob. "You can't just leave me alone like this!"

He grabbed me and roughly shoved me up against the door. I gasped in shock.

"That kid isn't mine. With the way you spread your legs, it could be anyone's kid. Keep your bullshit to yourself or else."

He threw me away from the door. I cried out as I fell to the floor. He didn't look back as he grabbed the door and threw it open. It slammed shut, leaving me with nothing but silence. I stared at the closed door in shock, unable to believe what had just happened. He'd threatened me. He wanted nothing to do with this child, whether it was his or not.

I picked myself up off the ground and walked to my bedroom. My entire body felt numb. I couldn't think properly. I thought Alex would be the easiest to tell. I'd hoped that he'd be excited and that he'd promise to stick with me and take care of me. If I had him, there would have been no reason to tell Adam.

"This can't be happening," I whispered to myself.

If Alex had taken it that badly, I could only imagine how Adam would react. He'd go ballistic, thinking that I was trying to trap him. When he found out that it might not be his, he'd probably tell me to stay away, too.

I hugged my pillow tightly against my chest and cried into it. I knew I had to tell him, but God, I didn't want to. If I hadn't told Chloe, I could've kept it to myself. I could've gotten rid of it before anyone found out. But I'd felt so alone and scared. I'd needed to tell her. I shuddered and clung to my pillow tighter. I couldn't have an abortion anyway. No matter how much trouble this baby was, it wasn't the baby's fault. It didn't deserve to die because I had been stupid.

The last thing that ran through my mind before I fell asleep was Adam and how much I loved him. But things would never be okay between us. Even a child couldn't fix that.

twenty-one

One Week Later—October

Los Angeles, California

I searched the airport, looking for Chloe's blonde head. I couldn't believe it'd been less than two months since I came out here to visit. There was no excitement this time, only dread. Everything had changed.

"Hey," Chloe said, suddenly appearing in front of me.

"Hi," I said as I tried to smile at her.

There were no shrieks of joy or hugging like last time. Chloe tried to smile back at me, but it fell flat. I'd told her how Alex had reacted, and she'd been furious. I knew she was worried about me. I was worried about myself.

The ride back to her house was silent. Neither of us knew what to say. When we walked in her front door, Drake greeted us. He gave me a sad smile before pulling me into a hug.

I gave Chloe a questioning look over his shoulder.

She shrugged. "He knows."

I tensed up, but Drake didn't let me go. "We'll figure it out, Amber. I promise. If all else fails, I'll tell everyone I'm the dad. We never should've had that threesome."

I laughed as I pulled away. I wasn't sure when I'd laughed last. "You must really suck in bed since I don't remember that," I teased.

He grinned. "Are you kidding? I've got some serious moves in the bedroom. Just ask Chloe."

I glanced over to see Chloe blushing like a fool.

"Will you shut up already, you idiot? Amber doesn't need to hear about your *moves*."

"What about that thing I do with my tongue that you like so much?" he teased, causing her cheeks to go even darker.

"I'm going to strangle you in your sleep," she told him.

He grinned. "I'm okay with that. You know I like it when you're rough."

"Oh my God," she mumbled as she covered her face with her hands.

I smiled at Drake, sending a silent thank-you to him. I knew what he was doing, and it was working. He was cheering me up and taking my mind off my problems. Even if it was only for a moment, I appreciated it.

"I'm going to take my stuff up to my room," I said as I grabbed my bags. "Try to keep your tongue to yourself while I'm gone, Drake."

He grinned at me. "I'll try."

I turned and walked up the stairs. I grinned when I heard Chloe smack Drake. He let out a grumble before disappearing into the living room. Chloe followed me up the stairs and walked into my room right behind me.

"He's an idiot," she grumbled.

"He's *your* idiot though."

She smiled. "Yeah, he is."

Chloe sat on the bed as I pulled a few outfits out of my bags. I had no idea how long I'd be staying this time, so I had packed light. If I needed to leave in a hurry, it would be easier to throw four outfits into my luggage rather than twenty.

"So...are you okay?" Chloe finally asked.

I sat down next to her on the bed. "Not really. I've accepted that it's happening, but I can't really wrap my head around the fact that I'm going to be a mom. I'm not exactly parent material."

"You're going to be a great mom. And if Adam turns out to be an asshole, too, Drake and I will help you. I'm sure your parents will, too. Have you told them yet?"

I shook my head. "No. I wanted to get all of this sorted before I called them. It's going to be hard enough to tell them that I'm pregnant. They'll be super proud when they find out I don't know who the father is."

She frowned. "I don't think they'll be upset."

I raised an eyebrow.

"Okay, maybe they'll be a little upset, but once they get over the initial shock, they'll be excited. This baby is their grandchild. I know your mom and dad. They're going to be ecstatic."

"They'd be the first," I mumbled.

She sighed. "I'm sorry, Amber. I know things look really crappy right now, but it will get better. I promise."

"I hope so," I whispered.

She pulled me into a hug. "It will. Do you know how you're going to tell Adam?"

"I have no clue. I don't even know how to get him to talk to me. I'm sure the moment he sees me, he's going to run like hell before I can get a word out."

Chloe released me and smiled. I didn't like the calculating look in her eyes.

"I can take care of getting him near you, and Drake can keep him from leaving."

"What are you planning?" I asked suspiciously.

"Drake can call him and ask him to come over. He doesn't know you're in town, so he'll come. Once he's here, he'll have no choice but to listen to you."

"What are you going to do to keep him here? Sit on him?" I asked sarcastically.

"If it comes to that, then yes." She stood and walked to the door. "I'm going to go ask Drake to call him. I'll get Adam up here somehow, so you two can talk."

"Now?" I asked, fear creeping in.

"If you don't do it now, you'll lose your nerve," Chloe said.

I sighed. "I know. I just thought I'd have more time to prepare."

"It'll be fine, Amber. I promise."

Then, she was gone.

And I was left alone—again.

"Why the fuck do you need me to help you hang shelves?"

I shot up off the bed at the sound of Adam's voice. *Oh God, he's here.* I wasn't ready, not by a long shot.

I'd changed into a white sundress that stopped just above my knees. Unlike most of my dresses, it covered everything. It even had straps, for God's sake. To me, that was like a full body suit. I'd left my hair down and put on a bit of makeup. It was stupid to worry what he would think about how I looked, but I did.

"Shut up and help me. Chloe's been bustin' my balls to put them up in one of the spare rooms."

"You're pussy-whipped, my friend," Adam grumbled.

The door swung open, and Adam and Drake stepped into the room. I didn't miss the fact that Drake had let Adam in first. If Adam tried to leave, Drake would block him.

Adam's eyes landed on me. He froze mid-step and just stared. I swallowed roughly as I waited for him to speak. He didn't disappoint.

"What in the actual *fuck*?" he growled as he turned and glared at Drake. "What the hell is she doing here?"

"She's here for you," Drake said. He crossed his arms over his chest.

"Fuck that," Adam said as he tried to move past Drake.

"You're not leaving until you two talk."

"This was a damn setup. Why?" Adam shouted at Drake. "I thought I made it clear that I wanted nothing to do with her."

"Because she has something she needs to tell you, and I knew you'd never willingly see her."

"You're right, and I'm not going to talk to her now. Move!"

Drake shook his head. "You're not going anywhere. Now, I can close the door and leave you two alone, or I can stand in here while she talks to you. Trust me when I say, you're better off without me. This isn't something that you're going to want me to hang around for."

Adam glared at him before turning away. "Fine. She can say whatever the hell she needs to say, and then I'm gone. I don't care if I have to take down your ass to leave. What the fuck happened to bros before hoes?"

Drake grinned. "I got married. Bros never stood a chance." He turned to leave. "Yell if you need me, Amber."

Once he was gone, neither Adam nor I spoke. I watched him as he glared at me. In that moment, I knew that he absolutely hated me for forcing myself on him. I could see it in his eyes.

"Are you going to stare at me or tell me what the fuck you need to say?" Adam finally said.

I looked away for a moment, willing myself not to cry. I'd done far too much of that lately. "I think you might want to sit down."

"I'll stand, thanks," Adam said sarcastically.

I fought back a retort. He was really starting to piss me off. "Suit yourself. But once I start talking, I want you to let me finish before you say anything, okay?"

He raised an eyebrow.

"I'm serious."

"Fine. Whatever. Just get on with it."

"Before I came out here last month, I got sick. I ended up going to the doctor, and he gave me antibiotics. The only problem with them is that they fuck up birth control. I forgot that." I sighed. "I'm pregnant, Adam. I didn't mean for it to happen, but I am. I know you probably hate me more than ever for it, but I can't change anything. And...there's something else. We had sex that night, but I had sex with someone else shortly after. I don't know if it's his or yours. I won't know until the baby is born."

He stared at me.

Then, he stared some more.

I fidgeted as I waited for him to say something, anything.

"Adam, talk to me, please." I hated how desperate my voice sounded.

256

"You're pregnant," he said, his eyes never leaving mine. They looked empty, like he wasn't even really with me.

I wasn't sure if it was because he was in shock or something else.

"I'm not asking for anything from you. I know what Hilary did to you, and I would never do that. I understand if you want nothing to do with this child, but Chloe thought you needed to know."

"Chloe thought I needed to know?" he asked, finally breaking from his stupor. "And what about you? Did you think I needed to know?"

I looked away. "I hadn't decided yet, but she made me tell you."

"Jesus Christ!" he exploded. "You're carrying my kid, and you thought I didn't need to know?"

"I don't know if it's yours! I would never expect you to take care of me like you did with *her*. I didn't do this to trap you or whatever it is you're thinking. It was an accident."

"I don't give a fuck if it's mine or not! I have a right to know!" he shouted.

"I'm sorry. I thought you'd tell me to get lost. I know how much you hate me."

"Goddamn it, Amber! This isn't about you! It's about that baby," he growled. "Have you told the other asshole?"

I nodded. "Yeah."

"And?" he asked.

I dropped down onto the bed. I wasn't sure if my legs could support me any longer. "He didn't take it well. He doesn't want anything to do with the baby, even if it's his."

Adam's nostrils flared. "Fucker."

"It's not all his fault." I hesitated, knowing I was about to dig my grave even deeper. "He's married. I doubt his wife would be cool if I moved into their spare room."

Adam's mouth dropped open in shock. "The motherfucker is *married*, but he decided to sleep with you. Then, he decided he wanted nothing to do with…" He ran his hands over his face. "I want to fucking kill him, and I don't even know who he is."

I sighed. "It doesn't matter. I can take care of myself. At least he knows, and now, you do, too. I don't have that on my conscious any longer. I can go back home and figure out where to go from there."

"What are you talking about?" he asked.

I rolled my eyes. "I have to find a doctor, tell my parents, and figure out what the hell I need to raise a baby. Besides the doctor, I have no idea how to go about any of that."

"You're not going back to Morgantown," he said furiously.

"What?"

"You're *not* going back. You're staying here with me. That could be my child you're carrying, and I'm not going to just let you walk away with it."

"I…you…" I sputtered, unable to form a coherent sentence.

"You'll stay with me, and we'll figure out all that shit together."

"But you hate me!" I blurted out.

"It doesn't matter what I think of you. If that kid's mine, I'm taking care of it. I want to be there for everything—every doctor's appointment, every ultrasound, the first time he kicks…all of it."

The emotion in his voice surprised me.

"He?" I asked.

He grinned. I almost fell over in shock.

"Of course it's a he."

I shook my head. "Adam, this isn't something to just jump into. We'll have to see each other constantly, especially if you expect me to stay with you. How well do you think that's going to go?"

He shrugged. "We'll figure it out as we go."

"And what happens if once *he's* born, you find out you're not the father?"

"Like I said, we'll figure it out as we go."

I felt tears welling up in my eyes. "You're really going to help me, aren't you?"

He looked uncomfortable as tears slipped down my cheeks. "Of course I am."

"Thank you," I whispered, my body sagging in relief. I hadn't realized just how terrified I was of doing everything on my own.

"Hey, don't cry." He walked over and knelt down in front of me. "Living with me won't be *that* bad."

I smiled through my tears. "That's debatable." My smile disappeared as I stared at him. "Can we try to get along? Can we be…friends again? I don't know if I can do this with you if we aren't."

He studied me for a moment. "Yeah, we can be friends."

I wrapped my arms around him, taking both of us by surprise. "Thank you."

He awkwardly patted me on the back. "No problem."

"Adam?" I asked as I pulled away. "Can I ask for one more favor?"

He eyed me warily. "What?"

"I know how you are with…women. I don't think I can handle living with you and watching you bring them home. Can you not fuck around while I'm there?"

259

He frowned. "I can keep it in my pants, Amber."

"I know. I just…" I trailed off.

He sighed. "I get it. Don't worry. I won't mess around with anyone."

"Thank you."

He gave me a small smile before his eyes dropped down to my stomach, "Can I…can I touch you?"

I nodded. He reached out and pressed his hand to my lower stomach. I held my breath as I watched him.

"A baby." He chuckled. "I'm going to be a dad."

I smiled at him, unable to speak.

He stood and held out a hand to me. "Come on, let's go home."

I never thought I'd hear him say those words to me.

twenty-two

Living with Adam was strange and awkward. I'd been staying here for two weeks. We no longer fought, but we weren't talking a lot either. Adam would keep his distance, and I would do the same. I was grateful that he was helping me, and I didn't want to push any of his boundaries. When we talked occasionally, we'd keep it simple, and neither of us would mention the past.

He would be gone a lot throughout the day, working on a new album with the band. I'd spend most days lying out on the beach and reading. I'd hated being alone in Morgantown, but here, I didn't mind it. I knew Adam would always come home. That comforted me more than I wanted to admit.

I'd called my work and quit a week after I'd moved in with Adam. I'd hated to do it over the phone without any kind of notice, but I hadn't had much choice. Surprisingly, Nancy hadn't been angry. It might have been because she had been too busy gushing over the fact that I was pregnant.

Telling my mom and dad had been much, much harder. I'd told them everything, including the fact that I wasn't one hundred percent sure that Adam was the father. They'd been angry at first, but they'd finally calmed down. Within a week of me telling them, they'd shifted from pissed to ecstatic, just like Chloe had thought they would.

Adam had paid a company to clean out my apartment. They'd shipped everything to his place. I left most of it in boxes, unable to bring myself to unpack. A part of me feared that Adam would change his mind and kick me out.

When I'd first found out I was pregnant, I'd been terrified. I hadn't wanted a baby. The thought of a child growing inside me had literally made me ill. I would've done anything to change that positive test result to a negative.

Now that I wasn't alone and I'd had time to come to terms with the fact that I would become a mother, my opinion had changed. Instead of feeling horror at the thought, I started to feel excitement. I was going to be a mom. I would have a precious life that I'd created, one that I would take care of and love. For the first time in a long time, the future didn't seem so bleak. Even if Adam decided to turn me away, I would still have my baby. I would give it the best life I could. I would survive.

"Hey, you ready?" Adam asked.

I looked up to see him standing in the doorway to my room.

"Yeah." I stood and walked over to him.

We walked out to his car side by side. My heart was beating in my chest like a hummingbird because of the fact that he was so close and because of where we were going.

Today was my first doctor's appointment.

"You nervous?" Adam asked on the drive over.

"A little."

"It'll be fine. I'll stay with you the whole time."

"Really?" I asked, surprised.

"Yep. Wouldn't miss it."

"Thank you," I whispered.

He sighed. "Quit thanking me for every little thing, Amber. No thanks are needed. I want to be here. It's not like you're forcing me."

Adam stayed true to his word. He stood next to me as I checked in at the doctor's office. When I was called back, he followed me and waited next to me as they took my medical history and weight. He even stood outside the door while I peed in a cup. I couldn't help but laugh at that.

Once we were taken to a room, the nurse handed me a paper gown. "Go ahead and change into this. The doctor will be in shortly," she said before leaving.

I stared at the gown in my hands, appalled. I looked up when Adam chuckled.

"What's so funny?"

"You should see your face right now."

"Shush." I held up the piece of paper. "There's no freaking back to it."

He laughed again. "And how is that different from your normal wardrobe?"

I flipped him off. "This is different." I sighed. "Turn around, so I can change."

"It's not like I haven't seen it all before," he goaded.

"If you want to keep your man parts intact, turn around."

He rolled his eyes before turning away. I stripped out of my clothes as fast as I could and pulled on the gown. When I looked up, he was watching me.

"You looked."

He shrugged unapologetically.

I jumped when I heard a knock on the door. A moment later, a doctor and the nurse from earlier stepped in. I breathed a sigh of relief when I saw that the doctor was a woman.

"Hi, you must be Amber." She smiled at me.

I nodded. "Yes, and this is Adam."

She glanced over at Adam. "It's nice to meet both of you. I'm Dr. Dover."

Adam surprised me when he stood and shook her hand. "It's nice to meet you."

"All right, let's get started." She walked to the counter and pulled on a pair of gloves. "We need to do an exam first. We'll go over a few things after, and if we have time, we'll see if we can find the baby's heartbeat."

"Exam?" I asked warily.

She nodded. "Yes. I'll be as gentle as possible, I promise."

She sat down on a stool in front of me and had me put my feet in the stirrups. Under normal circumstances, I would die from embarrassment, but with Adam in the room, it was ten times worse.

"Whoa, what is that?" Adam asked.

The doctor smiled at him. "It's a speculum."

"You're going to put that *in* her?"

I groaned and put my hands over my face.

The doctor laughed. "Yes. If you're uncomfortable, you can step outside."

Adam hesitated before shaking his head. "I'm not going anywhere."

One uncomfortable Pap smear later, I was able to sit up. I didn't dare look at Adam. The doctor threw her gloves away and picked up her clipboard. I listened as she explained how things would go over the next few months. I had about a million questions, but she took her time and answered them all.

Once we were finished, she smiled at me. "Let's see if we can hear that heartbeat. How does that sound?"

I smiled, suddenly excited over the prospect of hearing my baby. "I'd love that."

"Sometimes, it's hard to hear the heartbeat this early, so I can't promise anything, but we'll try."

I lay back on the table and closed my eyes. They jerked open when I felt my gown being lifted. I watched the nurse move it up until it was above my stomach. I looked over when Adam stepped closer. He took my hand in his, and he smiled down at me, excitement in his eyes.

I held my breath as the nurse put some kind of goo on my tummy.

"You ready?" the doctor asked.

"Yeah." I closed my eyes when I felt something pushing against my stomach.

The doctor moved it around for a few minutes, and then I heard *it*. My breath caught in my throat as I listened to a steady *swish, swish, swish* filling the room. I opened my eyes to see Adam smiling widely.

"Is that the heartbeat?" he asked.

"Yes. It sounds good," the doctor said.

Adam squeezed my hand tighter. I watched his face. His expression nearly brought tears to my eyes. It was filled with so much wonder and excitement.

"That's our baby, babe," he whispered.

My throat clogged with emotion. "Yeah, it is."

Too soon, the doctor moved away, and the room fell silent.

"All right. Go ahead, and get dressed. A prescription for prenatal vitamins will be waiting for you at the checkout counter. Take one daily. I'll see you two in a month. Call me if you have any problems."

"Thank you," I said as I sat up.

Once the doctor and nurse were gone, I dressed quickly. I didn't bother to tell Adam to look away this time. I knew he wouldn't. We left the room and walked down to the checkout counter. I set up my next appointment and grabbed my prescription before leaving.

We stopped at a pharmacy on the way home to grab my vitamins. The car ride home was totally silent. I glanced at Adam a few times, but he kept his eyes on the road. When we walked into the house, I headed for my room, unable to take his silence any longer. I had no idea what it meant. I was afraid he'd suddenly decided that it was too much to handle and that he wanted me to leave.

"Hey, wait a minute," Adam said as he grabbed my arm.

"What?" I asked quietly, praying that he wasn't about to tell me to get out.

"That was...amazing, wasn't it?" he asked.

Did I dare hope...

"Yeah, it was."

He smiled down at me. I sucked in a shocked breath when he pulled me to him and hugged me tightly.

"We're having a baby," he said.

Once I realized he wasn't going to kick me to the curb, I grinned, my body relaxing into his. "We are."

He finally released me after several moments. I stepped back, unsure of what I was supposed to say or do. I was so afraid I'd somehow mess up what little headway I'd made with him. He looked down at me, his face suddenly serious. He stepped closer and raised his hand to cup my cheek. I held my breath, not daring to move or speak. I watched as he lowered his head. When his lips connected with my forehead, I almost fell over.

"We're having a baby," he whispered again.

———— ———— — ——

"You awake?"

I opened my eyes to see Adam standing above me. I'd been lying out on the beach, hoping to get a decent tan before I got too fat to let anyone see me in a bikini.

"Yeah." I glanced down at my phone. "You're home early."

He sat down next to me and pulled his shirt off. My eyes had a mind of their own as they trailed down his bare skin.

"We finished up early. The album's almost done. We'll start on final edits soon."

"That's awesome. I can't wait to hear what you guys have. I'm sure it'll kick ass."

He smirked. "Doesn't it always?"

I stuck my tongue out at him. Things had been different between us since my doctor's appointment.

Another two weeks had gone by. We were talking more now. We'd even spend time together when he was home. I was starting to believe that Adam might actually *not* hate me. And my feelings for him had amplified tenfold. Seeing a softer, more caring side of him made me want him more than I ever had. I forced myself not to think about it. I couldn't. I wouldn't ruin everything—again.

He glanced down at the book that was lying next to me in the sand. "What's that?"

"A baby name book. I know it's early, but I figured it wouldn't hurt to start looking."

"Find any good ones?" he asked.

"A couple. I really like Gabriella for a girl and Jason for a boy."

He wrinkled his nose. "Why are you looking at girl names? We're having a boy."

I rolled my eyes. "You don't know that."

"Yes, I do. We're going to have a boy. We'll name him Adam Jr., and he'll be awesome. The end."

I laughed. "If it's a girl, I'm going to laugh my ass off at you."

"Let me guess...you want a girl."

I shrugged. "Kind of. I'm not really worried about whether it's a girl or boy though. I just want the baby to be healthy."

He reached out and took my hand in his. "I was thinking I could start on a nursery in one of the spare rooms. You know, set up a crib and all that shit. You can do the decorating."

"That would be nice," I said. I pretended not to notice the way his thumb was making slow circles across the top of my hand.

He sighed. "These past few weeks have been eye-opening."

"What do you mean?" I asked.

"Before"—he swallowed—"with Hilary, all I felt was dread after she told me the truth. With you, I don't feel that way. I just...I feel like this baby is mine. I feel like a dad."

"And if it's not yours?" I asked quietly. "What happens then?"

He looked over at me, a pained expression on his face. "No matter what happens, this baby *is* mine."

"Adam—"

"No, I want you to listen to me. I've been trying to figure out how the hell to say this since that first appointment. Be quiet, so I can make sure I get it right."

I grinned. "My bad. Please continue."

"You scare the shit out of me. You always have. The moment I laid eyes on you, I knew there was something different about you. I knew you'd change everything for me." He looked away. "And I was right. I didn't realize how much I cared about you until you told me you loved me. To hear you say that…well, it scared the hell out of me. I reacted badly. I know I did. I deserve a swift kick in the balls for what I said to you, but I only said what I did because I knew I loved you, too. I couldn't handle that. I couldn't handle being broken again. If I gave you everything, I was afraid you'd toss it aside like it was nothing."

I couldn't believe what he was saying. I felt tears spring to my eyes as I listened to him pour his heart and soul out to me.

"Then, I saw you out here with Chloe that night, and I just…I lost it. I could handle loving you if you weren't around to hurt me, but I couldn't stand the thought of having you near. So, I lashed out again. Then, I got drunk and acted like an even bigger dickhead. I've hurt you so much, Amber. I don't know how you can stand to be around me."

I sat up. "It's because I love you. No matter how hard I tried to hate you, I couldn't. You hurt me, and I kept going back for more. You broke me, Adam, but I didn't care. Nothing you said or did could keep me from loving you."

He shuddered, his whole body shaking with emotion. "I love you, too. I just don't know what to do with that. I never have. I can't stand the thought of losing you or this baby."

I swallowed, choosing my next words carefully. "I don't plan to go anywhere, Adam. I just don't understand what you want from me. If you want me to love you, that's already a done deal."

"I want you to be mine. I want to give you everything and never have it turned against me."

"Do you really think I'd do that to you?"

He shook his head. "Every fiber of my being tells me you won't, but...I'm scared, Amber. I'm so fucking scared of what could happen."

"No one knows what the future holds," I said softly. "What I *do* know is that I want you more than I've ever wanted something in my life. The way I feel about you...I'll never feel it with anyone else. You're it for me, whether you realize it or not."

He released my hand, only to raise his hand to cup my cheek. "And you're not scared?"

I laughed. "I'm fucking terrified of you, Adam, but I'm willing to take a chance if you are."

"Everything is happening so fast," he said softly.

"It is. Adam..." I hesitated. "Are you telling me all of this because we're having a child? Or is it because you really love me? I don't want you to feel like you have to be with me. I would never expect that from you."

"I'm telling you because I love you. I've wasted so much time with you because I was a fucking coward." He frowned. "This baby is more of a blessing than you could ever imagine. I don't know if I would've had the courage to tell you the truth if it hadn't brought us together. I might have continued to act like a dick until you finally walked away. So, part of the reason is because of the baby, but it doesn't change what I feel for you."

I felt a tear slide down my cheek. He studied me for a moment before grabbing me and pulling me onto his lap. His mouth sought mine in the sweetest kiss imaginable. I leaned against him, my fingers reaching up to his hand. I threaded them through, clinging to him for dear life. I never wanted to let him go. I never wanted this moment to end.

"I love you," he said against my lips. "I love you so goddamn much that it hurts to breathe. I'll take my chances on a broken heart because I love you that much." He pulled me tighter against him. "You're mine. You always have been."

He rolled so that I was underneath him. I expected him to kiss me rougher, but he didn't. He kept our kisses sweet, deepening them with each stroke of his tongue. His hands found the ties on my bikini bottom and undid them.

"Can we...I mean, will it hurt the baby? After she got pregnant, Hilary would never..." He pulled away and looked down at me.

As sappy as it was, tears came to my eyes when I saw the emotion swirling in his beautiful brown eyes. There was so much love and tenderness in them.

"We can," was all I said.

He nodded before pulling my bottoms away and tossing them aside. He raised his body enough to pull his shorts over his hips. In one swift move, he entered me. I gasped in surprise, my fingers tugging at his hair. His strokes were gentle and slow, building a small flame inside me.

"I love you," he whispered.

"I love you, too."

His restraint cracked, and he started thrusting harder and faster. I raised my hips to meet his every stroke as he kissed my lips, my nose, and my neck.

For the first time in my life, I wasn't fucking. I was making love to the man I loved more than words could ever express. When my orgasm crashed over me, I called out his name. His body shuddered above me as he found his own release.

When we finished, he rolled away and pulled me tight against him. I rested my face on his chest, lost in the moment.

"You're mine," Adam said quietly.

I traced the tattoos on his chest. "And you're mine."

As we lay there, he started humming. I recognized the tune, but I couldn't place it.

"What song is that?" I asked.

"'Angel' by Theory of a Deadman. Every time I hear it, I think of us. It's our song, our anthem."

I grinned, past memories flashing in front of my eyes. "I thought 'Turn Me On' by Royal Bliss was our song."

He chuckled. "It was but not anymore."

I snuggled closer to him. "I love you."

"I love you, too. And I'm going to spend the rest of my life proving just how much I love you. I'm never letting you walk away again."

"I'm going to hold you to that."

He kissed my forehead. "Please do."

In that moment, the peace I felt was like nothing I'd ever felt before. Finally, I was home.

epilogue

Eight Months Later

I screamed, every curse word I knew flying from my mouth. I'd never felt so much pain in my life. Dying would be easier than this.

My hand clutched Adam's, squeezing the life out of it, but he never once complained. He only gave words of encouragement. I loved him for it, but I also wanted to punch him in the face just because.

"Come on, Amber. One more good push," Dr. Dover said.

"I can't!" I screamed.

"Yes, you can. It's almost over. Just take a deep breath and push."

"I hate all of you!" I shouted before taking a deep breath and pushing. "Fuck!"

"That's it. Keep pushing," Dr. Dover said. "Don't stop."

I kept pushing until I felt like my head was going to explode. Finally, I felt the pressure release.

A wailing cry broke out, and it was the most beautiful sound I'd ever heard.

"Is the baby okay?" I asked.

"She's fine," Dr. Dover said.

"She?" I asked breathlessly.

Dr. Dover smiled at me. "Yes, she. You have a little girl."

I looked at Adam. He was staring at me in shock.

I grinned at him, unable to stop myself. "A girl."

He smirked. "I knew it would be a girl all along."

A nurse wrapped the baby in a blanket and carried her over to me. She placed my daughter in my arms, and I instantly started crying as I stared down at her. She was the most beautiful little girl I'd ever seen. She opened her eyes and stared back at me.

"Hi, Gabriella," I whispered.

Adam reached out and gently brushed her cheek. "She's perfect."

"She is." I stared down at my brown-eyed, dark-haired baby. In that moment, I knew that she was Adam's. There wasn't a trace of Alex's blue eyes or blond hair anywhere to be seen.

I looked up at Adam. "She's yours."

He smiled at me. "It wouldn't have mattered if she weren't, but there's no doubt about it. She's as pretty as her daddy."

I laughed. "Asshole."

He reached down and carefully took her from my arms. "Hi, Gabriella."

Tears slid freely down my cheeks as I stared at the two most important people in my life. I'd fucked up so many times over the years. I didn't deserve the happiness I felt right now, but it didn't matter. I had it. I had everything I could ever want.

"I love you," I said through my tears. "I love you both so much."

"We love you, too," Adam whispered, never once taking his eyes off Gabriella.

I no longer envied Chloe or Logan because of the love they'd found with Drake and Jade. I had finally found my very own happily ever after. For the first time in a long time, I felt peaceful. Adam and Gabriella were the only things that mattered, and I had them both.

I had everything.

The End

Broken and Screwed

Tijan

Chapter One

When I got to the bonfire, the smell of fire and booze filled the air. Underneath was the smell of sweat. My nose wrinkled up and I grimaced, but headed towards it. The guys had been partying all day since it was the last day of school. I was glad I didn't smell anything worse.

People swarmed in the woods as I continued towards wherever the fire would be. That's where my friends would be. Angie and Marissa liked to be the center of attention. Angie was the willowy blonde with a model's look. Her blue eyes seemed to launch out of her body. They were intense, smoky, and had ensnared most of the male population in our school. And Marissa rivaled her in the looks department. She was petite, with jet black hair, dark almond eyes, and a personality that dubbed her Sullivan High School's man eater. Even though we had finished our junior year and had three months of summer before we started our reign as seniors, I knew they wanted to start early. Those two were ready for the senior girls to leave so they could take the crown as the queens of our school.

"Alex!"

And there was one of them.

I couldn't stop a chuckle as Angie leaned over her boyfriend's shoulder and waved at me. She was so eager; she tipped forward and fell down his body and to the floor. She'd been standing on a truck and her movement sent a jerking movement underneath the rest of the girls who danced there. They screamed, grabbing onto anything to steady them. A group of guys stood around the truck. Some of the guys were ogling the girls, but some of them were chatting with their friends. More than a few jumped forward and couldn't hide their smirks when the girls grabbed them for balance.

Justin looked down at Angie on the ground, sighed, and continued talking with his friend.

"Alex!" Her shout turned into a whine and I took her hand. As I hauled her back to her feet, she groaned. "I'm so embarrassed."

"You shouldn't be." She'd done it enough times over the past year since she had started drinking. Then I glanced around. "Where's Marissa?"

"Where else?" She drew upright. Her tone turned snippy. "Trying to hit on your man. I don't know why she even tries. He doesn't want a girlfriend since he broke up with Sarah. Everyone can see that Jesse Hunt is the hit 'em and quit 'em guy this year. Seriously. He's hooked up with someone at every single party." She threw her arm around in a circle and her voice raised a notch. "And everyone also knows that if he's going to date someone, it's going to be you."

The slight enjoyment I had when I first got to the party died. "Stop, Angie. Jesse and I aren't friends. We're nothing."

She snorted.

"And if he was going to date someone, it would be Sarah. It wouldn't be me. He was with her for three years, remember? Those types of feelings don't vanish."

She snorted again. Her chest jerked up and down and she crossed her arms. "I'm going to get more beer. You want any?"

I shook my head.

She left even before she saw my response, but she knew I didn't drink. The only two times I ever had any alcohol were the two times I got wasted. Both nights intermingled with harsh memories, memories I didn't even want to think about now.

"Alex!"

This time it was Marissa. She had a bright smile on her face as she hurried around a group. She held a cup of beer in one hand and was wiping her face with the other as she stopped next to me. She panted for a second, but then flipped her black locks over her shoulder. Her hand went to her hip and just like that, her pose could've been in a magazine.

"Hey." I was half warm, half cautious. Was she going to talk about Jesse? He'd been her obsession for the last month. I knew she didn't want to really date him, but she did want to sleep with him. Marissa had always harbored feelings for him most of our lives. She never uttered a word to me until the last two months when she realized that Jesse and I were more strangers than what we had been.

She latched onto my arm. I fought from cringing from her beer breath as she fanned herself. "Okay, first: Jesse is an ass."

I relaxed. Finally.

"But, holy cow, that makes him so super hot. Am I weird? I must be wired backwards. I dunno, but I want him even more. I swear. Can you talk to him? Tell him I'm good in bed. No, wait. He has to know I am. I mean, hello." Then she frowned and her eyes crinkled together. "Wait. What was I talking about?"

"Marissa."

"What?" She perked up. Her nails dug into my arm.

"Let go of my arm."

"Oh!" Her eyes went wide again. "Oh my gosh! I am so sorry, Alex. Did I hurt you? Please tell me I didn't. I'm such an idiot. What was I talking about before?"

I peered closer. She didn't look that drunk.

"Oh, that's right!" Her whole body jerked up in an excited spasm. She clapped her hand to her cheek. "Please talk to Jesse. I know you say you don't want to. I know you say you're not friends with him, but I know you are. I know you both are still close, so do you think you could put in a good word for me?"

"I..." I had no words. Even for Marissa, this was more forward than she'd ever been before. She had to have been drunk because the alternate option was that my best friend was incredibly insensitive to me. Had she not forgotten about the last year? Or why Jesse and I weren't close anymore?

And then someone threw their beer on her. She was soaked in an instant. Her mouth fell open. Anger filled her face, along with shock, but her eyes were wide as she turned. Angie stood there with a smug smile and an empty cup. She waved it at Marissa before her hand fell to her hip. Both of them faced off against each other. Angie stepped close. She was taller and looked down her nose at Marissa. "Are you kidding me? You did not just ask Alex to put in a good word with Jesse for you? Are you serious? Seriously?!"

"You bitch!" Marissa screeched. She wrung her hands in the air, as if she wasn't sure what to do with them.

"Guys." I started to step between them.

I was hauled back by Justin; he bypassed me to grab Angie's shoulders. He turned her away, but sent a scathing look at Marissa as he did.

Her hands flew in the air. "What?" she snapped at him.

His eyes flickered once. A dark look was in them and her hands fell back down. She took a breath, looked at me, and took another breath.

I looked away. I didn't know what I was supposed to do. Comfort her? She was wrong. It'd been too much for her to ask, but she had a beer thrown on her because of me. I had no idea what I was supposed to do here.

And then I heard from her in a small voice, "I'm sorry, Alex. I wasn't thinking about you."

I took a deep breath. My stomach settled again and I shrugged. "It's okay."

"It's not. I was a being a selfish bitch. I forgot…"

My heart pounded. What was she going to say?

"Never mind. Do you want something to drink?"

I let out a deep breath of relief. She hadn't said it. And, like Angie, she left before I could reply. They both knew me so well.

Justin took Angie back to his truck and they climbed inside. Her arms flew around. Her face kept switching from outrage to fury and Justin kept patting her back. I stood there. I still had no idea what to do. They would reconcile in the morning. It was what they did. They would get heated, both of them were so honest and open. At times, the words weren't received well, but they always made up in the morning. When I saw Marissa with some of her cheerleading friends, I knew it would be sooner than that. She was biting her lip as she cast concerned looks towards Angie. She sent a few towards me, but her eyes fluttered and she looked away.

I made the decision to leave. This party wasn't for me, not that night, not with him there.

A few girls called out goodbyes when they saw that I was leaving, but no one stopped me. No one dared because the truth was that I wasn't close to any of them anymore. I had been. A year ago I was one of the popular girls. It was why I had become friends with Angie and Marissa. No one could rival us when we were together.

My phone buzzed as I neared where I had parked my car. I pulled my phone out and saw the text from Marissa. I'm sorry. I really am. Please don't be mad at me. I'm really really really sorry if I hurt you. I'm so stupid sometimes. Ok. All the time. This time. I was stupid this time. Ill make it r8t wth Angie too. Promise. Breakfast in the am? Barnies?

I thumbed a response back. Sounds good. Call when u wake up.

A second later. R U mad? R U hurt?

I heaved another breath. Was I mad? No. That was Marissa, she didn't think sometimes. Was I hurt? On this night, I couldn't breathe without hurting. I should've replied, told a lie to my friend, but I didn't. I pocketed my phone and kept my head down as I got to the car.

Everything slowed to a halt after that.

Nothing happened. No one made a sound. No one moved. There were no animals in the background, no smell that warned me, but tingles raced down my spine and I knew.

I looked up, swallowing over a knot.

There he was, Jesse Hunt.

His dark eyes penetrated me from across the ten yards that separated us. His black hair had been buzzed since that afternoon. His lips were curved in a sneer and he was sitting on my car trunk. His knees were pulled up as his feet rested on the bumper. He had on a sleeveless black shirt that was ripped at the ends. The tattoos on his arms seemed even darker from the moonlight. They were highlighted against his skin though he was golden tan.

My voice couldn't work. "What are you doing here?" I sounded hoarse.

My heart was pounding. I couldn't get enough air.

His top lip curved upwards in a smile, but he still kept the sneer on his face. I never knew how he could do that, but he had perfected it from when we were in junior high. "What? You got those virginal panties on now?" His eyes flashed a warning to me. "What do you think I'm doing here?"

I swung away. Why could he affect me so much?

"Hey!" He raised his voice a notch. "It's the big night for us, Alex. Come on. Who else would I be with tonight? Only you and me. We're the only ones."

I lowered my head. He was right. My heart slowed a bit. No one else could understand. No one else had loved Ethan like we had.

But that didn't mean I wanted to think about my big brother at that moment. So I swung back and rushed out, "I saw Sarah at the bonfire. She looks pretty." I wet my lips. When had they gone so dry? "Do you think you'll ever get back together with her? I think she still loves you."

He stared at me for a moment and then snorted. When he raised his hand, I saw the flask for the first time. He was drunk. Of course, he was drunk. I blinked back rapid tears. He only talked to me when he was drunk, but no—that wasn't correct. There were lots of times when he had been drunk and he ignored my calls, my looks, or my pleas for any comfort he could've provided.

"Are you serious?" He rolled his eyes and for some reason, it seemed savage when it came from him. He fixed me with another penetrating stare. "Come on, Alex. What are we doing here?"

"You're on *my* car."

He snorted again and raised the flask once more. "It's Ethan's car."

"He gave it to me."

I tensed, ready for a sharp rebuke, but it never came. Silence. My eyes snapped to his and I was surprised to see that he wasn't looking at me. He had turned away. I could see his Adam's apple bobbing up and down. The image of it took my breath away. He was beautiful in that moment. The moon was behind him, casting its shadow over him and when he looked back, he draped both his arms on his knees. His head hung down.

His shoulders drooped as he took a breath. Hearing the shuddering inhale from him, I clasped my eyes closed.

I heard the pain in him. My own matched his and I wanted to go to him. But that was how it happened the last time. Nothing good came out of that except more suffering.

I felt my wall crumble and whispered, "I'm tired of hurting, Jesse."

He looked back up. The cockiness was gone. The anger still burned in his eyes, but he had stuffed it down. I knew it was there, though. But it didn't keep me away. His torment was on the surface and he let me see that.

Tears burst from my dam. I couldn't stop them.

"It's the exact time that it happened, you know. Right now. It's 11:05. June 2."

The pain suffocated me, but I couldn't turn away. I nodded with my throat full. "I know."

Jesse sighed again and stretched his legs down. He slid off the trunk and leaned against it. The moonlight flashed over his flask as he raised it again. As I heard it empty, he tossed it aside and crossed his arms over his chest. Even though Jesse was lean, his biceps bulged from the movement. He had always worked out, but since Ethan died he had doubled his time there.

"My god. I fucking loved that guy."

A hand reached inside and squeezed my heart. More tears streamed from my eyes. I was helpless to stop them, but I choked out, "I know."

"Drive me home?"

My eyes closed again and I wrapped my arms around myself. There it was. That was the request I knew was coming. My heart thundered while I tried to think clearly. And then I said, "Yes."

The corners of his lips curved up, just slightly.

We didn't speak after that. We didn't need to. I went to the driver's side. He went to the passenger side and neither of us said a word as I drove past his black Ferrari or even when we pulled up to the mansion his father had built when Jesse's mother had been dying. As we walked through the hallways, up the stairs, and to his back bedroom my heart was calm. I was calm. And that made me not calm.

I shouldn't have been calm.

Jesse went to his bar and poured vodka into a glass. He slid it across the counter to me. I picked it up and waited until he poured one for himself.

It was the third time we'd done this. Ethan's funeral. Ethan's birthday. And now the anniversary of the day Ethan's car wrapped itself around a tree. He died a year ago and nothing was the same.

For more information, go to www.tijansbooks.com

Did you enjoy Tamed?

Check out some of K.A. Robinson's other titles!

Other Books by K.A. Robinson

Breaking Alexandria

Alexandria's drug-dealing boyfriend, Joel, isn't exactly the white knight she's always dreamed of, but she can't deny the crazy connection they have. She would do anything for him, including helping him sell drugs in order to fit perfectly into his world.

After catching Alexandria dealing for Joel, instead of turning her into the cops, Alexandria's mother forces her to move to her grandparents' farm in West Virginia. Spending the summer in the country, away from Joel, is the last thing Alexandria wants to do. But lucky for her, the sexy farmhand, Landon, who helps out around her grandparents' place, is a very nice distraction. She tries her best to ignore her attraction to him, especially since she still loves Joel.

When Joel does the unforgivable, Alexandria turns to her new friend, Landon, for comfort, and it ignites an undeniable spark of attraction between them. Soon, she finds herself caught between two very different men, and the struggles within her heart just might end up breaking Alexandria.

Breaking Alexandria is a standalone novel.

Shattered Ties

With a former supermodel mother and a rock-and-roll legend father, Emma Preston has the best of everything. Nothing is as perfect as it seems though. After her parents divorce, she's forced to live with her mother in a private Santa Monica community. Ignoring their parental roles, her mother becomes more focused on climbing the social ladder while her father is off on tour.

Growing up in a trailer park with his mother, Jesse is used to people looking down on him. When his mother begs him to submit an application for a scholarship to one of Santa Monica's top private schools, he never expects to actually get it. When he does, he is forced to attend school with a bunch of rich kids. He ignores their stares as they judge him for having tattoos and a less than impressive car. As long as he has his surfboard and the guys at the tattoo shop, he knows he can make it through.

When Jesse shows up on the first day of school, Emma can't help but be intrigued. Her mother would never approve of Emma talking to someone so poor, but she doesn't care because something about Jesse draws her to him.

Jesse tries to hate Emma, but he discovers that he can't resist her. Forced to hide their relationship from Emma's mother and everyone else around them, things start to fall apart. When Jesse's friend, Ally, decides to interfere, things go from bad to worse.

Can they survive their first love? Or will they be left with nothing more than shattered ties?

Shattered Ties is book one of two of the Ties Series. Book two, Twisted Ties, is now available!

Toxic: Logan's Story

True love is forever. After years of chasing his best friend, Chloe, Logan finally managed to win her heart—or so he thought. His world crashes down around him when she confesses to cheating on him with a local rock star, Drake. Unable to let her go completely from his life, Logan reassumes his role of best friend while he watches Chloe find her happily ever after with another man. Each day, he sinks further and further into his depression, and the kind, caring Logan he once was dies. When Jade, a member of Drake's band, inserts herself into his life, Logan never expects to fall for her. He's too broken, too damaged.

Jade ran away from home when she was seventeen, desperate to escape her abusive stepfather and her controlling boyfriend, Mikey. The only regret she has is that she left behind her little sister, Bethaney. When Jade's band, Breaking the Hunger, hits it big, she vows to go back to her hometown not only to reconnect with her little sister, but also to show her stepfather that she's not worthless like he said.

The moment Jade saw Logan, she knew she wanted him. Unfortunately, he was with Chloe at the time. After his world falls apart, Jade steps in to comfort him, determined to bring back the Logan she once knew.

Sometimes, you find true love with the person you never least expect. Can Logan and Jade heal each other? Or will they forever be changed by their toxic pasts?

Book four of the Torn Series, but this title can be read as a standalone.

Deception

Please note: This isn't your typical love story. Things are messy. Characters aren't always what they appear to be. Wrong decisions are made. If you're not a fan of the darker side of love, this might not be the book for you. Read at your own risk.

I'm strong—or at least, I want to be. I try to be. Oh, how I've tried.

But life screwed me over. When I was at my weakest and lowest, desperate and alone, he found me.

Robert changed everything. He gave me everything.

He was every woman's dream—rich, powerful, and charming. He made me forget the fact that he's twenty-four years my senior.

He made me feel alive, and for the first time in my life, I was content.

Until I met Cooper—his son.

And Robert? He began to change.

I'm despicable. I know I am. I'm ashamed of what I want.

Things are never what they seem.

Greed.

Lust.

Lies.

Murder.

Deception.

about the author

K.A. Robinson is twenty-four years old and lives in a small town in West Virginia with her husband and toddler son. She is the *New York Times* and *USA Today* bestselling author of The Torn Series, The Ties Series, *Breaking Alexandria*, *Taming Alec*, and *Deception*. When she's not writing, she loves to read books that usually have zombies in them. She is addicted to rock music and coffee, mainly Starbucks and Caribou Coffee.

For more information on K.A., please check out the following pages:

Facebook: www.facebook.com/karobinson13

Twitter: @karobinsonautho

Blog: www.authorkarobinson.blogspot.com

acknowledgments

I just want to send a quick shout-out to my husband, my son, and my parents for always being there for me. Also, thank you to my two best friends. Tijan, you're there for me every single day. I love you so much, woman. Life wouldn't be the same without our middle-of-the-night chats. And to my other best friend—you know who you are—you're always there to make me laugh and keep me focused. You know just what to say to pull me out of even the worst of funks. Love ya, brother from another mother.